BABY AND THE BEAST

Lonnie P. Anderson

Copyright page

Publisher's Name: Lonnie P. Anderson

ISBN: 978-1-962142-63-2

Dedicated to

Harold

CONTENTS

FOREWORD

L isten with your heart, open your eyes. Clamor your way out of hell into heaven's waiting hand baskets. Trust with faith, and examine yourself.

Do you deserve to go to heaven? Do you want to find your way? Is it coming? Is it here at our very doorsteps? Wait no more and make your way to God, Creator of us all. Some have turned against him and lead lives filled with disgrace and wickedness. Really? Now is the time to make your choice. Do you want to wait for destiny? Or do you want to find it?

Overcoming evil comes with forgiveness and internal rearrangement. Make your heart right with God; He is waiting with open arms.

Love the Lord your God with all your heart, mind, and strength, and love your neighbor as yourself. *Baby and the Beast* is a story about a young girl, Baby Pollyanna, who was abused as a child and throughout her young adulthood. But God kept his hand on her all through her suffering years and brought her through with shining glory. Magnified in comatose dreaming, she gets an inside view of heaven and all that is to come. Already, now, it is here at the doorstep—the Rapture. God's harvest is ripe and ready. The way is narrow, trust in Christ Jesus for he IS the Way. The way to heaven.

Many mockers will fail to win entry and be cast into the eternal lake of fiery brimstone, Satan's end destruction. Uphold Jesus, and not a hair on your foot will be singed. He is the way. *Baby and the Beast* sets the stage for illumination and glory, overcoming and victory. Seek justice every day. Do what is right with loving kindness, grace, and mercy. Demons will flee, people will be healed, and many who walk the earth will grow younger. It is magnificent. It is a miracle. Trust your gut, not the slander you hear around you now. Read *Baby and the Beast* and go on a journey from babyhood through growth and overcoming of the lost. Be nurtured by words of revival, hope, and eternal ecstasy. Heaven can be yours.

The Early Days

Sometimes it's hard to remember where you came from. Sometimes you don't want to remember where you came from.

Baby Pollyanna resonates with both of these truths.

She has mixed feelings about her past. Now a strong, mature adult, she seeks to heal herself from the severe abuse she felt as a child, which stayed with her through adolescence and into her adulthood.

Light is important to her. So is rest and sleeping. During the night, she talks out loud in her sleep, sometimes so loud and incoherent that her partner is forced to move to the living room to finish his sleep on the couch.

Her earliest fond memories were of sitting on top of the running dryer being jiggled around in her baby seat, being soothed by the sound of the dryer, and the sensation of the shaking world beneath her.

Mother's hugs and soothing speech came as a quiet comfort for her. According to her, this baby cried more than any baby she had ever seen, and she raised three of them. Pollyanna's sister's name was 'Rexi', and her brother's was 'Justin'. The three siblings were each one year apart, with Justin being the oldest and Pollyanna the youngest.

Dad seemed to harbor resentment toward Pollyanna from the beginning. But he was the only one who could soothe her in the evenings. He would lay on the couch, crooning with Pollyanna resting on his growling stomach.

She was an alarmingly cute baby. Sweet, soft, and a lusty howler. Baby Pollyanna was not deprived, but she felt as though she was.

Mixed up and confused, this baby was special. According to Mother she started speaking sentences from the beginning. She was bright beyond declaration, yet felt trapped by the constant competition with her brother and sister. This being Rexi and Justin who seemed to get more attention. Pollyanna often felt herself fading into the background.

Her loud, hearty howls often drew the attention she so desperately needed. Sometimes they ignored her until the crying had ceased. Her attentive, mother fed her with a spoon. Her father's name was Geoffe, and he was a belligerent monster. As time went on, she became aware of her father's dreadful behavior. She learned to use this knowledge to deal with him.

Everywhere she went she was shockingly shy, and deleted the memories she made as she went through life. Sometimes things are hard to forget, yet remembrance can come with great overhaul.

"Baby", as they called her, was the fiery underdog. Her brother played with feces from their dog out in the grassy backyard. He stank and stank and stank. He was grimy, gross, and unnaturally sadistic just like her father. Baby inherited her fearful outlook from them. She was highly self-protective. She had to keep her distance. Kindergarten was extremely fun for her, but her Dad's loud voice jerked her out of this reverie whenever he arrived home from work each day. No one had any patience for little Baby Pollyanna so she learned to entertain herself.

Through and through her babyhood seemed natural and normal. Rexi often showed signs of envy toward Baby. Baby was always just a little bit smarter, quicker, and more sure of herself. She came in a package with no instructions attached. Being the youngest, she benefited from experienced parents who knew how to bring up a child.

Sometimes she would play by herself, but more often with Rexi and Justin. Being so close in age, they knew how to react to one another with positive regard. This was the hand they were dealt in life, and they learned to live with it.

Justin was no ordinary brother. He chased Baby around the house and pinned her down with ceaseless tickling that made her scream. Mother and Dad turned a deaf ear, as this happened frequently.

Geoffe worked at a job that he hated, and often vented his frustrations on Mother and the kids. There was enough love to go around, but who got it all? Mother received most of the love, as the kids adored her endlessly. Enveloping their lives as young children, her love for them was innocent and pure. Geoffe's frustrations were a little bit harder to take, But he stood tall and demanding in a fatherly role.

Geoffe would make popcorn over the fireplace that burned in the living room on cold winter nights. The popcorn contraption was mysterious to Baby, who couldn't figure out how the kernels turned into such fluffy morsels of delight. They all ate it with happiness and Dad's abundant story telling.

The Christmas tree every year was exotic and magical with lights and strings of popcorn, numerous precious decorations from Grandma and Grandpa, and also baked ornaments that the children had made and decorated carefully. Every Christmas morning was sublime and absolutely dreamy. Everyone received gifts from each other. Mother and Dad always had plenty of surprises for them, as well as the stockings that were stuffed and hung above the fireplace.

'Corny', their big pit bulldog, always got a large, meaty bone that Justin had the privilege of giving to him. He was a naughty grey pit bull who loved the entire family, and was gentle and caring with Baby, for whom he had developed a soft spot.

Corny was a hazard when it came to leaving the pantry accidentally open. He would totally raid it and eat whatever he could, which happened about three times, conditioning Mother and Dad to make sure the pantry door was shut at all times, when not being frequented for food to make meals. The worst of times found Corny with a devoured loaf of bread and box of seventeen protein bars, wrappers on them.

Most often he was left outside where he pooped and peed in the yard and ran around barking at people with dogs passing by and at the mailman whom he hated and had on several occasions sprayed him with pepper spray at the mailbox that stood by the yard gate.

Corny was very protective of the three kids and lunged on the leash at other dogs when they walked together as a family around the small peninsula known as Park Haven on the waters of little Lake Recess.

Every year, starting with strollers for the young ones and tough restraint for Corny, the family walked around the park while the turkey was baking in the oven. Not only on Thanksgiving but at Christmas, too. It was a two-and-a-half-mile walk filled with fresh air, trees, water, and batches of poison oak off to the side of the path. There was a tree that had been struck by lightning and hung massively, broken midway up and crooked at this awkward juncture.

A nest of eagles dotted the view of the sky up above the tree packed interior of the peninsula. The walking path was smooth and covered with cemented gravel. Dad would carry Baby on his shoulders or in a backpack. Justin and Rexi ran along on their own as soon as they were able. The kids brought a rope, and Mother and Dad twirled it at each end so they could play jump rope. Justin skillfully controlled the soccer ball with finesse and playful energy, making it impossible for Baby or Rexi to take it from him. Looking forward to high school, he was the star player on the soccer team.

Reflexes

Every kid should regard childhood as a magical time of discovery and precious elation. Bolder and bolder they all got as years scrolled by on an animated level. Justin had a nasty habit of chasing Baby and pushing her down just to laugh and laugh at her helpless estate.

Rexi didn't know where she fit in, so she just did, making the most of everyday in her scheming with her brother and underlying envy of her sister. Immaculate to the last ball of dog hair on the floor of the hallway between the kitchen and the living room, Mother kept the "monsters" at bay when it came to cleaning things. The entire house was vacuumed from front to back and dusted at least twice a week. Mother was a neat freak and had a never-ending battle with dirt, and the feces that Justin tracked in from the yard outside. His little hands were covered in the excrement, and he rubbed it on his face. He was a little different in that his nerves were a little frazzled at the extremities making his hands and feet a little numb. He was also a little bit slow in his thinking, and had a habit of making loud noises that made no sense to anybody but Rexi, who understood her brother well. Baby was just a constant target for his need to corner and torture her with words and invasive, fathoming fingers full of faithless lust.

Despite his need to harness and harass her, Justin did love his little sister, Baby Pollyanna, and went out of his way to help her, like he did one day when she was coming home from school and got cornered by a big black lab. Frozen in fear, she watched as the dog ran back and forth in front of her, keeping her at bay and obstructing her way home. Justin, happened to be coming by a few minutes later and seeing the situation, he immediately charged at the dog, sending it away in shame with its tail between its legs. Justin took Baby's hand

and wiped away her tears. She hugged him and it felt awkward but nice.

Geoffe, the "monster" Dad, had a leather belt that he used sporadically on Justin when he got into trouble. Baby felt the sting only once, when she had lied to cover for her sister and brother about who stole tomatoes off the vine in the garden outside. Having seen what had happened she denied knowing anything at all. Dad finally got her to admit to the knowledge of the crime, ending up telling on her siblings. She had watched it happen; she had lied. Her punishment was for lying, even in defense of Rexi and Justin who had known better than to steal tomatoes, for which they were punished as well, for stealing and for lying.

All three stood at attention when Dad came home from work, making not a noise until he had settled in with Mother in the kitchen who would be making dinner. Dad sat silently in the living room, sighing big, huge sighs in his favorite leather chair with the leather footrest. Immediately the classical music station came on loud and obtrusive, as Dad hemmed and hawed away the stress from his day. He wanted more money. He wanted a better job.

Mother didn't have a job, and Dad wouldn't let her have one. She was a stay-at-home mother, who cooked and cleaned and kept everyone at peace with one another and entertained.

Each family member had a reflex behavior with regard to each other. It was almost better to be caught not doing anything at all, then to be caught doing something wrong or bad. Cherry picking came around each summer, and as the kids grew tall enough to climb the tree, they harvested cherries from the very highest branches of the tree filling buckets full of the big, bright, shiny, red and yellow Rainier cherries.

Corny loved to play in the yard with his army of toys and tennis balls. He loved to fetch. He liked swimming at Park Haven and chased the ducks all around. He torpedoed squirrels in the yard and attacked any unlucky cat that might climb over the fence. He had been known to kill two large cats. These had been a big, bloody mess.

Justin played with dog feces until he was eight years old when Mother's constant aberrations finally sunk in and Dad's belt had become widely feared. Somehow, he needed it. The feces, the naughty behavior that got him more attention. Mother was forever cleaning up after him and despised the house they lived in because it was "stained" with dog feces and other horrid messes such as dog vomit and bloody residue brought in from Corny's meaty bones. Also spills in the kitchen never quite seemed to totally disappear and as Mother said, the house stank with all that "shit and stuff". Everywhere in every room there was shit and stuff. The windows were streaked with constant wiping. Only when it was quiet, and the sun shone in could she relax outside in a lounge chair.

Mother cooked, did the laundry, dusting, and plant watering. She cleaned the kitchen as thoroughly as she could, and Geoffe, whom she loved, kept the yard mowed and the edges trimmed. She had her own glorious rose garden. She had a green thumb when it came to keeping the plants manicured and arrayed, fitting well in place. The garden was alive and beautiful.

Mother's favorite places were the kitchen and the elaborate garden. She knew the names of every flower blooming there, and that was not very limited. So many varieties of different types of plants made the yard a graveyard for the dead cats and occasional squirrels. It was a decorative place that the whole family appreciated with wonder and awe and admiration. So many colors, shapes, and sizes were the plants and flowers that only Mother could know the names of them all. She loved the weeding, transplanting, fertilizing and watering her garden of which she was the queen.

On one occasion a hornets' nest was found in the middle of a valiant purple dusted rhododendron. The nest started out very small and no one found it until one day when Dad was trimming the edges. As he neared the nest, he was surprised to find hornets bombarding him. One struck his forehead and stung as he ran around in circles swatting and screaming at the mad insects. Corny also got attacked, having dived into the rhododendron when he discovered their blatant activity. He was rewarded with a stormy cloud of tens of hornets pelleting his furry body and exposed eyes, nose, and ears. It was pathetic. He ran as far away as he could. Finally, the attack subsided.

The next day Dad bought a bottle of hornet killer and sprayed the nest. The hornets never came out again, and a week later Dad removed the dead nest and put it in the garbage can outside by the back alley. Corny forgot about the incident, yet remained ever wary whenever he neared that rhododendron bush.

Birthdays provided an exciting time for the family. Everyone gave presents, and Mother made each child their favorite dinner, plus a delicious birthday cake. The celebrated child would blow out the candles on the cake and make a wish. Then would come gift opening. This was constructively fun for everyone, and together they sang "happy birthday" to the happy birthday recipient.

Energy

Once in the life of each child, Geoffe would take a kid and go with him or her out for their "secret". When it came to Baby Pollyanna, Mother put the young child on a bus that she rode downtown. Mother told the driver where to stop for her child to get off. Baby was only eight. The bus ride was enthralling for her, and she bristled with energy when she saw her Daddy standing at the bus stop where he was waiting for her downtown. She hopped off the front seat and said "thank you" to the driver who waved goodbye as she clambered off the bus.

Dad and Baby Pollyanna's "secret" was to go to the market downtown and pick out some prime octopus meat with a jar of oysters, surprising everyone when they got home. Everyone sampled the oysters and chewed on the tough octopus meat. With much encouragement from their parents, the kids really liked the treat. "Oh, how good it was!" Sneaky, sneaky, each kid had their own "secret". Rexi got to tour a beer brewery, and Justin had a day at the local zoo. It was a proud family moment for each kid. No one felt slighted or jealous. The energy was positive and relational, due to obscure artifacts that were found along the way. From trips to the ocean there were sand dollars, shells, pretty rocks and photographs collected through the years.

One of Geoffe's mottos was to "make do with what you've got". So it happened that Justin once took it upon himself to demand a new, shiny fishing pole. He needed it to go fishing, he said. Geoffe responded sternly. He took a long stick, tied fishing line on the end of it, and put a hook on the line. When they had arrived at a good fishing hole in the river nearby where they lived, Geoffe, the monster, gave Justin a jar of salmon eggs. He baited the hook and dropped his line into the water. He did it mostly to please his Dad, not expecting anything to come of it. To his great surprise, he actually hooked a large rainbow trout and pulled it in. In all his excitement he didn't think to thank his Dad, but held up the fish for all to see. "Make do with what you've got", Geoffe repeated sternly and gruffly.

That same day, they looked up into the trees surrounding and saw a huge wasps' nest hanging there. Justin started to throw rocks at it, but Dad demanded the activity to stop and marveled at the nest so high and so huge. Having been recently stung in his own back yard, he ushered everyone quickly to the car before an angry wasp discovered them. "It's dumb to throw rocks at it," he lectured adamantly to Justin, who had no more hopes of going fishing. But Dad had proved his point. Justin was proud of his fish, his energy levels were high and excited. He needed encouragement at his age, being a little slow mentally, and dysfunctional with numbness at his extremities.

Life was really cool, but to be cool with his friends, he needed a new, shiny fishing rod and reel. So he saved his allowance money for a year and managed to buy one for himself. How he loved to go fishing with his friends Jeremy and Kyle. They were exclusively cool, except for occasional inclusion of Rexi in their forages of the deep ponds and fishing holes. Baby was never included. She was too young and didn't have entitlement to their coolness.

Baby had a disturbing memory of Justin exposing himself to her in the bathroom once. He took off his pants and told her to remove hers also. "This is what you have to do in the discos when you get a little older," he said and held out his hand wrapped around a little appendage between his legs. He wiggled it in his hands and thrust it at Baby's crotch. She screamed in shock when she discovered his intentions, quickly dressed and ran out of the bathroom leaving him in there with his own little disappointment. Baby was upset and wondered why Rexi hadn't been targeted in this "carnal" behavior, a word that she was too young to know or understand.

Baby's childhood was fraught with little favors here and there, as well as rejections and intimidating circumstances. There was the time that Mother got assaulted by a hapless roofer who was frustrated with his work and threatened to paint elephants on the ceiling in the kitchen where she screamed and violently pushed him away and out the front door. The worker never came back, and Mother never talked about the incident.

The house was filled with a creative energy. Rexi was a gifted artist, and ended up majoring in studio art when she went to college after high school. Justin, also, was a supreme artist and was able to draw anything and everything with expertise that no one could understand. He, also, graduated from the local art institute and dallied with architectural design. His cartoon drawings were spectacular, profound, and ultimately surprising. He majored in graphic design.

Counseling

Creative energy as well as barbaric lust cushioned and filtered throughout the rooms and the hallways of Baby's childhood house where she grew up. Despite their sibling rivalry, Baby and Rexi were best of friends, even closer than all their friends at school. They worked together, shared everything, and talked about everything under the sun. They spent hours in each other's rooms making up stories about whom they would marry and what to name their kids. They talked about Mother and Dad and the intense friction that tended to encircle their marriage and family life. Rexi felt sorry for Mother, the way Dad yelled at her as though she were just good for nothing.

Mother eventually burst out of her bind by enrolling in college and graduating from the University with a 3.98 GPA, majoring in intercultural relations. She was a natural, having moved to the U.S. with Geoffe when they first married. She came from Spain and learned the language and adapted to American culture.

Still, Dad was a threat to everyone's happiness for as long as he felt like an underling in the working world. He had his own consulting business and traveled a lot to different countries. Sometimes he would be gone for weeks or months, also being a sales representative for an assortment of curious products. Upon his arrival home, Mother bought lots of big construction paper, and the kids colored and made huge signs saying, "Welcome home, Dad!" that she hung throughout the house before he arrived home from his many trips abroad.

Corny got old and died from aging. The whole family was devastated at this loss. His body was left at the vet to be cremated. Baby insisted on getting two cats. Two so that they could play together and never get lonely. Mother and Dad gave in and bought two little tabby kittens with litter, litter box and food with a stern command that the kids take turns cleaning up after the little creatures. Geoffe found the cats repulsive, a nuisance, and critically dangerous with their sharp claws and teeth. Justin had an undying love for them, and Rexi tried to train them to do different things like sitting up and rolling over. Baby gloried in their soft and loving bodies, curled up all over her when she rested in her room on her bed after a hard day at school. Sometimes days were very hard. *Very* hard.

Baby grew depressed and no one knew why. Finally, Mother sought counseling for her. She had one on one therapy sessions for two years, exploring her feelings and avenues of projected betrayal. She felt like Daddy was mean and Mommy ignored her.

Her brother and sister were stoic pillars in her life, and she found that as she talked about them, she felt guilty about her denial of love for her family. It sickened her to be left out all the time. She had amusing friends in her bedroom, dolls and construction paper with scissors and glue. Paints, crayons, glitter, and colored pencils became the tools she wielded in confronting her inability to express herself.

Her counselor gave her exercises to do to improve her self-esteem. Baby was extremely bright in math, and her counselor encouraged her to join a math competition. She was good with computers, even from a young age she loved to experiment with Mother's Macintosh and cell phone. When she turned thirteen, she got her own first cell phone. Rexi and Justin each got one for their thirteenth birthday as well. Baby Pollyanna loved texting with her friends from school. Also, Baby took piano lessons and excelled at that musical endeavor. Her counselor instructed her to do exercises or join a sports team. Baby was inherently a below average sportsman in anything that required a ball. Her hand eye coordination was not very tightly mitigated, but one thing she became very good at was running. Long distance running that she could do by herself and still appreciate the toning and firming of her muscles, the health of her powerful heart, and peace of mind obtained from processing difficult emotions while on the road running to wherever she desired.

Baby's counselor also encouraged her to read books, and to practice reading all the time. So she did, and became fast friends with the library in town. Her grades in school were above average, if not perfect. Graduating from high school she left with a 3.5 GPA. This was an accomplishment considering all of Baby's shortcomings and emotional challenges.

She took anti-depressants throughout her freshman and sophomore years at high school. She successfully weaned herself off of them after that, and used running to deal with her difficult constitution and ensuing frustrations.

She was pretty, by all sorts, and not an eye sore to gaze upon. In fact, she attracted her first boyfriend in the ninth grade. This was during her first year of therapy. So, she needed a little boost into the world of adolescence, which included exploring cigarettes, weed, and alcohol. Her counselor was lenient with this behavior, knowing it would come to no harm, and deciding to advise Baby about the risks of addiction or illegal consumption in public places.

She was also encouraged to talk to her parents about these things, and to take advantage of the great love they had for her, and the many years of wisdom concerning the art of her growing up.

Finally, she realized that she did fit into the family, in her own quiet and wormy way. She clung to attention getters, and feel-good behaviors. She liked to make Dad smile, and tried to joke with him as he sat in his famous leather chair and listened to classical music. She would tease him and untie his shoelaces. She would pinch his knee caps and blow kisses at his face. She was rewarded with a clap on the back and an encouraging glance that forged a smile out of reckless leniency.

The davenport was another of Dad's most frequented spots. The problem was when he took off his shoes to lay down on it his feet stank, and the odor filled the entire room. Mother refused to let them tell him about it for fear of his own humiliation and embarrassment. It was worse in the fall, and not so bad at other times of the year. Pollyanna tiptoed quietly around her resting Dad, not wanting to incur a lashing comment about her supposedly naughty behavior, which was not really naughty, rather ingeniously explorative.

When she and Rexi had set up a beautiful and creative ranch with toys in the living room including horse models and Barbie dolls that had long hair they could comb and part and tie up in braids, and inventively color their faces with crayons like make up… Dad had no patience for the obstruction of living room space and angrily chased them and their creation downstairs to the basement play room which was nice but lacked windows to see outside. So, they would turn on the music down there and play the radio loud, turning it up with favorite songs and dancing and shouting and singing out of sight of Dad who permitted this reluctantly in a remote part of the house.

Baby's bedroom got cold in the winter so she would turn on her electric wall heater. Rexi prided herself on battling the cold and not turning on her heat to save electricity. Baby's bedroom was her sanctuary where she had her own bowl of goldfish and a radio with CDs to play. She was proud of her "library" of CDs, and listened to them endlessly. She also read while music was playing and created artsy crafty projects with all her coloring equipment and pads of sketching paper. Loving the cats, this was their favorite place to hang out. They would curl up on the bed, and stare rivetingly at the fishbowl. Baby's fish actually "danced" to the music she played. They kept her company. Justin was not allowed in her room, him and all his stinky cloud of dog feces. Rexi spent a great deal of time in Baby's room. Together they crocheted scarfs and hats like Grandma, on Geoffe's side, had taught them to do.

Baby spent twenty-three years in making a colorful patchwork crocheted blanket. When it was finished it was huge, decorative and beautiful. She was very proud of it. She kept it on her bed always, and loved lying on top of and under it. Rexi, being more skilled, actually crocheted sweaters too. Grandma had imparted this classic gift of learning how to crochet and actually excelling at it.

After two years of counseling, it all seemed to have helped, and Baby was a much happier person in the family. She learned to love going to school and working hard in all her classes. She was not the brightest of students, but managed to keep her grades fairly high.

Everywhere she went, there was an interminably curious cloud of followers all around her, who were attracted to her uncanny wisdom and deep insight into situations. She made a good friend to a lot of people, and knew, however, that no one was closer to her than Rexi.

Her first boyfriend was named Bryce, and he was an adoring companion who doted on Baby Pollyanna and kissed her in secret. By sophomore year he was old enough to drive his own car, which he had bought with his own money. He loved to drive around town with his "Baby" and stop at ice cream shops and burger joints and friends' houses.

They fondled each other in the car parked at Park Haven and had their first sexual experience in his bedroom at his house where he lived alone with his mother. Bryce's mother, Sarah, loved Baby and felt blessed that such a wonderful person was dating her precious son.

Bryce was not appreciated in the same way by Geoffe, the "Beast", who pounded on Baby's locked bedroom door and threatened to tear it down if she didn't open it up immediately. Poor Bryce crept out under the scathing eyes of Geoffe who held his daughter in esteem in a unique and jealous manner. What they must be doing played upon his imagination and his wrath was unforgiving.

From that day on they visited in the living room under Geoffe's watchful eye, who noticed every touch, smile, and endearing exchange with valiant overruling behavior, amusing himself by interjecting whenever he wanted with an obscure or disturbing comment. What sort of grades did Bryce get? What sports was he involved in? Did he go to church? Where did he buy his car? What did they have when they went out for dinner on any particular night? Was he screwing Baby, his precious daughter? At least, did he use a condom?

Baby was appalled, and poor Bryce took this intimidation by the Beast who atrociously attacked him every time they met. He ceased spending much time at Baby's house because her Dad made things so very uncomfortable. She was not to stay out past ten-thirty on Friday or Saturday nights, and she was not allowed to go out at all Sundays or weeknights after dinner. Finally, he relented and allowed Bryce to spend time with Baby in her bedroom with the door open.

Rexi observed the same rules with her boyfriend, Scott, who was a danger to society by sometimes driving when he was drunk. Sadly, he perished tragically in a car accident on his way over to pick up Rexi once to take her to a movie. The whole school was traumatized, and so was Rexi and her entire family.

Justin did not approve of Baby seeing Bryce. He was fiendishly jealous. He tried to humiliate her by accosting the two of them in the school lounge in front of a whole bunch of people that they knew from various grades. "Hi Baby, Hi Bryce!" he announced loudly standing between the two. Both targets being shy were mortified by public acknowledgement of their attraction for each other.

The discomfort passed and Baby and Bryce stayed together throughout high school, only separating when they went off to different colleges. This broke Baby's heart.

Sustenance

Mother and Geoffe did not go to church, except on Christmas and Easter services. They sent their three kids to Sunday school, however, beginning in the kindergarten. Every Sunday they would go to the neighborhood Presbyterian church and participate in Sunday school. It was probably the greatest gift they had ever bestowed upon their children.

Each Sunday they received education about the Bible, about Jesus, the Holy spirit, and God the Father; the holy trinity which was, in fact, One. This left the door open in later life for God to move on them, one by one.

Mother and Dad were usually cheerful when the kids came home, and asked how church had been. They never went to church services on a regular basis. Baby liked Sunday school and got on well with her teachers. The three took part in performances before the congregation at holiday services. They took turns playing piano while the Sunday school children would sing along with them. Piano was another gift of knowledge that their parents bestowed upon them.

Mother's mom from Spain, "Abuelita" was a widow and very depressed in her life. She visited the family on different occasions and would stay for a few or a couple of weeks at a time. Dad and Baby secretly abhorred Abuelita who was controlling and very verbally violent with her daughter. Baby had to scream out of her window once when the pressure got too great, and she didn't understand what they were talking about in loudly astonishing Spanish.

Dad and the kids knew a little bit of Spanish from school, and from Mom and Abuelita. The two argued continually, letting up for peaceful periods now and then where the house was at one with everyone and the processing of everybody was for the good of all.

One good note fell in that Abuelita loved the two cats to pieces. They brought her peace and contentment, and she spent hours sitting with them in her lap. She insisted on feeding, watering, and cleaning up after the cats while she visited. No one could complain about it.

Baby loved Abuelita, who had a Spanish Bible and read from it frequently out loud. There was something very spiritual about her visits. Although, she always held that Mom could've done better than Geoffe. She didn't like him and made herself known on that with intermittent comments and pointed negative ejaculations toward him. So Geoffe clung to Baby whenever Abuelita came, and kept her with him throughout the days as a buffer between himself and domineering Abuelita.

Poor little Baby was hungry often and didn't eat enough, or couldn't. Her favorite dinner, which Mom would prepare for her birthdays, was white rice, fried chicken, and artichokes dipped in a special white sauce, similar to Ranch dressing. She loved going out to pizza with the family. Mom and Geoffe made a practice of taking the whole family out for Vince's Italian pizza each time he came home from his business trips. There were a lot of those. As a mandatory educational exercise, each kid took a turn accompanying Dad on one of his business trips. Baby went when she was twelve years old. The purpose of these trips was to expose the children to other cultures at a young age. Baby and Geoffe went to Malaysia, Singapore, Hong Kong, Tokyo, and Thailand for a gap of two weeks. It changed her life forever. She settled into the lowest rung of the family's respective ladder.

Dad finally got another job, being a business professor at the local University. He remained reticent and withdrawn most of the years, paling at the image he purported as a young Dad with three obedient children.

Mother and the Beast were still together after many years of marriage. Justin is now married to Rachel with two kids, and Rexi has moved to Minnesota with her doting husband, Paul, and their three kids. They have two bird dogs and like fishing and hunting.

Excrement is no longer a fascination for Justin, just a consoling memory in the backyard. The cats remained alive for twenty years with Mother and Geoffe after everyone who moved had moved out. This incurs that Baby stayed living at home longer than her siblings as she attended University for six long years. Being broke, she practically had to live at home. Mother and Dad seemed pleased at this, as they hadn't counted on the pain of two children leaving the nest. One more gone would be painful for such empty nesters.

Baby studied to be a pharmacist. She also studied ecology, and environmental studies. She loved the outdoors and went hiking regularly in the mountains. She loved fishing in the hole where Justin had caught his first fish. She loved lying on park lawns and gazing up into the sky when it was blue, watching as birds circled higher and higher until they disappeared out of sight. Then more would come and fade above again. She liked swimming in Lake Recess, and learned how to windsurf there as well. She took lessons at a nearby recreational club. She had good memories of pedal boating with her best friend Lila. They confided in each other about everything, and told each other secrets that no one else knew about. She related to Lila about the incident with her brother in the bathroom when they were a lot smaller. Childhood incest. Sometimes she was gruesomely fearful of her brother, who still sought to corner and torture her now verbally and physically being intimidating in her face with accusatory sublimation that had no foundation. He would forever be a torment to her, and she wondered why Rexi was excluded from this ongoing punishment of character and hope. He amused himself at making her uncomfortable and feeling weak. He was susceptible of being a bully, a rapist, and a child molester.

Mother and the Beast gave no accountability of this feedback. Baby Pollyanna complained to her mother several times about the behavior, but Mother was in denial that any such activities would take place. The villain he was turned out to be the secret she kept, except for her friend and confidante Lila.

Baby and Lila spent nights gambling and getting drunk together. They trusted each other and weren't afraid of doing anything wrong. Or getting caught doing something wrong. They were oblivious to contra-adult expectations and did things that they knew their parents would not be approving of.

Baby squealed with joy whenever Rexi came to visit. Rexi understood about Baby and Justin, the conflicting feelings about wrong and right, yet she held to her own end of the bargain and had nothing negative to say about her brother. Why didn't her brother assault her? Baby would cry. In criminal regard he was guilty, having many times passed the line of acceptable behavior. In fact, in her late teens he had raped her abusively twice.

So, Baby walked around with a cloud of shame over her. Such a shame for such a beautiful woman. Exotic behavior was remorse in its constituent relegation of right versus wrong. Never before, and never after would the world of Baby be right to the text of the core. The unit of transaction between her and her brother was dark and desolate. Yet when he walked into the kitchen having come to visit Mother and Dad, there was a heightened sense of alarm in Baby that came out as a loud exhale and squeal of remorse. Mother and Dad didn't understand, but Baby flew into a rage and left the house when he was there. Yet still wasn't he just coming to visit his sweet sister and loving parents?

Dad had become a bitter man in his middle ages. What he had done to Baby on their trip to Singapore had been practically unmentionable. But it was tantamount and evident. He used and controlled her still, growling when she wasn't being positive, which she had to fake, but renegading her with guilt when she looked sad. What was his fault, what had he done to her? Where did this sense of wrong begin?

As the Beast took Baby on her assigned business trip, she cried out in protest. She didn't want to go and leave Mother. But it was her turn. Rexi had gone to France and England, while the Beast had taken Justin to Nigeria and then Egypt.

The Beast couldn't tame himself. His beautiful, innocent daughter, twelve years old, was so attractive and irresistible to him that he raped her. Her Dad drugged and raped her in the hotel in Singapore. She woke up in the morning feeling sick in her stomach, and Dad said it must have been something she ate. As they arrived home in the airport, Mom, Rexi, and Justin greeted them. Dad sternly told Baby to make sure she said that she had a really good time with Dad on his business trip. And that's exactly what she told them, having no lucid memories of the incident. There was no hard evidence that this was true.

Plentitude

No one ever found out, no one knew. But Baby harbored a mistrust when it came to her wonderful Daddy who always made her laugh and scream with delight. To an extent that was clearly unnatural.

Burdened with depression, she nearly committed suicide at one point, but found Jesus just in time. He saved her, coddled her, and took care of her in the home and wherever she went. One day the memories came creeping out of Baby in her dreams at night. They became more and more realistic as she had disturbing thoughts during the daytime, and she jumped without cause when Dad entered the room. Still, she smiled and laughed and "played" with him, making little ludicrous jokes and bantering about this and that. Together they watched football games and the Simpsons. They watched Anne of Green Gables together. Baby almost cried when she saw Anne kiss Gilbert at the end. Such a sweet and innocent life she had.

Still Baby didn't realize what had happened with her Dad in Singapore. She only knew that at some point in her youth she had lost faith in the world and construed her negative past to imprison charmed beliefs about the haven of her heart and the belittling of her unnatural pride.

She grew nonchalant and uncaring. But she loved the cats with an undying love. She took such good care of them, and laughed every time they assaulted the Beast.

Yet the hidden memory remained and came hurtling out of her into a standing up feeling of penetration between her legs as she leaned against the counter in the kitchen and her Dad sat at the table. The feeling was foreign, awful, and painful. She grew mad, and then mad at Dad from where the feeling was arising… and the next thing she knew, her mind was in Singapore with her Dad, and she knew it then. What had happened to disgrace her and make desolate her childhood? Perhaps it was the hotel attendants?

Baby was a changed girl when she came home from that awful trip. She couldn't play right with her friends at school anymore, and pretended to fit in but didn't. It became the story of her life, following her through high school and into adulthood. After expressing, the time came to accept what had happened and heal from it. She needed to deal with it. Her friends had just said that something was wrong, something was different about her. But what? She was careless about clothing and bought baggy garments that covered her in various colors that fit big and loosely. She started to wear high black leather boots and darker colors. Then she turned to light colors and wore a particular yellow colored sweater that she explained to her friend was to celebrate happiness. It was incinerating. A plentitude of faith concurrent with destruction.

She lost her childhood best friend Mariah who never understood why Baby had changed the way she did. Mariah didn't play with her anymore, and made fun of her in front of her friends. She just wasn't "cool" anymore. It was a sharp flip outward.

Dirty, marked, and controlled, her obscene thoughts took over and the memory emerged during Baby's second year of college. She presented it to her Mother who was shocked and distressed, in denial and vehemently disturbed. Mother told Dad, who stormed into the kitchen and screamed that Mother had told him that Baby said he had put a towel over her head and raped her in Singapore. He used the "f" word in his anger and stormed away again. Later in that evening Dad swore that if God found him guilty of the act, then would lightning come down and strike him. Baby implored God and sat in awe. Now she was wrong, now she was guilty of making up such a story. She cried out. She pummeled her Dad with fists and yanked at the hair on his balding head.

She swore at him, angry, bemused, shamed, forlorn, and broken. Her whole life was broken. Broken since that time after her trip abroad with the Beast, her Dad.

Not only did Mariah end their friendship, but she also became a lesbian and sought relationships with other girls that Baby would find impossible to be friends with.

There was a plentitude of laughing behavior and crying out with tears and distress. All over the years, her psyche had been processing her pain from the incident; dealing with the unacceptable nature of the crime, and the knee jerk denial reaction that happened after proclaiming out loud what had happened to her with her Dad. It hurt to the core. It explained her bouts of depression and need for anti-depressants during high school and years and then into adult hood.

Now having found God, it was easier to distance herself from the pain as the injustice healed and she grew into a person of pride and envy. No one knew her really, except for Lila and Rexi. Rexi was surprised at the news of Dad's raping his daughter, her sister, and told her it must not be true, and that Baby was breaking Dad's heart.

She grew guilty in her conscience and decided not to talk about it again. It was all told. Now let the healing begin. Up till this point she had been dealing daintily with this childhood obstruction, preparing to grasp it in all of its mortifying, consequential reality. Her inner turmoil was gestating in all of its oblique advantages, pairing up with an appreciation of nature and a good will with Jesus and all that he stood for in her life. She was forever grateful that her parents had sent her to Sunday school as a child. It made her ready to accept Jesus as her Lord and Savior when she was called upon and got older.

Enervating

very obscure detail of Baby's life resounded about before and after the incident. Having been a strong and vibrant youth, a great long-distance runner and avid sailboarder, strong swimmer and impressive scholar, she let her imagination fly as she sank into the world of books and reading. Her grades were better in college than in high school. Her most favorite college level class was an introduction to botany. In high school she favored chemistry and math. But it was environmental studies that really grabbed a hold of her the most. Then as a dream come true, she landed a job with a professional landscaping team. She loved getting dirty and working with nature, designing and caring for parks and other people's land.

Baby found the Beast intolerable, and never spoke to him about the incident again. It was buried, "forgotten", denied, and unreal. She was able to step back and see her Dad for who he was. She began to regard him with disfavor, until one time he yelled at her from the living room to stop treating him like "shit". He demanded that she come sit on his lap. And so, at twenty-two years old she sat on her old Dad's lap and consoled him, telling him what a good Dad he was, even though she knew he didn't think so. She sat there until he was quiet. Then she got up and decided to treat him cordially from then on. She wasn't the one with blame on her hands. But she did have the guilt, the pain, and the consequential shame.

As a child Baby had been energetic, proud, cheerful. She was afraid of nothing but continual assaults from Justin who cornered her and pinned her down more often than not.

Still the family was a unit, and Baby never again had to smile a fake smile. She bore the marks of remembrance to the evil perpetrated to her.

She married when she turned twenty-five, and had two miscarriages. She and her husband decided to adopt, but to wait for a while until the time was right, to be sure it was what they wanted. She got pregnant again and miscarried once more. So, her husband, Jeremy, decided to have a vasectomy. This was the same Jeremy who had played together with Justin and Kyle when they were kids. Jeremy never went to Sunday school, but Kyle did with Justin.

Somehow, Jeremy came to Christ in his early twenties as well, and was an avid Christian when he and Baby began dating in their mid-twenties.

They talked about Justin's misbehavior against his sister. Jeremy gave him a good talking to, and came home with a broken nose and arm that night. They never spoke about it again. Still, Justin cowered in the presence of Jeremy whenever the two were in the same room at family gatherings. Rexi had married two years prior to Baby, her husband was named Paul. They had met in college. They had three gorgeous children.

Justin, over the years, had somehow grown out of his need to assault his baby sister. They simply didn't talk to one another except in passing. At family reunions Mother and the Beast's grandchildren all played together as super-duper cousins who got along marvelously. Baby, Rexi, and Justin with their spouses sat around and talked and drank wine. There was little to be said between Justin and Baby Pollyanna. Rexi was adept at communicating around and between them to somehow keep the peace. Mother and the Beast, now a little older simply enjoyed being with family whom they missed so much after the nest had been emptied. Even Baby had moved out with Jeremy into their own place. Unsuccessful in having kids, they were the sore leg on the horse with the sob story of three miscarriages. They still hadn't decided to adopt. Instead, they had three cats, a bird, and a small lizard. Against all odds, Baby kept the home clean, sanitary, and pleasant despite the handful of pets. They loved their animals.

Pollyanna was desperate to overcome her drought of depression. Even Jeremy struggled with her base opinions of life at some points, and he knew to be there as a supporting husband, friend, and lover. Jeremy and Justin were now in- laws. Kyle still hung out with Justin, and Jeremy, but on differing occasions. They had all grown apart and struggled to keep the friendship's peace alive. Kyle and Jeremy were Christians, but not so with Justin who walked away from the faith early on from what had been learned in Sunday school.

Tubular vendettas flowed throughout the family. Baby was mostly quiet in their presence, while Rexi was logical and an apt communicator between the taut relations of Justin and Baby, who barely talked at all, their brother/sister relationship being tainted by violent behavior.

Only Rexi and Paul with their kids lived far away from "home" in Minnesota. Rexi understood her sister and loved her completely, always trying to bolster her attitudes and to lift her spirits. Deathly silent was the communication between Baby and the Beast. They leaned on everyone else to support their familial inclusion. Mother as always was quiet on the subject of the "incident" in Singapore that no one ever talked about. It was even doubtful that Justin had any clue about it at all. Still, Baby didn't like to dwell on her past, something her sister warned her about as being unproductive and of little help to her situation. Better to let go and move on, she said, whether or not this incident had ever truly happened or was it all a big story to get attention?

Faith and solace held hands with Baby, as she surrounded herself, her soul, her heart, her curious spirit, and even her body with healing from Jesus.

He was the only one who fully understood everything, even though Jeremy was also very supportive. Jesus was in their lives to the core. Subjunctive, imminent, and conducive dreaming at night woke her up crying out from horrid, explosive nightmares. She was stupid to herself, never giving herself much credit, and dying each day with the opinion that she didn't count at all. Her needs were not important. She could never do right by Jeremy, and her Mother and Dad just didn't know her.

So it was, that sadly, after five years of marriage, Baby asked for a divorce. She didn't know why, she just hated having to be falsely happy with her husband. She wanted kids. Not adoptive kids. Yet she didn't even feel as though she were responsible enough to have kids, thus labeling herself as a dysfunctional parent without ever trying.

Jeremy was so upset with the divorce, he moved away to live in Texas. Home, in the Pacific Northwest where he had lived his whole life was now saturated with sad memories. Point blank, he fussed over moving with himself. He knew he loved Baby Pollyanna, and that he couldn't make her happy, no matter how he tried. It was vegetarian lasagna in the fish soup. It didn't mix well with him in even the cookie dough batter with bacon and cheese and dill pickles. He wanted to vomit up his feelings of failure and be conducive to his delicate position. He couldn't please Baby; he hated her brother and was forced into the position of starting over somewhere else.

Flattery

Changes over time come to everybody. Even poor Baby, in her sad estate began to heal and turn over her place in life. Her divorce with Jeremy came as a surprise to her when she decided to do it. No matter whom she talked to, she couldn't change her mind about it. It was sad, but she no longer felt suicidal. Thanks to Jeremy and Jesus, she had made it this far. Jeremy was like a pulled sore tooth, crying to be evicted from the gum. It couldn't be replaced, but the sore could heal over through time. There would be no reminder of Jeremy at all, except whenever she saw Kyle with Justin. Justin and Rachel were a struggling happy couple. Their two children, a boy and younger girl were cute as could be and very well behaved.

Baby loved the little children, for as much as she silently abscond her brother. Now in Jesus, she came to accept and to forgive him for his provocative behavior in the growing up years.

Letting go of fitting in, she flattered herself in taking pride in her work, landscaping for a local community college and various business establishments. It touched home when work began at Park Haven, and she assumed the position of overseer at that job. She was physically strong, and working with plants, rocks, water, soil, every outdoor problem such as poison oak and out of control blackberry brambles as well as fertilizing and pruning back fruit trees became ambivalent, activity done thoughtlessly that gave her a chance to process and supplant evil thoughts for good ones.

She prided herself on the responsibility that came easily to her. She knew what she wanted and went after it. She was a delicious team worker, everyone counted on her to make the taste of the day more special and finished and successful.

Being outdoors so much was healthy for her constitution. She thrived on getting along with coworkers and people in positions of authority above herself.

She aspired to be working in the zoo around animals and tourists, but the job never arose for the taking. She made meals for herself and flattered herself for the success she had in this arena. She never put lasagna into the soup or bacon in the chocolate chip cookies. Everything she made complimented everything else she made. She experimented with various recipes, and admittedly missed making dinner with Jeremy. In fact, she did miss him. But left it at that. She was a failure, socially, morally, and instinctively. She was sad about the divorce but spent a lot of time with Lila and her family who had never moved far away either.

Lila comforted her when it came to the divorce and separation. She felt for her friend who struggled with depression and inhumane conduct. The Beast stayed remotely distant from his baby daughter. He never frequented her apartment, even when Mother would come by. Mother always brought a cake or a pie she made. She always remembered Baby's birthday, and stood as a huge support in helping Baby process through the divorce and aftermath. Baby worked full time. She buried herself in the process of working a full schedule and maintaining herself as well. Team working suited her well. She had fulfilling social interaction on a daily basis, and was proud to see a work when it was done.

Lake Recess boasted of a small rowing facility for the local community crew team. She would watch as the boats went by on both sides of the peninsula that made Park Haven. It was so serene and softly beautiful to see the people rowing in time with each other and gliding along in angelic design. Crew was something she wanted to try. She was a great swimmer, avid sailboarder, and this, this crew, appeared so enticing she could hardly keep from stopping there every time she drove by. She wanted to take lessons. She longed for it.

She flattered herself with her toned and muscular body that came from all her hard-working days. Her mind was basically peaceful, and she read books long into the nights. She had no urge to move away. She remained compliant with herself and prayed daily, involving herself with Christ and all his healing and loving effects. There was no one like Jesus, she knew, and believed in him whole heartedly. Beyond that, she found little belief in other people, except for Lila, her husband Rusty, and their two kids. She also struck a chord with Mother. Mother listened. She understood. She cried with Baby Pollyanna, but they never talked about Singapore again. Instead, they spent time walking together, crocheting together, baking together, and laying in chaise lounges together in the backyard while the Beast puttered around noisily working on projects about the house. He never finished. There was always something that needed to be made better, stronger, more aesthetically pleasing. Baby and Mother took care of the yard, the trees, the gardens. The newest arrival was a row of raspberry bushes. Everyone crossed their fingers for them.

Sometimes Justin and Rachel would come by, with or without their two kids who had school. Baby got along permissively with Justin who was extremely submissive and humble in her presence.

She felt a negative response every time she saw him, and regarded Rachel with a bit of humor and perplexity. What did she see in him? Baby knew. He was rapturously funny and loud, talking all the time and being bossy. He made a good head of the house, and she was respective of his natural but bullish leadership.

Justin was a staunch Dad, bossing his kids. Also, not a good brother to Baby. But it seemed, as time went by, and Baby was increasingly successful, that he worked on trying to talk with her, if only a little small talk to begin with. Baby's gut would writhe in fury with horrible memories of being pinpointed by him, raped, and assaulted. Maybe they were kids, maybe no one knew. If he wasn't sorry, at least he was remorseful and he idolized her.

Mother would watch the two of them with a little smile on her face. She knew something. Something only a Mother could know. She knew of Justin's slowness in thought and about his numb fingers and toes. His thoughts were thick, repetitive, forgiving, yet demanding as well. What he wanted needed to be done right then and right now. He didn't take well to rejection and felt abhorrent about his friend Jeremy marrying Baby in recluse of a foreign matter. Taking the twin turn around, he begot anger with suicide, and killed himself morally each day as a failure and a drunk. Jeremy, still in Texas, was never to return.

He was a failure, Justin, in everything he tried to do. Just opposite of his sister, Baby, he had trouble finishing projects, even if he tried hard to put his mind to it. Shaken up and condensed, his personality was pathetic, remorseful, stupid, "shitty", as Baby saw him, and boring, aesthetically repulsive, hindering to faith and everything he had ever learned about religion.

Several times he had tried calling Baby in her apartment where she now lived alone. Baby listened, repeated what he said in other words, and said goodbye before hanging up incompetently witnessing his faith and reserving judgment for later when she seethed with mild fury, that came out with a reading of Scriptures. Fornicating was evil. Her brother had fornicated with her abusively, with evil mandate and horrible, invasive intrusion.

Her shame relentlessly poured out of her as she worked every day and saved her money. As time went by, her creativity blossomed and her ideas on the job were quickly accepted and admired with audacity and reserve marked by beauty. This flattery poured healing ointment on her head, her body, her going in and coming out.

Fashionably compliant, she was a good-looking lady with serene aptitude shining from her glowing eyes of faith and eradication. She never eradicated pleasure, and found great satisfaction in running for miles and miles… in fact she ran a marathon, about 26 miles, and loved it so much that she ran two more and then once again every year that passed for the next ten years. She loved it. It made her feel alive, worthy, accounted for, and sublime. Her imagination took off with the pounding of her feet on pavement, through wooded areas, and across open fields and bridges. She admired those who did triathlons, but couldn't find it in herself to be so adept at swimming and biking. Marathons were her "thing" and she excelled at them.

She flattered herself with this achievement, with the moments that went by, and she could sense healing in her body and her psyche, her spirit and soul. Her heart was strong. She needed little other exercise outside of work, which kept her busy and intensely fit.

Even in the night when she had nightmares, her mind would go to running mode and begin to process through extremely painful mental data.

It wasn't for two or three years after the divorce that she even thought of herself as lonely. Her soul had been so slashed and burned for a long, long, time. Everywhere she went, her bruised ego tried to stand up for itself. She took revival from the Bible, which she made a point of reading from everyday. Along with prayer and church, her spirit turned over and over in interface with the Lord, making a spiritual soup of vendetta versus self-control maintaining a good human constitution or creation of God. She came to her maker in many ways on every day that came and went, and she blew like a feather in the wind.

Severely emotionally scarred, as well as relating to her body's physical memories she went around withdrawn into herself, a moon snail most of the time sealing her shell around her whenever she felt threatened. Baby also liked snorkeling when she would go with Lila to her family's retreat on Puget Sound. She spent many days there,sunbathing going in and out of the water, and eating and drinking like each day was a holiday.

Her tanned body so fit and toned was awesome to perceive. This also flattered her submissive ego and gently boosted it. Together they went hiking on the Olympic Peninsula to beautiful destinations like Lake Constance, and Hurricane Ridge. They did ocean hikes along the Pacific Coast and camped on beaches along the way.

Baby never really traveled outside of the Pacific Northwest. She knew it like the back of her hand and loved the climate and living there. Home to several ski resorts, Baby found her ski legs a little here and a little there across the Northwest, never really excelling but enjoying herself, nonetheless. She took lessons, but never really captured the essence of perfect skiing.

She had never seen a bear. She saw buffalo, moose, deer, elk, owls, eagles, and rabbits. She hated road-kill. Like dead dogs and cats and raccoons in the road. She saw garter snakes when picking berries, and envied people who walked their dogs. She had a grand appreciation for horses, although she knew barely anything about them. She liked going to the Washington State Fair and seeing the animals, art, jewelry, and rodeo as well as concerts in the small outdoor amphitheater.

Lila was her friend and companion throughout her many forages around the area, and they had dinner together every Friday night. It was Lila who suggested that she start looking for a "mate". Little Baby was shy and non-solicitous. She told Lila that her best chance at finding someone suitable would be in the church that she attended. Yet she didn't want to go advertising herself, and she didn't like the idea of initiating any sort of relationship. Maybe it was better to let go of the idea and pray to God about it.

Still, she felt like a sinking ship. Water was coming over-board and lapping at her toes. She couldn't escape the deep, and knew that her upset could best be treated with a therapist. Lila was fond of the idea. She knew her friend well, and all the ups and downs that she faced on a daily basis. She seethed with hatred for Baby's brother, Justin. Justin was a thorn in everyone's toe, causing pain and discomfort on a regular basis with all his complaining and angry demands. He was inconsequential and forlorn, helpless, and self-despising. His darkness was a funnel of hallowed ground chopped up and stirred down into a fertile well of water. He drained the joy from every situation, yet insisted that people listen when he talked.

Justin no longer went to church, and hadn't ever since Jeremy started to date his sister. His greasy, grimy hands needed to claim her as his own in every situation whatsoever. But Baby grew so standoffish, that he sullenly regarded to take in his abusive relationship with her as a galley in her sinking ship. They had a history of his abusive fornication with her. It supplanted immortality in her mind, and she doubted greatly that her brother would ever make it into heaven.

She was in check with his reality, and understood all his tricks and schemes. He was a local loser with a lost plate of cookies. No one liked him, Rachel barely tolerated him, and sunken deep into his silent repose was a deep and gallant hatred of himself. He was no ordinary hero. He was despotic and festering.

Baby and the Beast maintained a mutual silence and falsehood among disrespect and natural shredding of emotions. No one could make laughter in a room that they shared, and no one could understand the dark silence. Yet he planned and plotted.

Baby came to wonder if she could trust her Mother as well. Or were the two of them against her? How could Mother stay with this ugly beast? Growling, ornery, frustrated and contemptuous, he kept to his own quiet recluse of reading newspapers and occasional books. He still watched football. He still went for short walks. He hated her, that bitch, but didn't know who that was. It was just her. Her condemnation infuriated him. He found no consolation in himself. He refused to go to church with Mother, who neither went herself. Theirs was a sinking ship as well, although as by a tsunami, rather than a gentle closing of water over the top. Baby could still climb up the mast of the ship and hail to other boats to come rescue her. And this she did. So, she met William. They were in church one day and she had noticed that he was relatively new. She approached him to shake hands and introduced herself as Pollyanna, but that most people knew her as "Baby". William was touched by her soft demeanor. He was instantly attracted to her natural beauty, and her great self-confidence. As the weeks passed, he became proud to know her and made a point of sitting near her in the sanctuary.

Baby was thirty-three years old when this angelic relationship began. The two hit it off like the best of friends. He, too, had gone through a divorce, and his wife had died soon after. They were quiet and meek in each other's presence, and confounded their own consciences with belittling attitudes of tremulous avid constancy. Overcoming the nature of suicide, each had passed from hopeless to hopeful in life.

William was several years older than Baby, he was forty-three years old. The age difference didn't matter, and turned out to be a good thing for her in that he was mature and capable of understanding what she had been through in life till now. It was then and now, and now and then. For both of them. They could relate conclusively. Baby warned him about the three miscarriages. He didn't deny trying.

They would marry, but not yet. There was no need, and commitment was a hard subject to conquer. Every time they came to the end of a line, it seemed, a new one would arise taking them somewhere else both mentally and physically, morally, and with justice.

Their faith in God tied them together as equally yoked Christians. This was important to Baby who had depended on God all her life just to get through. There was nothing he could do to disappoint her, she was tragically disposed to everything around her and exercised her self upon the environment, rather than the environment preying upon her. Her world was small compared to his, yet his personality carefully crept around her with love and affection.

Mother met William and so did the "Beast", Geoffe. William took no liking of him, yet remained on good terms with Baby's mother. This was all for show for sure, yet expeditious or naught, there was little to do but show face and talk and smile and shake hands in the beginning.

Baby slowly crept out of her hole. Her moon snail self oozed out of its shell and put its fleshy lobe upon the sand beneath her. She loved it. She exceeded her limitations in love and in life, and found that life could indeed be beautiful. She flattered herself with love. She grew miraculously strong.

Baby prayed daily, she walked with the Lord Jesus. She benefited from his love for her, from his guidance and wisdom.

Baby knew her brother and Rachel and the two kids lived nearby yet they did not keep up relations. Only when Rexi came to visit with Paul and their three kids did the whole family get together. Baby shined with William whose gracious character was quietly serene and complimentary of everyone. Justin made an attempt to talk with William, and couldn't seem to shut up. The talking went on and on through the nights and days and nights and days. Justin couldn't figure it out. What did William have that he didn't? Was it just Baby? Who had his Baby Pollyanna? Wasn't she his to use? Where did he come from, so tall and handsome, educated and wise with a quick sense of humor that saved many conversations?

Justin insisted that William go fishing with him. Without Baby. Baby was no fun. She didn't get it. She couldn't cook dinner, and her words were stunting to him. Baby hated him, yet loved him in the Lord with all forgiveness.

William never did go fishing with Justin, just another insult added to his self hatred.

Insidious

Creeping like a caterpillar on a log, Baby's life had been long and laborious, yet as a caterpillar will morph into a butterfly, so did Baby grow beautiful wings of freedom. She hated suicide and was glad to glory that she'd never done it. Her life with William was far greater than anything she had ever known. They spoke of marriage and decided to wait and consider things. They wanted a foundation to build on, not to be thrown together illustriously. Their foreign intent was to please one another, thus receiving pleasure in thanksgiving and returned good will and joy.

Baby came to understand "joy". She wanted a baby but knew better than to try for that. She kept herself well protected. Sin came and went, for where there is true life, sin cannot factor in.

Glamorous and lovely, Baby shown like the sun on a beautiful day. She blew like the winds in the trees, and rippled like water touching sun on a lake. Her home was like the mountains bordering upon the lakes. Her waters were fertile and joyously bountiful. The outdoors explained all of her contemporary sadness with touches of betrayal. Her enemy came and went. It was a sad thing. Her need for love, and loving touch was a pleasure for William who gently held her, touched, her, and stroked her. Together they fit like crayons in a box. Yet with an eloquence that touched like champagne on New Year's Eve. It was a new life, a turning over of the good from the bad. An equality that resided against impertinence and ineptitude. Belonging to each other, they resisted nothing but the devil, which would always flee away.

The Beast couldn't believe his eyes when he saw the changes coming over his baby daughter. To him she was still a girl he could control and use, and keep quiet as with a fist in the mouth.

His repulsive action was to try and make William drunk in order to tease humiliation out of him. It never worked. The Beast would get drunk first, watching William work his magic with the Lord, losing faith in caricature and gaining leverage upon the nuances of trust and despotic opinion.

Mother felt sorry for Dad, and everyone wondered how she kept up such a good front. If not for Rexi, the whole family would collapse.

Disdainful and perplexed, reaching out to Baby became a favorite habit for everybody, who respected her firm resolve and wisdom with a listening ear. She always offered good advice and was an inspiration through the many achievements in her life. She knew how to speak and write a little bit of Spanish, and she was a cushioning welcome whenever Abuelita came to visit. Abuelita who died before Baby and William married, a sadness in itself.

Her ashes were dumped overboard in the Mediterranean Sea where her husband had drowned many years ago. Maybe her death was a great release. Without Abuelito, her life had been a long up going battle against everything that came her way. She could not find satisfaction anywhere or in anything, except for the Bible and its many teachings and wisdom filled content. Losing Abuelita was like losing a toe off of Baby's foot. It would always be apparent in her turn of history and memories of childhood. Something she missed when she thought about it, despite the many emotional challenges that Abuelita had set forth, when Baby and the Beast secretly despised her. She felt sorry about this now. Yet at the time she couldn't handle her violently emotional Abuelita who always said that Mother could've done a lot better than Geoffe.

Geoffe became sullen and grumpy as he got older. Every holiday resounded like a pain in his gut. He trudged through dry and dusty roads in his life, no oasis in sight. His only oasis was Baby, who seemed to have all his answers for questions he hadn't yet even asked.

Little Baby, was an aching fingernail jammed up with a tough screw fashioned with a bolt. He remained paralyzed in his ability to socialize with her and didn't understand where she was coming from whenever she addressed him. Her foundation was resplendent with forgiveness splattered with nullified relation. Perpendicular to her oneness with God, there was an elevation in her that he could not aspire to. She was happy and he was miserable. Baby was content with that.

The Beast and Mother always had a welcome mat at their door for any family members. Justin sought their company the most, and dallied for hours in the living room with Geoffe, discussing who knows what. They seemed to have a plan to travel the world together founded by and for Baby whom they saw and thought to undermine them. They took turns wondering at her strange estrangement. Why couldn't she sit around and laugh and talk with them, or glow like she shone when in the presence of William, her prospective mate who shunned them yet remained contemplative and cordial around them. Both Baby and William felt contempt for that branch of the family. It was in Rexi's presence that everything came together. She knew how to clap her hands and change the topic of discussion with lightning speed. She protected Baby, who, now, with her self assurance needed no more protection. She'd had her fill of taking shit from her Dad and her brother, and only kept the peace for the sake of Mother.

Lila stayed around forever. She was one of those who would not die on the way to heaven. She was ready and expectant of it. She prayed each day and into the night when she thought about Baby and William who were definitely saved also. Rusty was a wonderful husband to her, and her kids were a huge blessing. She felt for Baby who had no children of her own. Maybe it was best that way. She needed her self to depend on right now, and children just didn't fit the picture with her self-image.

Baby was strong and confident, and knew for a fact that she wasn't going to hell, remaining strong in position with her faith. Congruently disposed, she found joy in the morning and peace throughout her days. Her nights were sound, and she seldom had recurring nightmares anymore. She was fit and trim to a tee, and still made use of the library to sate her hunger for reading. When she was tired, she rested, when she wanted to run, she ran, for miles and miles. She liked riding on the Washington State Ferries as a passenger, and sometimes went back and forth twice before disembarking. She watched the seagulls floating above the deck, keeping pace with the vessel and swooping up and down with the wind on their wings. The sun on the water was beautiful, and so were the sailboats that dotted the scenery.

Insidious and encroaching on her perplexed vaunt of wisdom she mattered little to those around her, or so she surmised with an inherent bout of shameful demeanor. So she smiled at passing strangers and said "Hi" to people she met. Her childhood so viciously marked made her sure that she didn't want kids. She feared being a disappointing mother or inadequate role model. Her intrinsic behavior was God fearing and totally committed to a healthy Christian faith. Benefactor of wisdom, she crushed her foe, the disdainful energy with positive regard for everyone and everybody. She spoke and people listened. She cried and friends supported her. Her Mother was dominating to a certain extent. She was crazy and ludicrous with insidious façade and total annihilation of anything to do with Jesus whom she had never met and didn't want to give the chance for something so fraudulent and introspective. So she did yoga, book clubs, and group mountain hiking. The Beast read his magazines and newspapers. He refused to get a cell phone, and had never worn a wedding band.

His leaky roof sang of a lazy disposition, Biblically so. Even back when Mom was attacked by one of the many roofers who had come, the job was never successfully done. The house still leaks when it rains hard, despite whatever Geoffe attempted to do to it.

To this day he hasn't been struck by lightning as he had vowed so viciously long ago in the revelation of his misuse of Baby on their trip to the far East. He remained reticent and in control, or so he thought he was in control. Little did he see the unfolding of truths before him, wafting off to the sides and escorting him latently towards some unknown far off conclusion. He dug in his toes, but couldn't stop feeling like he was slipping and sliding.

Now adjusted to their "empty nest" Geoffe determined that it was time to get a dog. So he bought a Rottweiler puppy, female, and gave her to Mother as a Valentine's present. It was a delight for her, and she named it Strawberry. She walked Strawberry every day around the neighborhood and up into the hills. She came back feeling release of pent up emotions, unable to shake the worry that she was failing at something. Something wrong, something right. Her initial attempt to remedy this insecurity had been to seek counseling for herself. No one really knew Mother, not even Dad. She was so into herself, her disappointment in life, and she had a lack of any dependable male role model. Having lost her Dad, Abuelito, many years ago, she had aged with the wisdom of a bitter wife, cursory and ineffective. She hated Geoffe yet remained by his side and no one knew why or even to question it. Her paralyzing visual effect came in a competent and relentless ardor for her garden in the big yard where Strawberry now spent her days.

Mother was compliant about everything, and jocular about any sexual innuendoes. She knew that Baby and William were sleeping together, as if this mattered to her. She pushed and shoved her way around the house, making messes of all that "shit and stuff" everywhere. It had been long years since Justin had played in dog shit and brought it into the house all over his clothes and his face. Her shrieking spirit despised every move he made, yet he was her pride and joy, the oldest child and her only son. She doted on him and he turned to her like a child sometimes.

Wisdom filled the home whenever Baby and William came to enjoy dinner with the old folks. They did so more out of pity than obligation. Mother and the Beast made horrible hosts to them and tripped over every family rule, including everybody diving into the food whenever Dad said to "go for it!" Baby loved Strawberry and questioned her Mother as to why she had chosen that name. Apparently it reminded her of the days way back when she took the kids yearly to a strawberry U-Pick berry farm. It really was an island of joy in the loud sea of earthly trouble and familial stresses. The keepers of the strawberry fields where they picked had had a Rottweiler whom the kids had loved to play with. She had good memories, fond ones, and her heart spewed out this treasure in her daily walks with Strawberry. Things go wrong in life, sometimes, she thought, and had definitely gone wrong between Baby and Geoffe, on their token business trip. A part of her believed the story from Baby, yet her very stern opinion of goodness in life eloquently betrayed this opinion in ransacking and turmoil founded deep with hatred and loss of trust. But she had Geoffe under her thumb. He needed her. To betray the truth and set him free from his own negative conundrums. Every time he turned around he faced another obstacle, and often ran into the same obstacles over and over. Baby and the Beast never danced at Baby's first wedding. He would not be invited to her next one.

Baby had trust issues compliant by her Mother's remorse and faltering opinion of her. Everything pointed at Baby, in Mother's eyes, as being the fault of everything wrong in the family. She blamed her daughter for being deceitful and successful in the face of disrespect and violent abuse.

Baby had graduated from college, and was held in high regard due to this success. She had a profitable and fulfilling job and managed life like a pro, even cruising through her divorce, which had come as a shock to the family. The Beast held her accountable and constantly badgered her on this failure in life. To him it was a credible loss, making sense of nothing but the paranoid "nothingness" of his daughter who never laughed with him anymore and who brought animosity into his presence and even long after she had left. Baby wanted justice, for the horrible behaviors of her Dad and her brother. But she didn't know how to get it. She knew from the Bible that vengeance is the Lord's. So she loosened her grip from squeezing her heart in faith and love to realize the altruistic forgiveness called for in this situation. She knew that without it she would never overcome.

Mother and Baby didn't see things eye to eye, but they could focus together on the same things. Baby was perplexed and wondered if her Mother would make it to heaven. She was most certain already that Dad wouldn't. Neither would Justin. Was this punishment enough for them? Or did they recall from the hope and glory of witnessing to a faith that was stronger than any of them? Here she was, Baby Pollyanna. People looked up to her. People admired her. She was a shining role model for all kids of the younger generation. She even spoke kindly to Justin's kids, if not to him alone.

Baby's suffering had been so deep, she had developed an uncanny reality of being able to read others' minds to a certain degree. She knew what people thought before they spoke it. It was an ingrained ability, quite austere in the beginning, but building up to a huge factory of hope. It began with fitting in, to her insidious family cluster, and overcoming faith and destination with her purpose and content. She remained insightful, wise, as many could so attest, and afraid of virtually nothing at all.

Her clinging grasp to the Father in heaven, kept her on her toes. He spoke to her. She listened.

Life was no longer insidious for Baby Pollyanna and she blossomed with William in her life and by her side. They would talk for hours about many different things. They shared themselves, and they shared Baby's apartment, for William had moved in with her temporarily. Having always saved money, she and William now juggled the idea between them of moving out together into a country home somewhere beautiful and partly remote. William urged this change to happen, but Pollyanna was not yet certain of the idea. She loved her job. She loved Lila and Rusty's family, but she loved the idea of not being under her parents' thumbs more. Moving into their own home would give her a release from a sordid past, and distance from her brother. Even Rexi had moved away a long time ago, somehow knowing of the failures and despotic truths of the family, not wanting to confront it head on.

Baby's growing up agenda signaled for a great change in her life for the better. Her resolve to overcome made it necessary to overcome the differences she had with her Mother and the Beast. The insignificance of her removal placed her on a waiting list for assistance in her journey of life. She felt remorse, and cancellation of hurts, turgid and vapid emotional valor, and safe keeping of her witness through faith. To her own testimony she had more than two angel visitations that had helped her significantly. In her instructive medium, she kept to herself and talked to herself through a lot of situations. She factored with resistance and regurgitated hope from the many healings she had received from several of these life changing experiences.

Her hold on the Father was greater than her hold on anyone else. She saw it in herself to let go of the Beast, not to count on him in goodness for anything at all. Strange but beautiful, she overcame her fluid destiny before it reached her. Her boat never sank, she was rescued from above. She was compliant to nothing, suicidal in disgrace, and receptive of the nonchalant demeanor that oozed from the creation of her character.

She choked on the venom from her Mother and father, belching up great coughs of disgust and horrific, wracking cleanup. Her approach to life was to cleanse herself from the past, and thus put a cap on her healing, which would go on forever to a place of reprise, where healing would be manifest and forever impounded on her nature, belligerent to nothing else, and sacred and qualifying to her own abhorrence for the Beast. For Mother? She felt energetically forgetful. Her history for Mother had been detrimental to her character, and unable to qualify her for regress or solemn motive in the procedure of belonging. Her wasted approval often came as a joke, with a laugh and smile so convincing of her love. But was it there? Did Mother really love Baby Pollyanna? Her youngest daughter. Her hope for immortality. She knew somehow that Baby was her key to salvation. She knew not what or how, but rather sensed the value in her daughter that would equate to deliverance. Disrespectful demise formulated passionate opinion about the chance of recovery to hope.

She was expeditious about her prostration with the devil, not even sure if a devil existed in truth. Boring sometimes, her husband rarely put a dull hand on her. He seldom hit her. Never pushed her down. He was, however, verbally abusive to her. His bullying commands and lashings had taken a toll on her character. Baby wondered if there was hope for her Mother. She prayed for her. But she knew that Mother's deliverance was a question that could only be solved by her Creator and his gentle guidance. Mother never cried much, but when she did, everyone felt sad and guilty. She never spoke of her tears, but actually asked to be excused for them. She blamed herself. Her witness to the Lord was tweaked because of Abuelita's adamant faith. Perhaps there was hope. Baby encouraged her whenever she could, taking some of the weight off of Geoffe's nasty reprove and her sense of insecurity. Factoring in grace, there was a great flag of peace, a white flag waving in the breeze above Geoffe's home. It was deliberate and imaginary. Only Baby could see it. It was there because of Jesus, who would judge between Mother and Dad on that final day.

Their destitution and misconstrued reality was faithless and empty. Every now and then, Baby would invite Mother to go to church with her and William. Mother really took a liking to William, and in the end it was his charm that sucked her into it. She came to church with them one day.

The experience was outright and forthright. The mystery of Jesus fell like a shroud on her quiet, meek, and aching soul. She wept big rolling tears and hacked a cough in uncontrollable anger and sobbing. William put a hand on her shoulder, and Baby put her arms around her. Together they prayed for her. For her release from earthly imprisonment into a deathly calm that witnessed to the great and many wrongs she had seen in her life. She carried on like this for a good half hour. Finally she put her small arms around Baby and cried even harder. She sobbed violently, so that Baby felt fear at the release of evil coming out from her. Mother would make it. Mother would go. Baby knew she needed to talk to Mother about Jesus and the importance of knowing him in faith, believing in and accepting him as her Lord and Savior. Mother needed his love more than anything she had ever known.

Very astute and degraded, she felt pulverized after this huge break through. William talked to her gently, guiding her in her receptiveness of the faith. He talked to Jesus for and with her. He instructed her to acknowledge him, to open her heart to him, to allow his piercing healing into all the cracks of her bitter defenses.

Somehow Baby had stumbled upon something she hadn't known and didn't understand. Mother had kept such a secret of her fears and bitterness, her violent betrayal from Geoffe whom she had defended helplessly, but out of necessity rising to the hope of Jesus' glory. Never had she had a wink of peace since little Baby had come into the home. Baby knew it not, but she was adopted. Mother's sister had died in childbirth, and Mother and Geoffe had taken her home into their family.

Custody

When they got back to home with Mother, there was Geoffe, the Beast, standing at the door demanding to know where they had been and what had taken so long. Eager to have something to chew on, he blew off Mom as she walked past him into the house, and Baby and William followed, without a cursory glance to him.

William and Baby were on fire with the Lord and his presence in Mother. Baby suggested that they go walk around Park Haven peninsula to let their feelings free into the air, not being pent up in this spiritually lethal environment. Mom agreed and shyly suggested that they take Strawberry with them. Geoffe would have nothing to do with it. He wanted to work on the tool shed he was building in the backyard.

Mom sniffled and made little noises of defeat and overcoming. She looked sideways at little Baby and couldn't believe how strong and mature she had become. She was sick to her stomach about Justin and Geoffe and their impermissible sexual assaults on her. She had heard the stories. She knew what was true. She knew what to do about Geoffe, but that would be enough of that from then on.

Mom was delighted with William. Somehow his strength and courage matched his aggressively spiritual demeanor. He was honest and forthright. Dependable, forgiving, and building a nature of hope with her beautiful, adopted daughter.

Her respect and admiration for the quiet man were turbulent and roiling, built on his character, peaceful soul, gentle wisdom, and elite intelligence. Quite a step up from Jeremy, she thought. Little could she do in the face of Christ who swooped down now to her receptive faith and illuminated hope. She nested her head into his formal demeanor and comforting forgiveness.

His illustrious knowledge of her aching and suffering grew like popcorn into her inquisitive mind. She celebrated each victory with each baby step. She knew the time had come to tell Baby the truth, for the truth would set her free. She knew that Justin and Rexi were indisposed to the fact of her adoption. Nobody knew except Mother and the Beast, and Abuelita had known. This explained some of the arguing that went along with every visit from this estranged woman whose widowhood ate like a canker at her breast.

If only she had known. Maybe it had been wrong not to tell her. Maybe she was a flop and no good. She had carried this baby from birth into adulthood. Stops along the way had not been so good for the little one. She remembered the way Baby had slept so peacefully on Geoffe's stomach as he relaxed on the couch. What had gone wrong? Why did Geoffe abuse her the way he had? Whose fault was it? She knew. It was his fault. His nasty deception and rendering of assault upon a young child. Could he be forgiven? No. Was it really true? Would he take Mother to hell with him? No. He had already brought her there in this life. It was her turn, now, to rise up. To feel peace as she had never known it before.

She succumbed to the atrocious feelings of ugly decrepit heated pain that Baby had suffered. She knew it, had seen it, and didn't know what to do about it. She'd never known what to do. So now it was time. She must tell Baby the truth about her birth mom.

As they walked at the park, William maintained a steady droll of conversation, filling in weak spots and justifying ignorance with faith. Mother grew silent. Mother grew bold. She stopped and turned around facing her daughter. "There's something I need to tell you," she said to Baby Pollyanna.

"What is it, Mother?" Baby stopped and faced her Mother.

"Baby, sweetheart, you're adopted." The words fell like ice fall from a glacier into deep, churning waters. Then came the whales, strong, healing, peaceful.

"W-what?"

"Yes, my sweetheart. My sister was your Mother. She died giving birth to you, so I took you and raised you. You've come out really good, but I know your path has been awful, horrid, despicable. I know about your Dad, Geoffe, and what your brother, Justin, has done to you. I know about all of it. You might not remember telling me, but you've told me about all of it all through the years. There was nothing I could do. It hurt me too, but you had to live through it, and nothing can take away the championship that you own for being such an overcomer. Believe it Baby. I love you probably more than my own kids. You have always been my little one, my little Baby."

"Mother. Are you real, for sure?"

"Honey, I wouldn't lie to you about this. I love you." She said it. Words that Baby had wanted, had needed to hear her whole life.

Grandiose Regard

A tunnel of love appeared before Baby as she absorbed the information that her Mother fed to her day after day, talking to her like she never had before. Baby listened and smiled and cried a little. A little boulder had been put in its place in her heart, a rock of Christ, a hidden source of healing pacification.

Very construed and ugly in opinion, the very thought of talking to the Beast about this matter revolted her. She couldn't fathom the intense hatred that she felt for him. She had somehow, in herself, been able to forgive the man for the evil he had done to her, and she could not love him. The best she could do was to feel luke warm about him, and this atrocity the Lord would spit out of his mouth.

He spewed in rage against her when Mother sat the three of them in the living room to discuss the matter as William stood at a distance in the kitchen drinking coffee. He waited, and listened, and he prayed.

The Beast was staring at the ground beneath his feet, breathing heavily, and with inertia that pummeled him downward into his seat and cemented him there. He could not move, could not turn, could hardly breathe. There it was, the truth, and the Beast committed himself to it, with narcissistic denial of the disgrace in his own capacity. The evil that swirled about him was a horrid energy in the room. He could take it no more, yet he could not move. He was paralyzed in his own seat.

He tried to rock back and forth, but remained frozen like a statue, his mouth open and saliva running out of the left corner. He felt like a pigeon near a park bench. He felt betrayal capacity in himself and found lucid regard for the grandiose regard that Baby now took of him, grating her teeth and chewing on her lower lip.

Mom explained to Geoffe that she'd told Baby today about her birth status and custody with them. She told Geoffe to his pined and sorrowful face, smirking soundly and sagely taking grace from her opinion. It was the right thing to do, and he could hardly do it. He looked around warily. What had he done? His mind was empty yet terrified.

He growled and spoke ugly words of regression and gruesome ownership of their adopted daughter. She could cry all she wanted. She deserved nothing. She was no good.

Her elaborate portrayal of dignity socked him in the face with a turgid fist about to explode with delight. Her spiritual fist made mash of his face and in her mind she saw the blood running off of him. Blood she did not belong to. A wager that he had had, and that was all.

She grew bolder as time grew latent. The ongoing pressure of suicidal enigma that had always been hers in his presence since the business trip evaporated. Baby looked up and said, "Thanks, Dad."

He froze even more, swearing and cursing under his breath. At that moment William walked into the room with his cup of coffee and sat down on the couch next to Mother. His handsome and manly appearance took stock on the aging man who called himself Baby's Dad. Who had taken her and forced her into wrongful deceit, glued her mouth shut, and cast her into a furnace filled with dead bones and morbid grease. It had been her walk to deal with the truth and come to grips with it. And now, with the truth of her custody, she lifted her chin for once in his presence and felt the keys open her coffin of life. Now, just waiting for her to walk on.

She took two or three deep breaths and then breathed easily again. Aware of her breathing, she became aware of herself. Not even Satan could steal this certain victory from her. There she was. There she was, and now she could be.

Bathing in a river of knowledge and of truth, she grew vapidly productive in her thinking, hanging onto her belligerence as a guard, and meaning to hurt no one. Hurting someone at this point would be anathema to the situation. Here perplexity swooned with earthly pleasure. So there could be peace on earth, and she could see it coming. Bitterly reading her Dad's thoughts, the Beast's, she came against him in reiteration of his disgust for himself and everything he had ever tried to do. His wrongs out did his rights no matter what he did or how he tried to live up to Mother's expectations.

His bitterness ran deep and ugly. Mortification of death in consequence of denial. Revulsion described the hatred he felt for himself.

Fabulous entities tried hard to pry open Geoffe's mind in his base suit of revelation. He regarded cursory effort to bewitch the mind he knew, the fault he reasoned with, and the contaminated blushing that appeared in indignation about the truth of the matter. Baby was, indeed, adopted, yet she was quiet and shy and never took note of what was wrong in the house. Even in her bottomless effort for the truth to be revealed, she had never known the conditions of her birth, and her place in the family as cousins to those who had been her siblings. So Justin was not her brother. Rexi was not her sister. She had cousins that she grew up with, ignorantly so.

Twice despotic, and three times ragged, her mouth opened in a quiet holy hallelujah. There she was, foreign evolution to the Beast, not blood ties, no natural nurturing. Somehow her childhood had seemed normal, up until her horrid incident. Even then she was unable to see the differences between her "siblings" and her self. Quiet and understanding, she feared breaking this peace that had come open to her. She feared losing her way, all the accomplishments she'd made in life.

Her wisdom kicked in like a piston, and beat upon her efforts of horrid acknowledgment, and did Mother love her as much as the other kids? Dad was proud of Justin, always had been and didn't think about the topic of his abuse on Baby. Rexi was his shining star. Who, then, was Baby? Baby was the initiative problem, the source of sour pudding, the belief in gross disparagement and failure of prophetic witnessing.

Here he was, having walked all over Baby, the Beast and all his nasty belligerence toward her. His evocative suicidal nature was unhampered, for he knew he didn't want to die. He was afraid of death. He had no hope in the after life. His witness to foreign matters was pertinent in recalling juices of wisdom on Baby's little precious rose bud lips. Finally, it was noticed that when Baby talked, people listened. Urging on a scientific recovery for the reproof of her unnatural upbringing the turgid faith that denied evil wiped over everything. She was disgusted in her reprove of demons. She had suffered enough from them. It was time to expunge them from her world. Her negative world of hatred, expedient failure, and harmonic indifference. She quite hated a lot in life, but things had taken a turn.

No longer was she a public abuse symbol in compliance with the will of others. She possibly owned the most contagious faith on the planet, and rocketed into her life like a small engine that was out of control. Her grandiose regard to her failure in life was an outlet for the tears that would not come. Not yet. Today had been Mother's day for tears, and it would not be missed. Mother knew how to handle the Beast, and had been a pro at it for many years. She gave dog food to him for dinner, and he ate it greedily. Giving dog food to Geoffe was a normal procedure of hers. He thought he was getting something great. He was getting dog food. He ate hungrily till he was full of foolishness, and badgered the deceit with which he hated anomalies, not knowing quality from false appearance. Here she sat daily in the house, reading, and cooking, and taking pleasure in outdoor exercises. She came home to her hungry husband and mashed potatoes fell on the floor. She swept them up and fed them to Geoffe. He ate like an obedient child, only Mom's deceit for him was upgraded by default.

Looking past his stupid foolishness, she wondered why she had married and made a family with this piercing wonder of disgrace. She no longer loved him as a husband, but rather as someone she felt the need to take care of.

Obedient to everything, he no longer found peace in making his own decisions. He was publically abusive to Baby in the house, yet she did not mind anymore. She took it "like ducks", like water drops rolling off of her feathers. She quivered and shook and the water fell off of her like something she shook out of her sleeve.

It had been a hatred from the beginning. But she had gotten pregnant with Justin, so they married, and that was the end of that.

Rexi came along and the family was complete. One older son and a daughter. When Pollyanna came into the picture, there was nothing to do but accept her as part of the family. She was older now, for sure, yet without complications in her need for dignity and pasture to rest reasonably in.

Her brain had always been elusive to them. No one knew her thoughts. She hid behind curtains of socialization. She was emphatically shy, and questioned Rexi about being behind or in front of the social curtain. Rexi told her that, indeed, she was definitely in front of the social curtain. Baby was traumatized. Why must she be behind that curtain of socialization? She was quiet, never knowing what to say, and not making many friends in school.

Now with Strawberry, there was a chance for Baby and Mother to "catch up" by going for walks together. Immeasurably grateful for this chance to get to know her Mother's inner being, there was a trust that grew like a tornado and whisked about their gentle feathers. They hugged and cried and laughed. They walked along in friendship and not betrayal again. There was a chance to come to understand the "Beast" as Mother understood him. Baby began by giving her viewpoint. "He hates me, hurts me, and discredits me. He's ugly, mean, and stupid. He's disgusting in the way he handles me, and he's gross in all of his boring behavior." He had nothing to be proud of, he had broken trust with the family when he destroyed innocent Pollyanna on the business trip, which according to him, had been "fun".

Her whole world had been destroyed because of him. Her self respect had been mashed when Justin poked his middle finger into the pie of Baby's innocence. Rexi was her friend. Her cousin now, and not her sister. She squeezed out tears when she thought about this. Somehow her independence grew as her resolve and truthful satisfaction burned a brand into her soul. She was a witness to Christ. She absconded the delirious nature of lucid denial in her opinion of hate. Hate was reserved for the devil, and all of its stupid flings. It was harmonious and obtrusive, succulent and made like an imposter. Bewitching in nature, the resolve of goat's milk in her cup shattered her faith in ingenuity. She would absolve nothing in partaking of her generous freedom. She no longer had to treat her Dad like a "good

Dad". She no longer had to fake it and be internally revoked each time he came at her. There was nothing but preposterous glory in his hatred for himself. He could not climb out of the bowl of shit that he had sat down in. Now he was stuck.

Baby wondered and asked Mother if she might call her "Mom". "Mom" agreed with joy and laughter. "Of course," she said. "I am your Mom."

Witness

An accredited accomplishment had been made. The turning of oats over on the floor. Tripping, scuffling, walking daintily and taking broad, patterned and confident steps, Baby grew out of her hole. Like the Easter egg hunts they had had on Easter there was good mixed in with the bad. Dad used to bring home donuts on Sundays for the kids to eat before Sunday school. There was depression in the despotic attempts he had made to witness to his family of the depth of his patronage. His murderous cruelty had become a sort of buoy in the waters, to warn away on comers, and suggest the possibility that there was something, after all, wrong with his nature. He had been a bad Dad at that. There was misuse in his belonging to the family, and he ordered kids around sternly demanding obedience to his ruling hand. Rexi and Justin took it in stride, but Baby had always cowered beneath his reckless judgment and incorporate anger. They took it in passing, but she trembled in fear to be around her father. Her Dad, the "Beast". Baby and the Beast were at odds with one another. There was nothing doing that could not be done. There was faith and glimpses of goodness, but as time went on, Baby stopped cowering.

Delightful joy filled her to the brim in her loving relationship with William. He was so careful to her and let her understand the things she needed to hear, like revoking her father and letting go of the disastrous hold he had on her. William knew something of the past history in their house, the family being filled with family secrets that all told would shake the foundations of the universe. Well, at least their universal compound. Belligerent in nature, the trust effect that came with uprising and holding on to gentility, quickly resided that hope had come and made itself available for these secret keepers. Maybe Geoffe had some secrets of his own. Whatever they were, he was rotting in them as they inhabited his being, his place in the house, his degrading sensibility and his acts of passive cruelty.

Curative and seductive, he ordered Mom around who took it like ducks letting the water roll off feathers. She regarded with disgust her shame for Geoffe, for his inequitable hatred of himself and his own selfish glory. Pandemonium vacated the premises and the loud voice grew softer. No longer was there a spirit of hatred tearing everyone apart. Baby called Rexi and begged her to come home. She wanted to justify being cousins with her. She wanted her love and gentle prodding, the nuances of affection that had kept her alive in the growing up years. Now she needed a friend who had been through it all with her.

Mom added her vote to Baby's plea, and Rexi decided to come for a visit. She cried in Mom's arms when Mom told her about Baby's adoptive status. She couldn't believe it could be true. Yet in all her disregard and humble nature, she accepted the truth with a new and vigorous appreciation for her sister turned cousin.

"He hated me," Baby said to Rexi. Softly, quietly, and in a whisper. There was nothing to hide now. Baby asked if Rexi really knew what had happened to her in Singapore years and years ago. And why must she keep hanging onto it like this? There was nothing ingratiating about the disparagement, yet in eternal glory there was nothing but faded resolve. Rexi liked William the way that Mom did. He was such an impressive man who made people want to know him and be around him. He was successful in life, he was a prophet, a minister. Yet his vainglory was humble and great. He properly disposed of himself and made things right between people. He used to pastor his own church, but now was in between churches. His faith was extensible, fortified with hope. His peaceful resolve was irresistible, and in a calm quiet way he drew people to him. He had prayed long ago to find favor with all people, and the Lord had really come through with that.

Submissive hope and failed destiny came upon Rexi who knew she needed Christ, but how or why? She came to church with Mom, William, and Baby during her visit. She went home with a planted seed in her heart, that was a seed of faith and religion made of Jesus.

Foreign to her were the ugly days of Baby's resurgent gumption and need to put herself first for all the attention she could get. There was faith, there were nuances, she had hope. According to Rexi, Paul made a great husband and father, and their three children were growing up fast.

It was necessary that Rexi see her brother Justin on this visit. Justin needed to hear the truth after all. It was only the right thing to do to inform him about Baby's adoption. Justin ground his knee into the dirt when it came to listening to Baby. But he would pay attention to Rexi, his little sister too. Justin visited Mom and the Beast while Rexi was there. Even Baby made a point of showing up on time for dinner. She wanted to see Justin's kids, but he had not brought them or Rachel. Just as well. He froze stock still when Mom made the announcement at dinner. Baby was his cousin? With relief he passed the mustard to Dad who put some on his ham steak. Surely Dad would know what to say.

He sucked in his breath fast and deeply as if confronting a great wound. He was disbelieving at first. He came across as cocky but unsure of himself. He never felt right in Baby's presence, yet family was important to him so he broadsided the question of her family bond with a skewed partition of denial that he had ever done anything wrong. According to him, he had never sinned against his sister, now his cousin, and any claims that she made to that subject were falsehoods and fictitious stories.

Baby excused herself and left to go home to William. She shared the story of dinner with him, and Justin's insistence that nothing was wrong between them. She ached painfully in the truth of his resistance. She was unsteady for awhile, unstable. Talking with William she came into herself more credibly, inert in her ability to overcome what was not acknowledged. According to her, Dad was in line for lightning, and Justin would soon fall down a well.

Forgiveness reared her honorable head. William described the importance of forgiveness in this situation. Only then could she truly heal and move onward with her life. To add hope to glory, he asked her if she would marry him.

Baby howled and hugged him, squeezing him tight. She said "Yes!" This was just the turn of events that she had needed to move on. Despite her ugly family history, he still loved her, and retracted no guilt from her situation. She was believably a butterfly and would always overcome. She had seen the worst, been through the worst, and now she could glitter like sparkling sun on the water, to which she attested was the most beautiful sight of all.

Perplexed and dramatic, not sure of how to proceed, Baby let William take the lead and he drew her to him. They were together, and together they were one.

Copiously and confidently, they submitted one to the other and shared the possibilities of their future together. On the horizon there was hope and glory. A rainbow stood above them. The horizon unfolded into eternity, dragging with it the whole and committed people of Christ. There was nothing to be afraid of, for nothing could snatch them from his hand. He was whole, he was true, and his vainglory meant nothing to him. It was to absolve the faith of his destiny to keep knocking on people's doors. Infantile and sadistic, the narcotic emblem of joy and resistance came in resounding emanating spirits long locked up and now set free. The time had come for the Rapture, and was anyone ready? It was a steady oncoming, a process that took some time as aged people grew younger, and younger people saw the difference between life and death.

The dead in Christ would rise first. Then, the other followers of Jesus would rise with Jesus and join him in the clouds. Forbidden entrance, and disgusting ruse of oblong hatred. For how long had Jesus put up with the shit of this unholy generation? For whom had he died on the cross? Would a nebula of stars come crashing to the earth? Unholy inertia was an emblem of disgust in rationalizing the hatred of this anomaly. Holy hatred grasped those who didn't believe, and tossed them to the devil in his burning lake of brimstone. Forever.

Indisposed of narcissistic behavior, the turning about of notions in the mind of the weak began with cursory respect and regard. For God loves his people with unconditional positive regard. Those he took to him in their souls, making a minister out of a man, and a swan out of an ugly duckling. Elaborate and construed behavior was seditious and active in imaginative glory and suicidal regeneration by slowness and history. So it would begin. God would make a short work of it, but it would take some time. And time was one thing that Baby had to call her own. She regarded her faith as a healer and it made her strong.

Bitter reprove and enigmatic failure were absconded in foul mouth and natural resolve. Those without Christ would die a painful and unnatural death. Defeated by the wisdom of the Lord, they could not escape that fate in all of its vainglory. Those who denied him could not escape the rational rule of God's pencil. Writing to the scribe who would set his mind in all rationality.

Thoroughfare and thorough through, placated painted emblems passed as short prayers. Those who kneeled down in helpless remorse were forgiven. Those who turned a nose up to the Lord, himself, were socked in that nose and belligerently dragged over hatred and the disgust of reptilian feces. Oblong and unnatural, these caricatures came as the fact of hatred bred through lucid denunciation. Elaborately overcoming of nuances that pushed one towards the brink, those who called on faith were overcome with watchful forgiveness. These also must forgive those to whom they owed forgiveness. Perplexity and anonymity, bruised with talents and squeezed out of proportion, the faculty of injustice was just wasted time on useless victims. Sinful subordination matched regress with the fallen institution of faith for the faithless.

Holding onto the past, when these things were made true and benevolent, the unjust trusting of sinful demise became ugly to the eye and threatening to the spirits of the free. Overcoming negligence with proprietary and unfocused demise, the holy grail of inertia died in suicide with forgotten emblems of faith and seduction. Seduced and pounced upon, these unlucky fornicators seemed to turn up a nose to God all throughout their lives. There was little to live up to, without the triumph of a witness to the regard of doleful waste and injustice manufactured out of lust.

Creeping up like little critters in the face of jealousy, the vapid truth of ornery killing and in sinful malignance the truth of justice remained hospitable to those who were blinded by faith and knew not what it was that beheld them.

Façade and fractured immaculate glory would position hope into the injustice of faith made out of sight and positive resilience. Just to regard the elimination of those who despaired relief, the fact of faith could not be eliminated between cursory rejection and omniscient growling. The thunder of the Lord, the striking of lightning on earth in various places, the earth quaking, fire and brimstone, accrued to despotic fierceness in quizzical reliance upon the justice of the corner stone of Jesus Christ.

Belonging to fortitude and emollient texture, came the truth of fictitious belonging, the serving of faith with regression and denial in all behavioral quarters filled with death. No problems of religion, only the one true faith in the one true God set the problems right and began with miraculous healings. Letting go and hanging on to the rapturous thoroughfare of subletting denunciation, we make room in our hearts, preparing a place for the Lord. Psychotic wisdom filled with all manners of hope and oblivion brings about with it a talent filled with hope and truth. The talent of equitable flavor found in forced entry to evil conglomerate disgust… thoroughfare. Forbidden hope only justified the anomaly of distaste and puking disgust. Natural betrayal was found in the woods beyond the house, ignorant, sinful, and lusting. Reaching hands folded in prayer.

Wasteland

Waters beyond filled with scum and turned to blood. In effortless betrayal of forgotten sedition, the illustrious hope of fantastic persuasion came alongside the truth of perpetration and significant sins. Wasted and torn, ruined and denied, there was remittance in the fondling of skin in the dark as lovers made love in the nights and on their beds. Justin and Rachel were rapacious in their sexual patterns of behavior. She suited him not, and found no regress in herself for his wounded and ugly hands. His numbed fingers and toes belonged to his mental slowness, which was held in hiding and covered with an insolent outlook on life, and a bitter reprove of his knowledge.

All equivalent to a maturing world based on deceit and greed. Giving over to Jehovah's Witnesses, truth based on denial gave regressive results to formative opinion of the nature of disgust. Abounding in flavorful distinction, there was hope in the nearness of nature and the patterning approval of grace. The regressive nature of founding sin and glory became littered with progress that cut away freedom and brought imprisonment to the smallest of souls today that lives in reparation of doting despair and autonomous and feeble secular religious antidote.

Affluent religion based on retrieval of hope and the sightings of miracles traces back the temper of nothingness, which exceeds all fault and behavior in denial. Programming knowledge with denial and absolute deficiency, there is ultimate resolve to overcome differences and accept each other. Without hope, without faith, without truth, there is hopeless despondency, and fingering religious articles of nothingness in all stupidity.

To describe the sin but waste it away in a place where it has no hope there is letting go in all subjunctive acrimony for the belligerent "Beast" who has no hold on Baby Pollyanna. We forgive, we forget, we set ourselves free in a nation that breeds populace and understands that life is hard. As Abuelita once said to Baby, "Know that life is hard and accept that, and then it won't be so hard." Take your time, fill the equations, and sublet your mind to innocence and peace. Disgraceful quality in enervating substances takes nutrients. Food for the stomach and the stomach for food.

Holding onto joy is good. It brings faith and saturation of the weirdness that escapes our ongoing problems of forbidden defiance. Paperweight, nudging our toes, and fact finding all hold onto one truth. Weight is better than nutrients. It is the survival of all. Clarity insidious to sin, makes mortal the enmity of justice relying on sedition to prove it wrong. There is no such thing, since we have a conscience. We know when we are doing wrong, and when we have made a mistake we can immediately recover by not blaming ourselves and inserting a do over. We can find forgiveness, not rotten sublimation.

Tooting your own horn cannot be a bad thing. Good things need to be recognized and handled with an equitable hand of downward wisdom and proprietary insolence. Chasing anger and handing down guilt, the justification of ground black pepper on eggs is like a clam in the bucket, overcome with grace and nervousness.

But Baby is a happy girl now. A young woman free in the faith of Christ Jesus. No longer does the Beast pose a threat to her wellbeing. She has given up on the vulgarity of Dad and Justin, and absconds with the diligence of trust that she has with William, who harbors nothing but love and goodwill for her. He trusts her, he believes in her, and he doesn't give the Beast a second or a quenching thought.

Her detrimental demise is found in lost faith recovered, new to her like ice cream on a cone. Sweet and soft, crunchy and deliberate. Positioning herself with aggravated guilt, she gives over to the obliteration of disgust. The Beast can hurt her no more. The wisdom of her faultiness in all persuasion of the good goes along with all that which describes natural faith in her own genetics, and she knows she is well made, if just substituted for another Mom. She has asked her Mom who her blood line Dad is, but received no information on the matter. Just as well, the therapy she received in high school kept her guessing on whom she really was, to what extent did these great thoughts of "not as good as" keep her in a jar? A jar of alcohol, which she does not use anymore. No more drinking to get drunk, just one glass of wine in the evenings. Her mood swings are in tune with the many facets of her belonging on earth. Here she was and here she is and here she ever will be. Niceties are good, forgiveness is gentle as a passing feather on the wind.

Crunchy snow beneath her feet keeps her careful where she puts her next step. Running through meadows like a child, her playground is what this earth has become to her. Now there would be no more suffering. No more idiotic lost and degenerate creations wasted on resiliency upon a wasteland of fortitude and unnatural eviction.

Turpentine is poignant, is poisonous, and used to clean up messes. Baby always thought of herself as a "mess". She clung to Dad in hopes of approval, who gave her nothing but moldy cheese to chew on. Disgusting, sickening, good for nothing but mice in a trap.

Little mice between her toes, crawling up her legs, she behooves not the indecency of internal ineptitude to fortify walls around her precious insides. Not only that, but with exploration of her mysterious disgraces and tangy icing on her lemon cake, with intrigue she discovers hope and renewal to believe on the Lord Jesus Christ and makes him the Lord of her heart.

Crime and indecency are formal in effect. Not only is the truth twisted around gliding, slimy serpents, there is unnatural opinion about the others that are "out there". Forbidden knowledge to be had when its time had come. Nobody knows, nobody does, and nobody can relate to science in this monstrosity. Quibbling with Creationism and the "Big Bang" theory there is justice in sorting out the truth. What does the Bible say?

Littered with lost function and undermined capacity, through and through there is joy in the reception of equality. Equality between races, sex, and leadership. Who can guide but one who knows how to use the whip without seriously hurting anyone? Cancel discrepancies through holding onto indignity and fornication, lustful loss in juices of apparition. Fairly holding on, and giving leeway to the masses, there is approval to those who do good in the Lord. Leniency and forgiveness do justice to all.

Leaning on the apparitions of hope sluiced with a butter knife, the gentleness of Christ's rule comes with his faith and glory, the undercutting of religion found in compliance to sin. Butter knife or no, there is obliteration in separating the good and the bad, a nuptial and a tradition based on negativity and approval, bequeathing the aftermath of forbidden failure and ignorant supplication. Based on facts of religion and oppressive dominance, no one on earth has a right to go to heaven except those who go with Jesus Christ who is the Way, the Truth, and the Life. Flying like eagles on the wind, rejoicing comes with the paralysis of truth, its most benign and possible repose, giving hope to nuances of faith and crust to the demon in hell. Aggravating hope and contentment big with gestational fluids there is rebirth in the nature of Christ who came to save not to condemn. People condemn themselves when they reject the truth of his Lordship. For he is true and faithful. Mighty in regard, and significant in sin.

Bringing about illustrious sin again, there is Baby faith and there is faith in Baby. She loves to play everyday on her earthly playground that she has earned through longsuffering and true, unquestionable faith in the Lord. Bring about recluse and she is finished with our society. Belonging to the Lord, she is a princess. In factors of disguise, the belittlement of faith in her altruistic appeal gives a notorious consequence to the rejection of liver on a toad stool. Poignant, yet reverted.

Twisted Words

Garble, garble, garble. Thick and twisted, inert and functional. The levitating surprise of clouds on the horizon keeps a glare of the sun from burning too much. Saturated hope and instructional demise, there is little to watch for but sardonic horrible oblivion that sacks truth and lives a lie.

Crunchy, crunchy, crunchy. Little or nothing with sweet repose, the fabulous enigma of church on the horizon, swallowing the Word of God and riding in line with significant and well behaved horses. Gutsy and enthralling, the bitterness of the emblem of faith twisted in words of loss and truth, the absence of mortality and the beginnings of the foundation of God through and through hand over popularity to goodness. Faith and reprise, the glowing and arbitrary nurturing are winded with unsteady lungs, hapless future and forgone glory.

Beginning again and again, the time has come to begin again. Merciless and true, the justice of erotic, decrepit forgiveness lies in wait of optional opinions and disturbing faithful glory. Saturated with hope and effect, bitter niceties and hopeless, vapid dust in the wind, we find nothing but the relation of guilt toward suicide. First gone, and last to arrive, insidious hell and leeching suction of grass in the night, cold fields of glory and hatred, benign flowers and flowing streams disgraced by peppered narcissistic hope.

Cosmic hilarity dusted in the nose of absurd sniffling, quieted by grace and humiliated in function, the loss of servitude twists around with words of faith and lost opinion of jarring disgust. Planting flowers around the room and pieces of pie remaining in the oven leftover, where is room for the necessities of life in functional virtue? Leotards with no feet sewn on, and ball room dresses spinning round and round, devices of giving are too ludicrous to believe in all the hating hell of dastardly subjugation. Forced entry, pushing and pulling, comes out a new creation, believing in ecstasy, criticizing natural betrayal, putting forth the foot of redundancy to sublime incrimination of due justice. Baby is sure that her life will improve and continue to improve for all time. With William she is complete, without the Beast, she is common and desirable. Fashions of faith and reiterating glory are confused in her abject humor and faultless incendiary magnitude. Parallel with discrimination, she finds the future is not so ominous after all. She glows with insecurity and knows that where she is weak, the Lord is strong, and that makes up for all of her doubt in religion. Faithless and true, conglomerate with repetition, false failure regurgitates somber infection and littering with wasted twisted words of negativity that wrap around the soul and cling. Clinging with disgust and hatred, warping the natural song of decency, and obliterating newness with oneness… peaked interest derives quality from abstract opinion.

The Beast goes on quiet walks by himself. His shuddering soul and pounding heart take subjugation by the hand and worm it around his trafficking mind, colliding with every step he takes into a wall of weary reprise. He has no hope and doesn't understand justice. He can't count on his fingers and toes the times he has been truly happy. Perhaps when Mom got pregnant with Justin and bore him a son of whom to be proud.

Liquidating infectious spoof and conglomerate tendencies abstract the lion of growling ferocity and the figurative undue disgust found in his own underwear.

Beautiful like the morning is his wife. So sad and sorry, so regretful and full of shame. His morose and ongoing saturation with piety strings him to the cross of negligence, one that bends over and breaks apart on the ground, grinding his forehead into the dust.

Quaking with fear, he does not know what he is afraid of. Losing hope? He has none. Dying? That time is on its way in a truck load of bouncing citizens of earth who did not make it through the pearly gates. Dying and deception. Failure to call on God in time. Filled with hatred, filled with obsession. He clings to himself. His ego retracts and trips over logs in the way. He counts trees on his fingers and gives up counting. Has his life no meaning at all?

Pushing negativism away from him, with twisted words of waiting and sublime apology, for him it is too late. It's sad to watch a loser lose. Wasted, gone, being sucked together in nothingness. Baby has instruction to be there for him, but she can't. Her puzzle pieces don't fit into his puzzle. They have two different views. Hers of glory, his of condemnation. So sad, and so sadly seen to the effect of reality, similar to watching a criminal on death row being executed, only there is no in between where forgiveness was a possibility. Cavernous darkness surrounds him and favor loses his discredit. Opinions waver as the truth comes out. Baby doesn't look too closely, for fear of being sucked in. She won't pray for him, it is too late for that. The humiliating incidence of his portent destruction is able to overcome nothingness with surmise.

Resounding waters that die imminently keep hatred at bay, and overturning twisted words of hope. Glassy lakes without fish in them. During which time the oblong ecstasy of Christ goes crazy with redemption and forgiveness.

Lucid hope and betrayal come to nothing at the river where life crosses over into death. Never to return and without a drop of water to cool the tongue. Reparations are made in forgiveness, yet it is always up to the maker and the made.

Ourselves, a creation of witnesses and hope, made in God's pleasure, and sucked up in remission of glory with sustenance are like pleasure and paddy cake brim stone forgiveness. Keep on forgiving for as long as you can, thinks Baby, and don't follow the lost nor let the blind lead the blind.

Watch out for holes in the ground that speak of death and absolution. Wasted despair, congruent denial, and figurative anomaly can't stand the wisdom of losing in all of its foolish vendetta. Beyond reiteration there is the loose tooth that must not be set before it is time to go.

Passion and faith and glory count numbers as they come flying by, turgid with hope in the epitome of faith crying out for acknowledgment. Futuristic surprise is wet like the nose on a dog, and the long pink tongue licks up water. Crying in faith you can be a little bit ornery. Do it twice and the twisted words will vibrate in your mouth where the tooth is loose.

Fractured and broken, bodies will heal, faith will grow as injustice fades away. Peaked by performance and growing in eternal light made not by the sun, we come to weakness in knowledge. Patterns of hypocrisy and talents too great to lose found major disgust with patterns of familiar acquaintances. Holding onto the Lord is well done and pays greatly. Symbiotic resilience and negative attribution give greatly to the patterns of hope and denial. Infiltrated by disgusting hatred and motivated by lost sperm on the ground…bitter and concealed. Hatred by confusion, gone in glory and forgiveness in rape. But to do so to one of God's little ones, it would be better to be thrown in the water with a millstone over the head. The justice that stands in the calling of grace pays a heavy pardon. No one likes to see it when it is here. By grace it follows a forbidden path where destruction and demise equal one.

Foregoing turgid waste and proper poignancy, functions are disgraceful in the forgetting and letting go of the past. Thanks to heaven there is goodness for all God's little ones. Even the little ones that are still in the big ones, for we all have an inner child. Musically suffocating, chemically debauching, we find favor with God in the new time, where justice lives on hope, and perpetration obeys no knowledge.

Through and through, the heavens that remain are unimaginable. Superfluous and bruised with the pounding on the doors of our coffins waking up to find yourself not dead, there is resounding applause in heaven. For those who died and for those who won't.

Configure the gestation of hope and find knowledge in truth, for truth is the spirit, gentle in touch but forbidden in evil where twisted words warp our knowledge and it all leads to an untimely death.

Tremulous

Shaking like a leaf in the breeze, falling like a leaf in the storm, and standing tall like the tall oak or cedar, is justice in all of her outstanding glory. We cry out for faith, for something to believe in. Baby knows, she has been there, Baby Pollyanna. With regard to mistrusting the aberration of faith, she has witnessed and overcome life with greater life and eternal life. Submitting to nothing, but God and her husband to be, she is grateful to have such wisdom provided for her, and makes her a joy, a hope, a steward, and a helpmate.

Ingrown toenails on the foot can cause you to trip up and slow down. The race is on, and we must all run like the runner who wins the race. To set your eyes on the prize, there is faith, hope, and glory. We witness by what we see, thus the "eye witness" in the news. Which tabulates and turns us around, informing us day by day with news stories that fill in the gaps and the turns and the skips and the hops that are all going on out there in the world.

The truth is that oblivion sets her sights on regard, and nests in the waters of lily pads. Not drowning, but gently waiting as the world turns. Faith and flowers, both beautiful. One is forever, the other ends in life, in the end of its life. Super hero manufacture of wisdom and grace and polished silverware and destroyed paintings, the loot of furniture and unturned tables remains for the having, for the "haves", and the "have nots".

Destroying public property is wasteful and destructive. It is a lack of respect and a hardened notion of too much of not enough. So it goes in the tremulous leaves on the winded trees there comes in foregoing a cataclysmic and regressive contorted destructive habit. Habitation in its own seniority lives to fight for the death of the lost, the betraying, and those with no regard for the Holy Spirit. Which, in turn, acts upon injustice and glazes our eyes to the spiritual nature of the world. There is too much goodness and glory to fixate on the lost and destroyed. Not to bring it back, to grieve, and to let go. And then, to go with God. To know the flow and to go with the flow.

Turning over again and again in the wind, like a shirt unbuttoned and another one beneath it, we are weary of wearing our earthly garments of sex and wealth and jeopardy. To lose and to hope is to give again into the sin of denial of that which is prudent and just. No one knows the difference until they get there, and see that their skin is losing out on life obtained and growing younger in these last days.

Encroachment bowed down on regressive sin can obliterate the calling that we have in life. Baby doesn't spend too much time thinking about the Beast and his ill fated destruction. Maladapted, she doesn't ask "why?" is he this way, or what made him do this. She knows he doesn't understand Jesus. Reason tells him that he is different from others who can't stand the way he is, yet treat him kindly to a point. Lethargic reactions to this reason keeps him afloat with his wrists bound together in a jail cell of murder and deceit. For this is his place. For how long, who knows? How many times has he cheated, killed spirits, overturned Bibles and in frustration denied himself the only one way to everlasting goodness?

Wary and dumbfounded we approach him yet do not reach out to touch him. He must pay for his faults, and that justice may be done. Turned over, paralyzed, filled with poison, and gone.

Tremulous and wary fingers write this letter himself. There is no dancing in heaven for him. No ball room dresses twirling around. No food on the table in the presence of our enemies. Is the Beast the enemy? Ground control supplicated to annihilate his historical faction, ludicrous and cross. Crossroads and switchbacks. Jesus died on the cross to save those who turn to him away from sin. His function is not to die again, never, and to give life eternal to all who qualify. Breaking not the dungeon gates in rare perplexity but unfounded with knowledge and with hope, the rare anomaly is answered and construed with frustrated opinion and fathomless disgrace. Baby blames all of her unhappiness on him. The issue of her adopted history, it must have been a big decision to take her on with Mom ruling the fold, and Justin and Rexi, just too young to understand.

Everywhere she goes, she is afraid of something. She is afraid of happiness and doesn't recognize it when it falls upon her. Her ghost is in heaven, the soul she lost as a little child, coming back now to the guest house of her haven, the window open for true nature in sublime repetition to come home.

Even in the places where she is exotically dumbfounded, the resurgent and overcome places of death in her life have hobbled on to this glory, this significance. Refracted and cut loose, the condemnation of justice is wired by nasty and festering cuts on the skin. Holding onto glory, the absolved and redeemed put faith where it belongs. Not in hope and glory, but in Jesus Christ himself. Where He is, there is hope and glory, and we can go there, Baby knows, and celebrates eternity with William. Never again to be chided and accosted by absolved and reticent enigma. Paralyzed to fate and costing a fortune. God's house has many rooms. There is one for you and for me, Baby thinks to herself. We are wired for pardon and reprise, the most significant perpetration of leadership found in hope. Secure and insignificant, Lord of all rules all and determines every destiny. Yet, like knowing the numbers of our hairs on our heads, every point of truth is given to him without quibble, and leadership gains control.

Suicide and lackadaisical nuance betray nothing with hope and invitation. Lessons learned are mighty in the meek, and forbidden in the lost and the true. We find matter of fact knowledge in the faith of Jesus Christ, turning about like the earth on her axis. We are foundering, cost worthy, and effective as nature denies absolve and figuring costs the credit needed to hanker an opinion. Bitter resolve and fashioned hope meet head on in nature and all of her beauty. Catching up and hanging on, the deceitful will be cut away and lost from glory. Never again to raise a head of despair, and not to exact a cost from the Creator.

Oblivion and sensitivity create desperate demise in the forlorn and the lost. Registered in safety, the fight is not with the nuance but for the regressive element of truth, which is Spirit. Under ground and forgotten about, the skeletons of many who have died will rise again in a breath of hope and figured opinion. Nobody knows the will of God, the time of day, or the grafted symbolic servitude which lusts to portray heavy fate and delectable taste with necessity and justice. Portrayal of the heavy fate is lost in coming about in opinion of hope and justice and negativity. Thanks be to God that we have the power of prayer. Baby knows to use it. She relies on it. Not in Justin, not in the Beast. Who reject prayer, who rely on stenciled apparitions in the air that imprint our faces, coagulant and true.

Bitter in enemy, bitter in justice, and oblong in fate, we are reactive characters to illuminate the world on a plane of hope and mercy. Doubtful to the tee of fortune, there comes a rescinding paralytic crying out for hope in mercy. Mercy is great and mercy is true. Mercy swings justice completely around on the swing set, without unseating the occupant. Delirious with hope and affection, those who have hope can see into injustice and change it.

Bitter resolve, the quaking of opinion without letting go makes carnal our rescinding alliances in fate and mercy. Letting go and being faithful, there is justice in recluse, in pondering, in making right the wrongs.

Totally defeated in gestures of despair, the lost and foremost destiny of fate in its grasp, its vice like grasp upon wisdom and conjecture. Trying too hard and forgetting opinion is suicidal to hope. Believing in the truth, the regard of nature formulated the Adam's apple in regression of turgid evolving separatism. In watching out for the lost, for the true, for the innocent, we commit great deeds of glory.

Suffering in a mishap of rescinding patterned betrayal, the nothingness of hope and miserable repetitions. Puking unnaturally in drunken oblivion, the misery is great on our personal conscience and diabolical cavernous disgust. No more waiting for the truth, the diabolical personage is manufactured in fate and gloom. Darkness, cold, luke warm potato mash and hopeless defeat by tender victuals and twisted turns of glory come lost in reticent surmise.

Bringing about the sordid opinion or ruined mash and upset plate carts, the denial of destiny is in our foundation of knowledge. Baby is humble and knows that she doesn't know too much to be disregarded by the angels of heaven. Golden glory and twisted deprivation obey the rules of heaven on the globular planet that twists and turns in ruthless madness and forgoing of rejected opinion.

Maddening and lustful, broken, despotic, criminal and unfair are those who have held us down for too long. In the making of crematory powder, there is rejection in sin and forgiveness of letting go. No one dies to the nuances of fate and turmoil. No one lets go without hope of being caught in the hands of the great and faithful. Oblivious to opinions, the cathartic and despicable nature of wrongness on our food trays poke at nearness of recovery to the naturalization of turmoil and foundation.

Nobody knows, when, where, and for how long will this Rapture last. Fate, striding with populous, and internal healing of organs plagued by cancer and any fortuitous disease makes mash of disgusted and wasted acrimonious celebratory design and settled jurisdiction.

Pow! Goes the washcloth to wipe away disgusting build up in unnatural puking. Fortification of injustice and contrary to the arbitrary necessity of blame, we are carnal in our natures yet the spirit of Christ overcomes. Even in celebratory inertia the trust of truth fathoms all ridiculous faith and perpetual suffering. Waiting for your turn to be healed, you may recover in pureness of belief. In turn, your pureness of belief can make you immune to deceit and fashions of betrayal in the doctor's office.

There we go again with the high tide of costly medications and do they really do the job? Yes. No. Imminent depression of lost hope and giving up. Yes medicine is good. How does it help? Are we lost without it? There are hopeless glories out there that do justice to the system, where rhetorical disgust makes side effects worse than the symptoms. Then it is necessary to decide which road to take. Thank you, Lord, for the power of prayer and healing.

Fairy Tales

Pot of gold at the end of the rainbow? Truth or fairy tale? Rescinding with golden glory, the aggressive union of fate with lost tales of fate design pardon for the unforgiveable sinner who sinned too much and for too long without acquiring resort and perplexity in unity with surprised endings. Contoured and misplaced, the broken old wives tales are rich with venom and curative disorder. God is not a fairy tale. Believe it or not, he is rich in truth. Overcoming is belief in the Holy Spirit sent to earth to counsel us. We pardon sin and give up on denial. Faction and truth, the destiny of apparitions and declaratory passions freeze where they stand in mercy and obedience. God desires mercy not sacrifice. Meaning stand still and paint faces on the walls of mirrors, that they may reflect the cost of doom brought about with forgiveness and sanctification.

Lost and threatening, peals of thunder fortify earth with bolts of lightning. Pouring down rain obliterates necessity and transparent puddles on the roads. Like the deer that jumps out in front of your car on the highway, injustice factors away road-kill, and someone gets to eat it.

Problems with salting it to taste come in truths of passions and glory riding high on vinegar and burnt flesh. Designed to nourish oblivions out of hopelessness. Thanks be to God that we have the power of prayer and forgiveness. Forgoing evil and justifying truth, the fairy tale of counting sheep at night might or might not work but it is harmless. Some people are challenged when it comes to sleeping at night. Count sheep? Or get sleeping aids?

Glorious hope comes with the truth and despairing nature of carnal wisdom, to which clings the biology of credit versus denial. Competition and readiness is good. Prepare for your challenge like

Baby prepared for hers in battling with the evil nature of her adoptive father so gruesome to her to be called the Beast. Baby and the Beast clash.

A hit man doesn't last for long in this world if he is troubled by deception. Putting the target in the line of sight is quick and dead. Bottomless, falling forever into darkness, doom, hatred.

Without regression with apology, comes the truth that forgiveness is retaliatory and perfect in the nuance of hope. Don't plagiarize and don't give rebuff to the particular natives of this country, those that were born here. In totalitarian and fostering responsibility, the fate of nature is that she wars with the cold. Brought about like butter on the knife, spread onto the toast, and coated with honey, there are miracles of fate that watch the altruistic portent and knowledgeable disagreements with fairy tales and nature. Sucking on sin, finding faces in the clouds, have mercy, and not to require sacrifice in belittlement of rejection.

Putting the carrot before the donkey is a good way to get it going to pull the cart. Upset carts drag on the ground. Donkeys trip and fall down. Everything can go wrong with this rotten demise we call purgatory. Don't believe in purgatory and you will be right. You can control your thoughts and choose what to believe. Baby knows this for she is very critical and tempted to wish the Beast evil. But she does not, for there is enough evil in the world already.

Disappointment and hope go hand in hand. Obstructions of justice come with fairy tale dreams. Already peace binds the process of becoming immortal in a challenging room of resistance and a fashionable flavor of al dente. Just right, just done. To the kissing point of satisfaction. Plural disease with healing hand in hand, kiss grace for it is sufficient for our needs. Wanting and registering hope on betrayal is like falling on a rotten log. It hurts, you resist. Baby doesn't like to think about the Beast and what will happen to him. She shares no askance of his future, and denies having any responsibility to his deformed nature.

Plausible and regressive, the totalitarianism of fate must truly be right, without the hit man falling to pieces. Justify fate and you justify love.

Preposterous hope and believing in fairy tales like the Easter Bunny can be fashionable with fame. Equity and compliance come with the sharing of this Easter egg hunt tradition. Who hides the eggs and where is justice done? Why celebrate Easter? Is it fashionable for fame, or just an illustrious way of covering up Jesus the Christ and his ascension into heaven?

Boredom, denial, whatever. The Easter Bunny is fun to believe in and totally harmless. It is like a game that nobody really knows why they play. It is a highlight in the calendar year. Significant, sweet, and loving. Coloring eggs can be so healing, handled with tender care and creativity.

The hunt is the test. Good to make a map or list of where all the eggs are hidden. The rotten ones are on a list of dissimulation and portentous reprise. Faith in God and faith in hope.

Derelict and despondent, the noisy cluster of angels in heaven look down to smile on those of us who are having a good time. Fostered with fate and glory, many meaningless and disastrous hopes forego the inclusion of mandatory hope and sweated expunging to the pile of waste. Stinky, smelly, rotten garbage and shit and stuff go beyond the necessity of devising hope in a corner of oblivion. Mass suicide is not an accident. It is a running from fate into a terrible derelict faith of retardation and repressive enigma.

Battered and torn, the demise of reliance on grace is a gift and justifies mercy in place of sacrifice. Religion is not so hopeless and boring as it might seem. In fact there are many different religions, only one worshiping the Lord Jesus Christ and his Father, God, in heaven with the Holy Spirit.

Bitterness

Wasted reprieve, broken bonds, saturation with ignorance. What on earth does it take to bring back sweetness and pleasure? The horrid doom of homeless, broken down people now appears hopeful. There are many "mansions in heaven", and God has prepared a place for everyone on his list in the Book of Life.

Regarded with immanent glory, the surprise of true faith is that you can never be disappointed in God. He suffers seduction with hilarity, despising the very hands that wrought deceit in the world. Lewd and obstructive, the very nature of faith gives denial to questions of deliberation. Faithless and confused, comes with boredom and a question of aberration and unjust glory. Hanging onto forgiveness, saying "sorry" to those you need to apologize to, and allow the emotional emollient of sweetness to ride along your tail, and envision the proper retardant to incapable hands.

Interest in belief, getting past the "getting", and lording over the despondent nature of grief and recovery we find that very many things have very many rules that have all sorts of behaviors. In witness to recreation, the somnolence and outspoken words of truth are heady in reception by those listening. In portrayal of destiny, the sugar on the head was meant to repose in lighted danger and suicidal apportionment. Never on forgiveness. Only a little to dabble in, the rest for sweet history.

Matters of the heart are digested and sweet with rust and knowledge of sin. There is hope, we don't have to be rusty. Practice, practice, practice. Practice and overcome.

Naughty, naughty, naughty. Giving into temptation and foregoing the illustrious, obstinate sin cries out for mercy in our own uncharted futures. Picture the disgrace of mankind. It lies in the wicked. Fortuneless, pummeling in danger, and servitude on the road witnesses like faulty acid on white cotton paper. Pressing decency into hope maligns the fortune of the altruistic, although justifying disease cannot make regret with failure. Failure with redeeming repose, failure with blaming the devil.

Found in sin, found in uncovering blinded eyes, and purporting analysis with frequency into gestation and surmise, the beatific, unclouded features of God's face multiplies our rows of defeat and unnatural ecstasy. Waking up in faith and pushing forward with mercy, we grow proud in this loophole of forgiveness. There is time, there is hope; God gathers the clusters of his people from near and from far and puts them on a shore of destiny. Unfounded faith and deliverance with happiness and glee, there is ceremonial brigade loosened by qualms of the furious.

Gestational wisdom comes with the natural hope on the world, not a nasty, disgusting uncovering of destiny with a microscope. Bringing along the dead in wasted freedom helps to hold fast the security net of singing in the shower. Be brave, don't deceive, and don't play the fool. Resounding in nature, the bottomless religious factor of faith shows its faith in regeneration down on the line. Giving up hope and holding onto reality means you have gotten there. You don't hope for what you can see, rather for what you can't see .

Unnatural glory and stupendous demise gives obstruction to paranoid confusion and dazzles the fate of the world, our world, with reasons to go onward and upward in faith. Holding onto reliability, you find nature in repose with fortune, and the wicked don't go free.

Resolve

On account of ability and fortuitous behavior of the lost, there is a hand to hold onto that won't let you go. There is destruction in the lost where the wayfarers give up on timeless beauty and give into the suction of faith and superfluous destiny. Nobody else knows what you have been through. Egging on destiny defeats the purpose of religion and faith in peppermint drops. Destruction and accountability remain defeated in the will of the Lord, whose hands are not tied behind his back.

Grace and partition to the lost gives hope to the weary. For the trusting of nature and unnatural resolve holds hands with the ugly and the stupid.

Don't forget that the plain and stupid have faith too. And rejoice in it due to their injustice on this planet. Breaking up into little pieces, and then putting them all back together rights the wrong and cleanses wounds of sickness baited by deceit. Broken and unknowledgeable destinies requite to give absolve to the factions of industry that rely upon effort and restraint in the giving of hope to the unnaturally sardonic or deceived.

Picking up on cubes of frozen ice and rolling them around on your belly is a means of distracting you from suicidal thoughts. It is a frenzy, and a vendetta towards religion that stupefies greaseless foregoing apology and unturned leafs of new ways. Waking up in intrinsic nature, there is to absolve and resolve. Quaking with denial, the factor is true that God tests us but doesn't tempt us to do anything bad. Those are rotten hopes of forgotten glory that once seemed right but ran out of time. Even in the turning of the moon through the night across the skies of open destiny, we forsake gloom and Neanderthal development. Giving goodness to hope, and walking a straight line you follow Jesus who never misses a step. In walking he makes a Way to follow, and lives as the Truth and the Life. In him surpasses the public opinion of digestion and foreign inebriation. Plastered to the wall, sick with disgust. Redeeming failure and pruning our unnecessary parts, we live in cursed glory and phantoms of moonlight that sways the tides. Upheaval to glory gives fortification that lasts through the darkness of night. God made light to shine into the darkness, not the other way around.

Plagiarism and indecency is disrespectful to society. So short on hope and significant in paradigm. Crossing the t's and dotting the i's we submit to insignificance and focus on the puzzle pieces. It is right to do things right, and not to destroy the work of others. Resolve to do the right thing and you are on your way to wisdom and glory. Perpetuation of the needed instinct pushes past resolve for futuristic glory. Let glory be, here and now.

Not all that is good can be bad. There is right and there is wrong. Sometimes it hurts to be right, yet feels good to be wrong. That is quaking in sin and you should not do that. The Beast is wrong in his arbitrary demolition of his young adopted daughter. She is quick, she is faithful, she knows justice. There is justice and instinct, and unnatural gumption. Righteousness is good. It feels good, it sounds good, and it looks good. Looks goodness right in the eye and feels good about it. Unnecessary tokens of justice repeal the hands of fate on maturity. Broken and incessant are the cries of the wronged, who suffer sordid defeat and loss at the hands of the wrongful giant who stands taller than he is.

Justin no longer calls upon his sister, Baby Pollyanna, due to the discourse that is in him when he goes his own forbidden way. The truth is, he hates her just as much as he loves her, and hate is easier to grab a hold of. Unnatural and deniable gives fate to glory, in the instance of repose, a natural yet foregone character. Demise is destruction and it comes swiftly upon the wicked who will suffer in due time.

Uncommon hatred and sweated denial live in grace with the hand caught in the cookie jar. Too sweet to let go, yet the fist won't fit back out with the cookie in hand. Crumble the cookie and pull the hand out and it is spattered with cookie crumbs that fall to the floor. And wipe away guilt on sweatshirt and jeans.

Unpopular gives disfavor to the resolve of guardian versus somnolence, whispers in the ear that are no longer sweet nothings, but threats to kill, maim, and destroy.

Sweet nothings in the ear are forbidden for the sake of sanity. Only those words you were meant to hear will be sounded within your range of hearing. What if you cannot hear? Or what if you hear too much? In itself an oxymoron that dilutes character with praise.

Significant failure lost to disrespect comes with the truth in burning glory of failure due to sin.

Sin, the big "S" word is not a stupid word that someone just made up. For the purpose of its meaning, it describes what unnaturally we should not do.

Repose is qualitative and ugly, overcoming in blessings and purported on faith destructive of the elegant. Walking a straight line makes your path straight and easy to follow. Truth enlisting with behavior and confidence, allows for freedom to walk through the door. And who doesn't want that? Crazy as it seems, the superfluous describes hatred in all of its unremitting crooning coming through the windows left open at night. The wind, the earth turning, the beauty of the stars in the sky, by nature is the earth stupendous in glory made by one who knows exactly what he made and has no apology for it.

Resolve for opinion is belligerent and disgraceful, pruning the factors that waste energy and grafting in the branches that provide hope and glory to the engine machine too tall for twisting branches to take down.

Glowing with rescinding fate and absolute turntable justice lies with faith in the resolve. It is a treasure to practice from your heart. For where your treasure is there is your heart indeed. Focus on sustenance, thinks Baby when she falls down in her walk of faith. For her it is like the worm in the dirt that is spared from the shovel, too small to be applauded yet peaceful in thought.

Resolve is unfocused energy brought to a point. This is significant in failure free of sin. The word again. Too altruistic is it to have a word that names our "sins". Regretful but true, there is apology and forgiveness for sins that can set you free from it all. All of it. The grasping branches in the Lord's tree of justice brought about by illumination of glory in the heart; it feels good, righteousness, and should not be denied.

Discredited by maladjusted preposterous aliens, the fingers of the Lord write names in the sand. Bending over backwards, the salient revisions of sin are stupendous in facilitated depression, like the depression that has haunted Baby all her life. She still takes anti-depressants and finds no shame in that. William loves her and the time is soon approaching when the two will marry and become one in the Lord. True she was married once before, but to her analytical thinking mind she finds repose with the quality of divorce versus eternal unhappiness.

She found faith, she found glory. She resists bringing him to visit Mom, but he goes anyway, not wanting the Beast to get away with anything unnatural or nasty, if even a bad word or undeserved repellant thought.

Repellant thinking, she decides, is a good way to ward off the enemy. Tangible and true, our thoughts are movements in the mind. Breakable in the broken brain. Fed the wrong foods and drinking that which is too salty or too sweet.

Infectious laughter comes to Baby when they get home from a visit. William is egging along their probable move to the country for a house of their own, away from the Beast and from Justin, who only hold her down out of guilt. Yet Mom needs her, she knows this, and so hangs on to the hand of her supermom. This galactic surprise comes as a mystery to all of them. Why does Mom stay where she is?

Truth, faith, and destiny keep her from sinning against her husband. Although she is tempted, she does not break him down or overturn his wheelbarrow in the yard. Inflicting danger on him, like she yearns to do, would only pollute a bad thing into something worse and bitter and not reproving. Swift and crappy dysfunction comes upon him as he gets older. He turns taciturn and untraceable in his evil ways and pathetic limping around the house. Too beautiful to destroy, yet impotent and unstructured. Defeat does not fit his character, and diffuses into the rottenness of his injunction and elaborate hateful patterns throughout each day, no one knowing him completely, yet not wanting to.

Grave and disgusted, paralysis of contribution merges with his savior's approval, yet his wickedness is undeniable in all its portentous hate and glorification. Factored out of altruistic disgust, no noble thing will rear its head above him. Even Strawberry keeps her distance from him and follows Mom around the house.

Perfect and gentle, obedient and kind, she goes on long walks with Mom, but only the two of them and Strawberry. The Beast finds too many reasons not to go. Geoffe cannot be a husband to her, for he forgives nothing and gives arbitrarily without meaning and resolve. Too much hatred, too much impenitence.

Trustworthy

Observant to quality and natural turgid hatred and disgust, the viral truth of inept fornication of the mind goes hand in hand with the easy disgusting habit of asking for things. Sin, sin, sin. Arbitrary and convenient. He is disrespectful to Mom, yet gives her easy feed back for her continual caring and contribution to his unfeigned happiness. Grueling and reproachful, the suicide of his danger is maniacal with regret. Like fallen flowers in the snow, where did they come from? Did someone drop them on the way to the cemetery? Who will put flowers on his grave? Who will watch him go? Who will save him when he can't come back? Then who will call to him?

Cranial disgust and demise, the prolific entity of despair, and the conjugated opinion of honoring the most dishonorable, it is mad suicide.

Hateful back handed shit and stuff, according to Mom who hasn't given up on Justin either. The two of them come in one pod. Both are wicked, and both are destructive. Anomaly beyond consent there is resistance to the slipping and sliding feet in the mud as failure retracts and doom takes over. Baby is resistive, yet strains madly against denial of hope. A part of her loves what was her dad, what began as her brother, so she feels sinful in her guilt. Yet the quaking denial of the cold and oblong necessities of cranial hatred booby-trap discovery is a shadow of what is to come. Only in the belonging of fate to aspiration does the minute hand keep going round the clock.

Destructive in reality and paralytic in hope. Truth versus denial is unacquainted with suffrage and opinion. Put all the votes in, yet God makes the decision in the end. This is alluding to his behavior of loving assistance and graphic reduction of the flood that will never come. Not according to God's promise with the rainbow, (Genesis 9:12-16).

The rainbow stands as a symbol to God's promise to never flood the earth with water again. We wake up in despair, people drown in the waters of earth. Pointedly, and ignorantly, the faith that sucks down on seduction balances hope with negativity. A brat finds a trap and must find her way out. The behooved swallow whole that which is caught by the fly swatter. Ignorant in sin, the unlucky give justice to name of their favorite character, and why. No one loves to give insolence as much as a patterned and effective way of telling the truth. Annotated perjury presses indecently upon the warped and misleading characters of injustice and defeat. Even somnolence, in the night, revision of the disgusted betrays patterns of squeaky feet in the hallway. No one knows for sure how it goes, yet it remains that you learn to identify who it is by the sounds of their feet. Some scuff, some slide, some clip and some pop or stick until lifted. Sounds and noises of feet let you know you are not alone. Barking up the wrong tree is malignant and oppressive to your turntable justice which refuses to remove destiny from hoping and learning about residual anger.

Pop and turn, press and squeak, scuff, scuff, scuffle... each one is different, and Baby has recognized everyone's footsteps in the house where she grew up. Sometimes she gets tense, other times she relaxes. Probably the sound of Rexi's feet is the best for her.

In this new haven of her apartment with William, she celebrates each day with a positive thought about him. Even internal combustion of her placid emotions, she recognizes death before it is made real to her. Never giving up, sometimes she replaces negative thoughts with broken yet positive ones. It is being quiet when there is so much to say. It is just.

Venom and capacities of disrupted behavior forego the crematorium with riches of grace and glory. Disgruntled and preposterous design give up hope when nectar doesn't come. No one betrays Jesus and gets away with it. Of this she is sure, and overcomes her nonentity of survival with a talking twist of fate. Fat and overloaded, the discriminatory obsolescence of denial twisted with defeat hobbles on broken hooves and lacerated paws.

Criminology and defeat and destiny. There is hope and faith in denial of the twisted truths, that those who are trustworthy will not give up or give in. It is lewd and preposterous in the fated angelic patterns of forgiveness and miracles.

Take away the bad and you destroy hope, for there is no longer any need of it. Suffering on suffocation, nothing forgives as well as the penitent heart and the aberrant mind. Nothing breaks the penitent heart but a lie from the enemy.

Yet God prepared a feast for the just in the presence of their enemies. Forgive your enemies and it is just as pouring coals of fire onto their heads. Resolve to be trustworthy, keep trying, and you just might make it.

Elaborate and qualified truth sticks with gusto to the right and good, picking up on broken vendettas and putting grease to the squeaky wheel.

Nothing is so glad as the heart that has been blessed by God. Not by Geoffe, for he has no blessings to give and he neither receives any from anyone else. He is tolerated to the end by his wife. His son reveres him like a God, and his daughter Rexi puts up with him, but Baby neither likes nor discards him. She is leaving his destiny up to God, and she will not intervene. Mapping out the territory of the twisted and venomous mind, we find capability put to no good use but to irritate others by constantly deriding them. It is as though he gets pleasure out of irritating and disrupting others in their thoughts, interjecting discouragement and bad luck energy. Both of which can be wiped away quickly if practiced, and both of which are a waste of heaven's gifts on earth.

Injustice and benevolent hand and hand retardation give a quip to the reality of instance and repose. Nobody narcs on wisdom or forgets an apology. Twisted faith and patterned necessity are too forgiving to be real. There is a werewolf world with lechery and blood sucking. Not real, but hating it in the inception of evil into goodness. Phantoms of the night, hatred during the day. Two very appropriate evils that have escaped into our earth. No one knows it, but they are real. They take what they cannot have, give faith to the true, and let go with evil reprise. Negative glare and angered resistance obstruct apology and plot evil while lying down all day, submitting to opulent build up of the body, and weakening of the lungs.

Trustworthy Baby hates to see her Dad like this. He is like, and is, a Beast sucking on the fat of others, even when he can't quite reach out to get it. He sucks and sucks and sucks and blows hard, yet his elevating blood pressure pushes him into the cushions so soft yet worn down.

Trustworthy Baby makes notes in her mind about how to get around trusting her Dad each time he betrays her with inception and botched goodwill eaten by moths. Forgiveness in her is decent and palpable, yet she bites back now and stares at him with leery eyes.

William thinks it is a waste of time to see him, for he only brings out the worst in her, and beats her down like a fallen rose to the ground, stepped on and squished.

Mom is grateful to see Baby when she visits. She has her own life now and is able to pick up the strings and go along for the ride with Geoffe. Tentative, mistrusting, she juggles on her feet to shy away from his avid bow and arrows of poison which he aims to for the heart. The Beast knows how to get what he wants, but he doesn't know what he wants and is in random betrayal of himself. Needy and greedy. Supplication and factions of demise. Glory to God for the worshipping of Jesus. Incentive and altruistic resolve.

William, too, is trustworthy. His love for Baby extends to her family, but not pointedly to Justin or the Beast. Baby grasps with pinching fingers to pull out the good from the bad. She overcomes justice by tattered resolve and penitent futuristic placidity. Quiet in repose, and bending over backwards, the trustworthy William baits his time and climbs out of the shower with forgiveness on his barren heart

.

He is greedy for the supply of love that comes from Baby to him, for God's eternity, and the special gestation of overcoming guilt with surprise.

Founding in faith regressed with sin comes the supplicant and dastardly submission of the fool. Broken and slow minded, nasty Justin feeds on blood sucking like his Dad. Together they watch football and make grunting noises.

Active and coagulant, despair and reproach, the nasty with the wise is not a good combination. Featuring lust and maligned wonder, the justice of faith and rescinding allocation of the opposite wonders we find mercy in strings of gold cast down by heaven to lift up the weary. Baby is weary, yet she cannot give up the fight. The fight of figuring out who she is, what she wants, and how to achieve success in her life.

Composite realism finds alienation to be too subversive for anyone's good. Crafty and cutthroat, the center of pleasure for the Beast is his own imagination. Here he creates what he wants while wasting time on not getting it. Subversive pleasure picked up while sinning cannot go on. In time it will become the fool's demise and the factoring in of sin will only bring him down harder than before. Each time he goes down, he goes deeper, and his eyes are growing very dark. He can't see the rainbow, but would hate it anyhow.

Blasting through repugnance for sin we come upon the miracle of fate found in destiny. Knowing how to hold on to suggestive remittance, quiet crying betrays nothing and is healing for the soul. Laughter is healing for the soul, yet there is no laughter in the Beast's home, only barks and gruff attempts at conversation when it comes to needs. Thankfully Baby doesn't live there. The poison seeps through the walls and the paint on the house is covered with moss. Breaking down of the walls and entering into his studio of messes, the breaking challenge of reissue comes as a surprise to his arbitrary madness.

Functional, yet sublime, and only in reason and glory, the operative factor of somnolence plays on the Beast's forgotten mind as he pummels the walls for pleasure and satisfaction and disgrace. He needs angels, he gets demons.

Tension

Disparate tensions swing back and forth on the chandelier in the living room. Geoffe has a dartboard that he plays on between moments of neophyte retardation of his mind. No one can beat him at darts, yet he uses them for entertainment anyhow. Not even then can he take pleasure in success. Baby hates the dartboard, and has always hated the dartboard. No one has ever been hit by a stray dart, for none of them go astray. He plays with darts and collects guns and knives. He has a big chest full of his expansive collection. Once a target shooter and deer hunter now he lies in rumination with his memories. Satisfaction does not imply to him that he is happy. He can't read his life well enough to know if he *is* happy or not. Fateful and foolish, he manages to smile when Mom brings him his daily cup of coffee. He sweats and stinks. He is repulsive to her.

Everywhere she goes, she is trying to get away from him. What can she do? Move in with Baby and William when they get their new house? Could she leave Geoffe? Just up and leave him there to waste away in his own hatred and disgust?

Making up for building tension between everyone, there are the holidays that stand for Christ. Christ who forgives and forgets, as far as the east is from the west. New to him, the Beast, is his seemingly unable reproach for getting what he wants. As he sinks deeper and deeper into the couch, he breathes fate with glory and finds the devil parading around on his werewolf belly needing bloody road-kill to perpetrate the lemon headed obstruction between his mind and his stinking, rancid soul. Bloody in all of its jaded scraping of the walls, in desperate confusion, not knowing how to escape the falling in of the roof, and the tattered rug beneath him. He falls deeper and deeper. His eyes get sore and tired. His breathing labored and studded with drool.

Perpetrating in his mind is a concubine nymph sucking on his sweet breath, polluted by sugar and filled with animosity from his undone religion. Plastered like grease on the stove, he ruminates with his head between his knees, plowing through rows and rows of planted tares. He has no harvest. He belongs to no harvest. He will not be harvested. Only in the opening up of his soul can he let in the light of day, yet he refuses to do so. Bumping along, the ego in his brain tells him he is miserable and he does not know why. His sinning fingers manipulate the remote for his wide screened TV. His demand for coffee comes right on time at two o'clock every day even when Mom is not there. This puts him through the roof in a rage and carnal disgust for this aberration of a wife that he puts up with. He is blinded by fate and sees not what once was so beautiful, for their love is gone.

Wasted in inclination and patterned resolve, the ugliness of his fate becomes a weight on everybody. Yet Mom shoulders the burden, keeping him comfortable with an illness he can only know as self hatred, and he does not know this. His weak and feeble knees ache during the night and he whines getting in and out of bed. Mom has put up a cot in the bedroom and will not sleep in the same bed as her husband. This only makes him confused.

Pride and hatred come in short quality, where dissertation and opulent disgust filter through with his disgusting armpits and smelly bottom. His hair is a greasy mess, and he only showers twice a week. The dog ignores him, just as Mom does. It is her defense against him. For what he did and what he does. All the time a new thing comes into the house each day. Mom and Baby put their heads together and decided to invite the pastor from the church to come over and have a little talk with Geoffe. This he was willing to do, unaware of the circumstances.

Upon stepping into the house, he feels the negative energy, the rank odor, and something sweet, but he does not know what it is. He steps into the living room, and there is Geoffe sitting up with sweating palms, breathing heavily. The pastor is short but sweet in his stay, for he knows the problems here lie deeper than his resolve for the day. Something evil is at large and he does not know what.

He sits down in an easy chair and greets Geoffe with a smile, reaching out to shake his hand. Geoffe lets the hand fall, and neglects to reach out and shake it. He is quivering with something satanic, but not to his knowing. He only knows that he doesn't like visitors on account of his social inebriation or rather, his inability to give and take. He receives this guest with a gruff hello. They talk. Geoffe meanders through thoughts of discomfort and inability to feel God. He asks the pastor if he is doomed, because he feels that way. He complains about his ornery daughter, Baby, who scares him. He is in need of rejection, but he doesn't know why. Fate has taken hold, he thinks, as the lost intelligence in his mind fails to reel in the hope and forgiveness of Christ that the pastor bears. He smiles, a rarity, and makes a stupid joke about the son of God, and how his own son is just as good if not better. His twisted reality falls on uneager ears, lifting fate and fortune into manipulative patterns that resurge with gross indolence and broken spirit.

Somehow, if only he would pray for healing for her husband, Mom eagerly fills in details from day to day routine and obsolescent scales of propriety that drop on one end and leave each day with a few small tears.

What can she do to help her husband? Won't he recognize the hand of Jesus to take hold of? Ornery and belligerent, Geoffe shoos the minister out of his man cave and insists that Mom sees him to the door. Why this disruption for all of his daily blindness brought to bear before his seeking eyes?

Sadistic in hatred and controlled resolve, the fire in his eyes is ugly and obtrusive. Pimples on his chin are growing in number, and he scratches and whines about the discomfort. What oblivion is this, he wonders? Where can his passion go if it is not for the fireplace across the room, and the insensitive TV that laughs at his emotions. Quibbling with restraint, positive in coming undone, his broken fingers keep trying to turn pages of a book. Not a good one, but he reads it anyway. So many pages to turn, nothing doing.

Broken chimes in the yard are ambivalent against nature, yet their constant ringing soothes his weary soul. Little does he know that he is already condemned. He does not know that he is not in the Book of Life or in God's hands. God does not want him, yet he lives on in serene opulence and purported behavior. Sucking, sucking on bloody incinerated thoughts, he can't remember why he started feeling this way. In truth he is in denial about his condition, a wasted breath of life, only to retard forgiveness in his insensitive condition. Baleful eyes hate the walls that surround him as he looks out from the bottom of a pit he has somehow fallen into. Or did he dig it himself around him? He's lost, confused, and upset. Everyday the same thing. And then his chin. Ouch! Mom urges him to wash it with water and soap, to cleanse his whole body in the shower more often. Dreadfully despised by his condition, the shower only means more disruptive activity to an uphill battle that is rolling down like so many logs. A king's legs are longer than the hooks in his fingers, which manipulate something at all times. Even if it means to manipulate himself into resurgent broken down sexual hatred.

Nobody knows, nobody cares. It is his doom, his fate, his repulsion from the world that will not walk with him to his eternal doom. Damnation. The end. The kill, the rotten insides that take over and defeat him. Nebulous, recharged and in maddened disgrace, his suicide would do him one last good turn. Yet he waits and waits daily. Not knowing what he is waiting for. In regret he quietly wastes away and Mom begins to lift her head again. She finds flowers in the garden that she doesn't remember putting there. She picks up after Strawberry every day. She walks her everyday and sometimes takes her on trail hikes where dogs are permitted. Everyday she practices her yoga, she reads interesting novels and she thinks about Baby and William, two positive pillars in her life. She thinks of them and swoons with ecstasy that they are there to help her bear the load. Rexi doesn't even come to visit anymore. She's too busy working and taking care of the family. No one understands why she refuses to come, but Mom somehow thinks she does. She knows it is Geoffe, who yelled at Rexi last time she visited and called her an ungrateful child. This she could not take, and did not visit again.

Mature and hopeless, she finds enervating energy in the eclipse of her sodden days, dank with the moisture of the fields of glory that surround Baby, who loves still to do her landscaping. Here and around and around. Mom knows she doesn't want a baby, and understands this in her daughter. Who would think, that the one adopted would be the one most faithful? Her hands are tired and she cannot help them, yet with remorse she realizes that suicidal sin is not a pleasant energy to be around, and causes great tension in the air. The Beast now plays with himself regularly. Just a bit of release to tend to his rotten constitution.

Regularly, the act of submission to his body keeps him bored and longing for something more. Something he can't quite grasp and that is slipping away from him. He rarely gets off the couch now and sleeps there at night. The bedroom makes him claustrophobic and he can't breathe in there, in there where his two full blooded children were conceived. He hates that Rexi won't come. He shudders and quakes whenever Baby sets foot in the house. Often times she brings him donuts. Frosting covered donuts that taste so good. Only to leave again with Mom on a walk or a trip to the mall where they can wander about and buy new things.

Nobody understands why faith stands in the way of rape, of evil done not to be forgiven. Chided by his wife, the Beast roars in anger at her only to be scolded in his big, massive, ugly face. His sneaky eyes veering from side to side, making little contact with anything on the walls, just the TV.

Rape and then rape again. Giving into suicide would not behoove him in his foolish pride. To him life is neither good nor bad. It just is.

Little by little the Beast is slipping away in madness and defeat. Quibbling over nothing, he cannot resist his punishment. Giving over to faithful compliance with his watch that he looks at every five or fifteen minutes. He is counting the time… till what?

Unfinished servitude, molesting and raping his daughter, his precious Pollyanna. Every one laughs when he says the wrong thing. He is ridiculed, he is despised. Foreign relations are astonished at his gross encounter with fate, when he curses God and throws mental shit at the savior. The savior who sees him exit life one last time, forever to live in shit and hell.

Never to return, never to see anyone again. The tension is high in his mind as he thinks on thoughts he can't find, and flows with the standard judgment that has come against him. Querulous in retard, his insignificant judgment can only pale at the oncoming anxiety and paranoia that he feels in his last days, breaking down into crushed enigma, and fortune telling of his remote constitution.

Then Mom comes into the living room one morning and finds him dead on the couch. She screams, shrieks, and calls 911.

Overturned

Thankful for each day she has before her, Mom no longer suffers through her days. Geoffe was dead and buried before she knew it. It accosted her with pleasure, and she woke once more knowing again that each day will be crawling out of this hole, this pit she had inhabited through the life of Geoffe. Dead and gone. No more moaning and crying over every little movement. No more blood sucking breath over her hurting soul.

She turns around and starts over. Against the wind, she forces her life into an overturned position. Thanks to Jesus she is free again, and she welcomes him into her home, where the stench of Geoffe rubs off on everything until she realizes that she can no longer live in this house.

Overturned, her faith multiplies as she recognizes the hell she has been through, putting up with Geoffe. Broken down and wasted, gone. She finds herself smiling into the mirror again, and the loss of her husband comes as a relief to her. Not only her, but Baby and William rejoice together. Justin is pitiful in his weeping and grieving over his lost role model. To Justin Dad could do no wrong, in fanciful behavior and backwards sin. Justin's mild mental slowness is not a complement to his personality. Rachel skates around him, and works as a busy Mom.

Enthralling energy slowly begins to rise in Baby, Mom, and even Rexi, who came for the funeral and stayed a couple of weeks. She resented having missed his death, and now rejoices with Baby Pollyanna who is set free from demise.

Strokes of the clock wind happily into the chilling fortitude of her dreams. At night she sleeps happily with William, and together they make a union of sublime and ultimate perfection. Work has no hold on her, she has a hold on her work. Every day she feels Satan slipping further and further away. Satan and his kingdom come at last to total annihilation. Nobody sees Geoffe, and he sees nobody. Fretful and nervous at first after the death, Mom is getting a grip on her life as well.

The flurry of butterflies in her mind is gentle and intricate. Each butterfly has its own patterned wings, and gentle dust clings to her mind in their play.

Resurgent and obtrusive, quacking like ducks on the water, Mom's opinion about herself is sordid and proud. How she did it, she did not know. This Beast, this Beast, would it forever haunt her?

Munching on man cave energy, the walls suck up the aura of Geoffe that stays standing in the living room. Everybody hates it, no one can stand it, except for Justin who worships it. In his denial of Christ and his humiliation being pardoned in intricate despair, love for Mom reaches inside and spanks his weary soul, for he too, is wasted on his journey.

Everyone knows the fate of shit and stuff. It is no more. Strawberry growls at Justin and keeps her distance.

Passion Rejected

Obsequious maladjusted disappointment shadows Justin's every step. He is being followed by hell and does not know it. Every time he turns around he sees something else, something new. It blinds him in his slowness and absconds his feeble mind that is fat on taking advantage of people. He succumbs to the lethargy of burnt crosses in his living room. Burned in the fireplace standing up one at a time.

Justin inherits Geoffe's knife and gun collection, and he is quick to take the dartboard too. This makes him smile with an evil, sickly grin. Overboard on luck, he makes mash of millions of pesticides in Baby's closet, which she keeps in her mind away from people. Here she prays to her Jesus, her Lord and Savior. Pregnant at last, she prays to hold onto this baby.

Futile in her own collection of bad memories, she knows that the Beast will haunt her no more. Never will he see this grandchild, who, thank God, has no blood relation with him.

Foreign intrusion brings fate about with regression, as the anomalies of fitting in at church take over and she realizes that a wedding would be proper.

She forsakes her dignity and decides to wait with the wedding. To her, she's not ready yet.

Poor William is at a loss. He fears for the baby that Baby might miscarry again. He can only hope and pray and dote on her with every good thing he can think of. She is agreeable to his love, and affection in every candid moment. Life eternal is grand indeed, she realizes, and knows that she will keep this child. If only it were true.

Nasty thoughts pry at the corners of her mind as the Beast gradually suffocates in her presence and leaves her hurting soul.

No more Beast, says the Baby, the one and only adopted daughter in the family. So she clings to her church family as well, and Mom, too, is coming out of her funk.

Rexi is forbidden from coming into her prayer closet. The one she has in her mind. She doubts that Rexi is saved, yet she can't be sure. She resolves to bring this up with her sister (cousin). Fruitless and hopeless, she miscarries yet again. Tears fall freely, the song in her heart is turned towards hope and happiness, not regression and failure.

Baby likes coming out of the closet, and doesn't blame God for her own bad luck. In decency of opinion her passions reign with the Bible and her day to day activities. She swoons into religion, admiring every token of Christ on the cross. For by his stripes we are healed, she recollects from the Bible. (1 Peter 2:24, Isaiah 53:5) Now she is doomed for her destiny, a frog in the water, and a fish on the line. Justin betrays her every chance he gets, always fanning the flame that reaches out to her soul. She absconds his presence in her life and can't wait to move.

Mom and Baby have talked, and she agrees it would be good to move in with them. A great weight has been lifted, and she sees no point in living alone. She loves her adopted daughter, Baby, and treats her with special regard and hope for a beautiful future ahead. She no longer has mercy for Justin. She doesn't know why, but the thought came to her not long ago. When she sees the way he treats Baby, tricking her and hurting her every time she gives up hope for his future, she wonders why she has ever put up with him. A disgraceful child, bad manners, sloth ridden speech, a carrier of depression and demise. His first instinct is to shoot down that which is good in the world, perceiving it all as the enemy. Disgraceful, subjugated, pressed into place, his happy religion of death and demise feasts helplessly on Mom and Baby. Rexi now hates him too, her childhood companion.

Betrayed and awakened, the formula for peace comes with reprise and obedience to the Lord. The Lord who loves Mom, Baby, and Rexi and her children, as well as William and Paul, and Justin's confused children and diligent wife, Rachel. This is the family that the Lord loves. Some behavior is irreparable, and now there is nothing left to suck on for Justin. He betrays himself and goes walking at night, in front of buses, and then dodging them just in time.

No one knows why Justin is so evil. He ranks in sin and falls out of the family, yet his wife and children remain. For this he hates and despises them, and takes out his anger on them. He tries to do evil in return for their goodness. Even Paul knows that Justin's children have the hand of Christ on them, and that they need to be rescued. Rexi prays with Paul, who has always been a Christian, and she accepts Jesus as her Lord and Savior. Now she, too is saved, yet again mincing on Justin's feet and pulling him down lower and lower. Munch, munch, munch. Justin stuffs his face at meal times and gives ugliness to his wife, whom he once loved, and now can't analyze what sort of relation she is to him.

She cries out at night, in blistering forgiveness of his rude behavior. She reaches out to Mom, who put up with Geoffe for so many years. Together they plan the way to treat Justin so nobody gets hurt anymore. First of all, stop doing him favors to please him. Next let him make his own dinners and other meals. Then to keep him away from his children so as not to do harm to them.

Both Mom and Rachel agree that he is a runoff from a very wicked father. One who agreed on everything mutant in the world, that faith might slide down the ladder and get lost in decrepit holes in the ground.

Passions rejected, uphill battle that it is, the nuance is to take control of Justin and reject his awful behavior for the sodden ignorance that it is. He blows his own horn, yet demolishes his chances for grace in line with throwing goodness out the door, and throwing darts at the dartboard. Quiet at last, Mom's house needs to go on the market. She wants to get an apartment, but that would not work with Strawberry to keep on.

She knows that the sale of the house would give her enough to buy a small house in the city with a yard and a mailbox. She goes looking with William, having decided to get her own place, and he wants to make sure that she gets into a good home, not a rundown piece of shit. The last thing Mom needs is more shit and stuff.

They find a house at last that meets all the check points on their list. Clean, well kept, nice yard, two bedrooms, two baths, roomy kitchen and living room with modern appliances and a fireplace. Laundry room downstairs, back porch, driveway for the car, and affordable.

"Let's take it!" shouts Baby when William informs her of their find. "Before it's too late." Mom is lucky to be able to afford it. With Geoffe's pension and her own social security, she is in good standing. Every body loves the house, even Rexi who comes to see what all the talk is about.

Moving day comes and every body pitches in. Soon Mom is moved and unpacked, taking her time to put things where she wants them. She needs new furniture, anything that doesn't have the disgusting odor of Geoffe on it. Her kitchen supplies are radiant and fairly new. Stock and still, she runs around putting things in place and aerating the house to bring fresh air into her home. Strawberry loves the yard and plays like a puppy outside.

Mom has a house warming party and manages to do it without Justin but including Rachel and the kids. He is not welcome there and knows it. Mom gave him a good, firm talking to not long ago and bashed him with her goodness and faithful enmity. She knows what he did to Baby in the past, and the awful way he still treats his own adopted sister. She wins, he loses.

Vibrancy

So Justin is now estranged from the family. This blatant rejection to him somehow hurts his ego. He faints and fawns himself, knowing that if Dad were still here everything would be right.

His nuptial agreement about sex is that he fornicates with his own wife, taking her when she is not ready, and using her body whenever he pleases. The danger in this is that his concupiscent attitude toward his wife, Rachel, covers her with sin and hurt and grief. She is not strong like Mom and can't vow to stay with Justin till the end. How long would that be? And he hurts her? To her heart he is a poisonous arrow. Sufficient for sin, yet she knows that Jesus can help. With the strength of Baby she can do this. Baby divorced quite a few years back. Of course she had no kids, yet the situation was right in that the yarn they spin is neglecting of reticent sin and obnoxious behavior. Jeremy didn't exactly hurt Baby, but she knew then it was not what she wanted.

William helped her be strong. He knew about Justin and what an awful character that he was. He knew that Rachel was suffering at the hands of her husband. He was guilty of abuse, and needed to feel her rejection in bringing up her demand for a divorce.

Justin went through the roof when she first told him. She questioned him. Would he do it? In his narrow minded head he could not believe that this was real. It was just a stone in his narrow path that he walked, forcing him to go around it and only push her into the wall. With seething breath and muscled arms he beat her and beat her. Now she can see, he says that there is no divorce and never will be.

Rachel calls the police and reports to them about the abuse of her husband, which extended to her poor and frightened children as well.

Baby prays with William that all will go well and according to plan. Rachel gets the divorce and full custody of her children, plus a restraining order on Justin to keep him away. After spending some time in jail, followed by a short term in prison, he is escalated to a rude and profitless place in life, morose and helpless when he gets out, and in need of counseling.

This he refuses, yet takes as an ordinance that forces him to seek knowledge of destructive tendencies in himself. He is pitiful, he is reticent. He throws his darts at the board in the small studio apartment that he obtains upon release from prison. He has a small lump sum in the bank that he can live off for awhile. Rachel manages her burden with a childcare babysitting job at home.

William and Baby are glad when this has all worked out. Baby knows that Justin is just seething with rage, yet he works diligently at his daily factory job, polishing pieces of metal to be used in airplanes and wheel chairs.

He succumbs, he submits. He cries and he walks through his daily regime, forcing his petulance upon the derided cover of dirt that traces him everywhere. Still he thinks of shit and stuff and the way his mother had hated it when he stunk up the house with his precious dog feces. He thinks back on Corny who was a good dog for the family.

He drinks at night after work, yet controls the amount he takes in. He has been inebriated and vomited enough times that he knows not to go overboard, and he wishes for Rachel to "come home" to him, where he promises he will be good to her. Rachel doesn't take his phone calls, and gets a new phone line.

The kids are a bit disoriented, not putting up with the abuse from dad who used the belt freely on them. Jesus has stepped into the picture, and Rachel is extremely well suited for her job, taking in up to seven or eight children at a time.

Expressive and despotic, Rachel goes through each day feeling better all the time. She is clearly responsible enough for her duties, and begins attending Baby's church as well with her kids and William and Mom. She bares her soul before the church who takes her in with open and loving arms, something she has never had before. She's always been shit on in this life, and her purgatory went on for many years before she got saved, and clear with Jesus Christ. It is a religion that she absolves, turning the universe around to face her this time, and knowing that her walk with Christ will make her stronger and bring healing from her sordid past.

Rachel especially likes Rexi, who relates to her well in account of their respective children. The little ones are all close in age and respectively love their cousins.

Baby creeps up on William to see if he wants to try one more time. For her sake he says "no", not wanting her to go through another miscarriage to which she is unnaturally prone. She is sad. Yet she doesn't want to adopt either. She satisfies herself beginning with childcare at the church, and filling the nursery with her positive loving grace and care and her heart swollen with goodness bringing peace to all the young ones under her watch and biblical guidance.

Contrary to her new beginnings, the once abused Baby is not at all abusive. In fact she has more love in her heart than a room full of average people. She shines above indecency, and carefully minds the children in her care. She is obedient to sin because she denies it and abstains from it and never says a bad word to anybody. Even to Justin in the end who could not raise an eyebrow to her. She forsook her sin, the sin that was placed on her, and has risen above all that was once wrong. With William she is eternally hopeful, and knows that life ahead should be full of mysteries and many turns of events.

Gracious and loyal, she keeps an eye on her Mom, and visits once or twice a week. Together they work in the yard and Mom's green thumb is comparable to Baby's.

The whorish feelings in her has disappeared now without Geoffe who used her much like Justin used Rachel. From the beginning it was bad and she wanted to get out, yet with Baby coming to them and the two other kids in need, she didn't think to divorce, but abided by her wedding vows, something noble to do, but definitely not necessary. She has joined a support group for battered wives, and it is on her plate to heal.

Tag Along

With inertia being as heavy as can be, there is no newfound opinion deserving the respect of children, who are laid up and not ready to revive. Rachel's children are extremely obedient, to the point of unnatural fear. Somehow they play well with Paul and Rexi's kids who visit now and then. More often now that Geoffe no longer resides there, and even Justin is lacking from the picture to the disgrace of Rachel who strives hard to overcome.

In nature, people naturally come to people they respect and enjoy. The tag along appearance of broken children is faulty and impure. Some lash out, some cower. Some are just angry and afraid and have this conditioned into them.

Everywhere she goes with them, Rachel's kids begin to heal as well and open up to their Mother, who has not always been able to be there for them by the abuse of their father. Who was neglectful and put great strain on his expectations of them to do exactly what he says and when he says it.

The newfound opinion in her life is that her children love her and need her and give her the respect she deserves, as well as helping her around the house and contributing effort for the childcare babysitting job that Rachel runs successfully.

Eloquent retardation from guilt and despair comes to a point of remittance and subjugated reprise deigned to be with the ignorance of reprise. Functioning in warbles of birds at the window, there is grace and hope for the despairing and those who have been soulfully suffocated.

Baby has come a long way since her horrific incident at twelve years of age. Now, the Beast is gone and is slipping and sliding out of everyone's memory. Even as she hopes to recover, Mom is successful in her support group and makes a handful of new friends.

She resolves to get better every day, and minds that she walks her dog each day for both of their benefits. Strawberry is a polite and loving dog. Her big head can be frightening to see, yet her demeanor is so sweet and gentle that she comforts all who are uncomfortable, and rejoices only as a dog can in the presence of healthy, whole people.

Bring about faith and the story gets even better. No longer are the destructive elements of the family in control. With faith and resistance and healing, the coming of age in this town for these people is reliant and absolutely admirable.

Everyone in this family has a place and a memory and a joke to tell. When Geoffe rises up, someone puts a foot in that hole and suffocates him to death. Everywhere he goes in the memories of each person there is death and hatred and uncommon resolve. He hates to love death, yet none of him remains. Only a resolute disturbance that can't be avoided due to such an animalistic tag along. In fact, the Beast tags along quite often in Baby's thinking, and with Rexi and with Mom. Justin whines with her on the phone when he deigns to call her, begging to see her, yet she won't.

Obtrusive and despairing, the insolent fiend readjusts his focus and concentrates in his menial job where he must go and show up each day but not on the weekends. He has, in fact, never seen Mom's new house. And neither is he welcome there.

Careful and random come the clues of destiny that will fall upon listening and attentive ears. Prorated to justice, the winning hand in the game goes to Baby, Rexi, Mom, and Rachel, those most affected by the Beast in his stay here on earth. Sublime religion and expedient perplexity bring new faith to the hurting souls who so need Jesus and his love. The Father deigns to comfort his loved ones, and brings about change for the futile hope that resides in them. Even though his toehold on destiny is bright and shiny, the imposition of evil spirits carries demolition for the fried and attributed nuances that disgust nature.

Oblong and afraid, stepping into new life, Mom resists her authority and doesn't use an upper hand with any of her kids like Geoffe used to do. As time goes by, she realizes more and more about the living hazard that he was. Everyone remembers him, and his evil spirit hangs on in destiny and tribute. Tribute to the absolved and discomforted people that knew him even when his character was charming and reserved. He never gave place to hatred, but consumed it in his own personality.

Broken in opinion and residing in glory, the true faith of Christ comes wafting into the deliberate resolve of forgotten anger and untouched sore spots. Mom is covered with those and seeks a therapist on top of her support group. Very good, she thinks. I can get a lot of help here. Her opinion is good natured, in belief that the bad must go, but she must process it out of her. She has no kingdom of faith, yet belongs to the kingdom of faith. Exuberant in the touch of healing, she falters a little as her "sore spots" reveal themselves to the eternal world.

God will wipe away every tear, and take every last pain away from those who believe. Who believe in the sacrifice of Jesus Christ on the cross, Who paid ransom to our debt inceptive of the Father. Counting on religion to count, Mom goes through some really rough spots and starts to drink a little too much. This unwanted behavior is nipped in the bud as Baby finds out and advises her adamantly not to do that. She keeps it up anyway, the depressive part of her healing taking hold of grace and giving into gratitude. Her perplexity catches wind of her wisdom, and taking her daughter's advice she stops the excessive drinking but allows herself one or two glasses of wine now and then.

There is a rescinding pattern of disgrace coming along with the nuptial attitude of faith in Christ who comes to his Bride, which is the Church. Finding contentment in a welcoming Bride, there is disgrace that must be contained to make her spotless.

Everything about her is good. Leading people to come to Christ and delivering from sin those who are forgiven. Condemnation falls upon the deceitful and wicked who remain. There is no hope in that corner, leaving out the compliance of those remaining who see Christ and lunge toward him. He is faithful to those who love his Father, and who love one another, the two greatest commandments in the kingdom. Those who discard this as unnecessary or unfruitful, deny even the faith of fortitude, found in enigmas of ascertaining guilt and mashing on suicide.

Suicidal images are portrayed as unwelcome and disregarding of propriety in justice. Where justice is fanciful and forgotten, the scrupulous remain in decent remission, giving trust to the negative who need help in deceiving the Lord with quickly forgotten love and mercy. The merciful regain the vision of hope that obtains power from Christ Jesus in all his goodness, being faithful and true. Those who were promised him obtain him inside their selves, as the truth of security becomes impotent in passion degrading guilt. The funnel of love sweeps greatness from compassion and resides in acquittal of absconded Jesus. Torture and prevailing impotency of true riding in the dust can compare to guilt being removed due to sedition and grace. Christ's attitude is one of a winner and an overcomer, a savior and a King.

Glorious despotism fries out the unnaturally impure, who have been tainted by evil deposition to the annihilation of disgrace. The pigeon toed stand on twisted feet. Yet Christ gives grace to the forlorn and unhappy.

Happiness stresses tension on the foundation of the rock, the rock which *is* Christ. Winning and losing, as God meanders through his harvest, he throws out the tares and brings the wheat into his barns.

Forever in deceit, those of the wicked who have escaped wickedness find decrepit bemuse and prolific anger. Fathoming the junction of disgrace and hatred, there is disgust where once there was fear. Nobody fears anymore, for Christ is come to earth and fills hearts with notable propriety and deliverance. Pondered over and consumed, the ecstasy of a promised fate of glory keeps at bay the losers who now shriek in terror, within themselves, not knowing what and where this fear comes from.

Tantalizing and true, the disruptive nature of congruence of opinion lies tattered with regress on sinful aptitude and standard forgiveness. Yet God knows each one down to the number of hairs on their heads. Forlorn and despotic, the weak find merciful healing beginning where once the devil had an unnatural and hidden hold. For perplexity the very ponderous of hope keep abject technology on graces and opinions of nature. Do-gooders and non do-gooders shine in blatant reprise, sick with the sin of guilt, that derides and overcomes acknowledgement of despair and faltering approval. From God comes the faithful seed, planted in a receptive heart, fearing nature without him, and not understanding what this all means.

The menacing regurgitation on reprise of benevolent approval disguises abhorrence and bitter acid in the mouth. Brought up from the stomach and expelled in the earth where she stands upon moments at a time.

Infiltrated regression and bottomless repression are forgiving in Mom who now shares with others where once she stood with stoic resolve. Scarred and new to her healing, she overcomes *with* Christ and carries him in her heart. Painful evenings and joyous mornings keep her going day after day in guilty reprise, not knowing she is saved, yet understanding that the earth is changing and she is thankful that the Beast is gone, gone away. Somewhere she knows not where, but doesn't give it too much thought. Her oblong regression of faith grows torpidly and profoundly as she finds herself on a weekly pattern of attending church. Little does she know that the Church is the Bride of Christ, and who can understand that?

Is he come to take on a Bride? Will he lead her to fruition? Can he comply with the wilted and broken whom he knows, those who are just gestating faithful reprieve and configuration of destiny? No longer is he alone, and never was he, for he had his Father always, except in the moment of his death. When he finally gave up the ghost, God immediately brought him home. To be impacted on earth as having risen from the dead in three days. Precious and guided attempt believes in the hope of the followers who disgrace neither sin nor forgiveness. Trial and tribulation will befall everyone, yet one who is God's will he never forsake nor abandon.

Discarded

Make do with what you've got. So Dad taught his kids when they were young. Also, don't mess with a hornets' nest but keep your distance. Even Justin when he was young had a little bit of good in him, from which he abstains daily and resolves to do evil whenever he can if he thinks about it.

Too much hatred brought into the family by Geoffe's discredited sin on Baby brought with it a fungus that will not die, that Justin basks in in his eternal hatred of glorifying the devil, yet doing so anyway to contend with sin. Flavorless and despotic, the luke warm taste in his mouth is enough to cause vomiting. Banking on denial and acquitting grace due to remittance, the loved still love and the hated still hate.

Passionless repression of a gangly nature keeps servitude as a lure to bring more into the fold. For doing God's work you will be rewarded, where there is no more sin, nor hurting, nor hatred.

Symbiotic lessons of reprieve count for something in the makeshift hold of Christ. He both gives and receives. He does not tender with inefficiency, and contends with the gracious and the meek. Satisfaction flies into his arms when he comes for his church, for he will lead them into the new era, foundlings and chicks, babies to God who loves all of his newborns.

Disgraceful reprieve and seduction on nature are particular in disguise of reticent hatred and glorification of the evil and the wickedness that strains to climb up out of the sinking sand to where it has fallen. With chains around their necks, and bolted to the surface, they remain lost in a mire from which there is no return.

The discarded come up empty, the witless do evil and maintain this destiny. Overcoming lost and fruitless observers, there bribes only evil stench with the loss of forgiving and congruent natures. Pitiless and unfounded there is death that remains and life again for those who are saved into the after life where heaven receives those who have "made it".

It's not easy, but the reward is eternal, and little can be done out of the necessity of faith and its eternal reprieve. Induction maintains a foreign glory where glory does not shine, yet lures prisoners who go after the false light. Jesus comes as the light of the world. Where He is there is no darkness, and that is within our own saved souls. Baby has never been so sure of her faith, now that Rexi has "made it". She won't be discarded, just as Rachel is patterned to make it too. Even the elephants will make it to the new world. Something of grace and dignity to the arbitrary and intelligent.

Fluorescence shines everywhere. Into the hurting souls, and all the people who are getting younger and younger. There is oblivious reprise to the fate of the narrow gate, that is the gate so small, yet open to heaven.

Retracting in anomaly, gruesome and chiding conditions become obsolete and done with. Hanging onto nature is good. Singing in the shower makes music to the Lord. Saturation with prescription drugs that work and do the job is a fulfillment of joy in complimenting science and its retrieval of sin, yet goodness shines on joy with the elements of the earth, and taken down opinion receives a breath of fresh air, numbskull, fastidious.

Reproved and mated, there is no longer a need to get married. Gracious and indigenous faith comes along with a broken need to retard growth. Destruction complies with disgrace, and the church opens up her doors wider than ever before.

Compliant with sin, the servitude of grand force comes with the Christian warriors who go to battle in spiritual warfare. Significant but sinful are the retreating cowards who shrink in the sight of the image of God, belonging with justice to the beginning of Creation. Thinking is latitudinal, longitudinal, circular, parallel, and twisted painfully around drowning captives of the quick sands in heaps where there is plentiful stardom, and sugar dust falls from the sky to bring remorse.

Tremulous dilapidation comes with a turn of events that equates joyousness. Profound, reticent, defunct, nourishing, healing, and rebirth, there is a pattern to turn losers into winners in times of the harvest of God upon his earth.

Characters of faith fashioned with demise on the church gives plenty agreeably where spiritual water came from. Water turned to blood, and water turned into wine.

Wearisome

Take on the yoke of Christ, for his yoke is easy, and his burden is light (Matthew 11:30). Come all you wearisome who are burdened and stuck, keep to the nature of Christ and find in his oblivion a world free of expectation and significance. Hatred refuses to do right, and does not belong in the church. A disgrace of wearisome travelers on this journey to hell keeps upwards and onwards for those who overcome and step aside from that way. That wide, wide way that simpers the lost with delusion and temptation to give to sin the solemn equation of goodness.

Fanciful and free, the wearisome who come to Christ will be replenished and filled with hope. No more deceit will rule in the world, for forgiveness has pardoned the hatred of the dead with those who were lost to sin and perdition. Betrayal at all costs is receipt of hell for those who tinder the flames of death into pieces of remorseful hunger. Platitude and omnipresent, there comes a device in the way of the Lord that does not turn to superstition. Quaking with guilt and remembrance, the wars of this world continue on into the new kingdom, which must pull itself up by the bootstraps.

Easygoing love and eternal design beyond our greatest imaginations becomes little in the face of glory and guilt. No one overturns guilt rather guilt turns over the goodness to the death of the kingdom in those the Lord discards.

Quiet again, and then peace comes with every breaking off of the wicked. Gracious affections sublime in righteous glory renders the sinners who sinned to a forgotten place of sinning no more. Copulating brings injustice, brings surprise, brings rebirth, hope, and glory. Just enough to bring us joy and glee, the touches of affection wipe away the tears of abuse and long unrighteous imprisonment in this world.

Disgrace along with fortitude brings a little denial along with it, for who would not admit that with loving care and affection, sex can actually be a great thing?

Sinners in repentance have come a long way, and now the ground is solid beneath those who have received the mercy of the Lord and Savior, Jesus Christ.

Take care to bring joy to the hurting, thinks Baby who once needed more help herself. The equation of guilt versus servitude keeps the anomaly at bay, of what can be done to further the kingdom of God. He replaces guilt with reparation, with naturally overcome suicide, with forgiveness and disgraceful rapture. Problematic and sufficient for sin is the way to overcome it, and to achieve grace without perplexity. Founded on truth and wisdom, the first two steps of going somewhere starts a journey. Broken and mistrustful, the honest learn to trust in the Lord. Finance or vacations give grace to the pardon of sin and the mercy found with serene wisdom. Platitude and merciful grace are indignant and protruding from wormholes of ecstasy and satisfactory compliance.

Wherever you go, there you are, even if you've never been there before. A suppliant of guilt in exchange of wounded healing, brings cosmetic devices to cover up our scars. New attitudes, the science of forgiveness, and forgotten ears of corn bound to grace.

Looking into the fathomless grace of virtue, we wind up with a lot of bread in our basket. Entreated: Those who have gathered much have none left over, and those who have gathered little are not at a loss. Fortune finds everyone in every circumstance, even if it is imaginary. Loopholes reign everywhere, fondling with despondency in our pants with sweet and tender fingers. Keeping plowed up with decency, the formulation of distant mortification alive gives hope for the despondent and those addicted to sex. It is a no good thing to be so addicted, for it brings abuse, as was the case of the Beast, and Justin with their wives and complementary both to Baby. Sugar and sin and disgrace.

Turning the sin over a new leaf and wiping dry the dewfall there on, we have madness and conjecture that wipes away tears of injustice.

There is little faith to madness, yet the true hang on even in the blizzards of confusion. Scientists say that there is healing in medicine but also that attitude is important too. Configure with total lackadaisical mistrust, we sometimes trust ourselves before we trust our doctors. Maybe this is the right way to go. Were we supposed to live longer? Or did death come at the right time, for those destined to die? To die no longer means you will go through "the change" into everlasting life. What can science say about that?

The total inscription of madness and anomaly and aggressive discarding of the hopeless and lost, there comes the cucumber of faith which leaves patterns of destiny on our parted lips, with slices covering our eyes, blinding us, yet soothing us.

Bakery and efficient crossing into the world of baked goods gives credit to the baker who made the baked goods. We are like so much as bread baked in the oven by Jesus, the ransom for all sin, and saving.

Turning nebulous with parted lips, we breathe in and breathe out, sometimes weakly, too wearisome to go on. Now have faith, for when you have done all you can do, you need only to stop and stand still, and Christ will come knocking on your door. It is fighting the good fight of faith. (1 Timothy 6: 11-12)

Holding onto nebulous Jesus, the figure, the spirit, the apparition flaked out on wasted gestures of guilt, the weakness causes us to whine and worry. Yet fear not the coming of the Lord, for he is already here among us, tweaking us here and tweaking us there, making us ready for the grand opera of music in heaven.

Wireless controls were meant to make life easier for us. Consequentially our figurative fights only mean that we are blinded by disaster before it comes.

With pig-eyed faith and misfortune, our luck turns to disgrace where the believing is not the sin, but chewing on it brings a present. Who doesn't like to give or receive a present? Jesus Christ is our gift from God to us. The lost and regained life of his Son, that we would be pardoned of our guilt and sin. Forbidding ecstasy, forbidding love, these are not good takes on life. Whatever turns over the hungry feeling to a level that makes one desire to give in return for the feeding, it is humorous that faith would not let go of destiny and inscription for foresight found among the lost.

Paralysis in inscription founded upon mutual destiny there is there a place where there is. It goes no farther than that, for luck brings the over change of the guilt faction that is fastidious with remorse. Blistering fields of despair were not meant to be crossed, rather, coating us with the living water of the Lord, the healing waters of life found with grace and secrecy. Popular wisdom would define this as unnecessary, and scientists say it would be impossible. But drink up when it is your turn to drink of the cup that the Father gives you, for that is your accommodation in life.

Bitter reprieve, suggested emotion, fires like the burning bush of Moses keep us alive and ready. It is then time to "take off your shoes", for you are "standing on holy ground." (Exodus 3:5).

Deceit and sin call for a stand of attention, the wasted lessons of which abound in guilt and clarity. The wounded heart will heal, the broken soul will recover, and sin vaporizes like a wisp in the sky. Tattered and torn, the broken soul needs love and encouragement. Just like "Humpty Dumpty," the egg which fell off the wall and broke and all the king's horses and all the king's men couldn't put it together again, only the "King" could. It's just another fairy tale with emotional importance.

Dirty and fallen, broken and aching with reprise, the involvement of danger in healing comes with misreading the signs due to gestational dignity. Perplexed, symbiotic, retrieving lust with hate and expunging them from our journeys, the hell you've been in will all disappear. Baby's faith is great on the journey that she has been on since her birth into the world. Never did she suckle. She was removed from her Mother who died giving her life. It is an overturning of kaleidoscopic parchment written with words of love, turning pages, pages, pages in the Bible.

The greatest love letter in life, the only road map to heaven written down. It leads, it fingers, it points. Go here, go there. Take this, take that. Receive and give freely, remember it is better to give than to receive. Bless others with the love of Christ, for they may be ignorant. Put on your shoes again, for according to the Bible in God's armor, the shoes are fitted with the deliverance of the Gospel of Christ (Ephesians 6:15). Bringing peace to avid listeners you are God's favorite steward if you spread his word around. Faithful and overcoming, faithful and true. Kingdom come. Come Jesus.

When we enrich our lives with the truth, there is no subletting of the intelligence that gives us conjunction with grace. The knowledge of guilt is only an experience. Our lives are a journey, lived for the glory of God in remittance. Not so that we learn and forget, yet the charisma of finding faith brings what you remember to remembrance, and then it is time to act.

Broken, partitioned, neglected, faithless and broken down comes with mercy and pleasure, sweet as milk and honey. This taste in the mouth so glorious in itself, not like the bitterness of pickles which are salted in vinegar, they are bad if let to rot. Rotting pickles stand in conjunction with vomiting and rejection. Think of the bad things in life, says Baby, and treat them as you would a rotten pickle. Expunge them and carry them to the dumpster, the purgatory which holds all disgrace to be embalmed and destroyed, carted further and further away from you. Solid destruction implies annihilation. As far as the east is from the west. Forgotten.

Rejection

Demolition! Time to clean out the closets and revisit places of love. Take a turn to the right and a turn to the left. Go straight and back up. You can't go wrong when your feet are on solid ground. Standing on the rock of Christ, not shifting sands. Build your house on that rock, and the storms will never cast it down. Yet the house on sinking sands will fall and break apart.

Letting go of life is imprisonment in itself. In faithless necessity, the feeling of letting go can be forgiven and interjected by faith. Always faith! Never let go of faith! Don't give up on hope, either. The two together spell comfort. Is there a more welcomed word to counsel? Rejection comes with embitterment, and wipes away tracks of tears on the cheeks. Reject hatred, bitterness, evil. Cling to that which is good and never let it go.

Only in the garden of Eden did the world ever learn pure peacefulness other than the lurking evil of the serpent, that Satan who tries to hurt us any way he can. He sneaks away when the Father commands him, yet right now he lives, not forever.

Pierces of arrows into many hearts brings the glory of perdition with the resolve of might and tainting upset pictures with ugly colors. So some of our lives have been. Something about ugliness calls for rejection, for it is equated with evil doing. Our scars are ugly. Our sinning is ugly. There is ugliness in this truth. The truth can be ugly, distasteful, foreign and searching for rejection out of despotic circumstances. Grace, kingdom, clowns. Behavior that is sweet and rejecting by popular demand, retrieval here is bought only by pumping out our fluids and starting over. Grace and imminent glory resound with the washing of the soul that has spent time in hell, only to appear ugly and distastefully touched with many scars. Only God can heal, and he works in many different ways.

We plant the seed, someone else waters it, and God can make it grow. You are a hero in the Lord if you are trying to make ends meet, using what you have and can rightfully obtain. Liquor can be sinful or medicinal. Again, addiction is the unwanted word.

Floral scenes are beautiful to the senses, but not in real time if you are allergic. Coffee brings goodness, but a headache if you have too much. Smoking is up for opinion, again, moderation here is the key, for senses are particular and fragile, needing to be watered with the grace of glorification.

Synthesized exuberance is elated in all the forgiveness of neglecting respect. Patterned graces conniving and conditioning, are upset in repugnance of an ugly face on a dog. Cute as a puppy, what happened when it grew up?

The Bible says that dogs will be outside of the city of the kingdom of God, the New Jerusalem. The Bible says many things about the new world, but most of us cannot imagine it, it is so great.

Something so great has been so neglected by many. Where will we be in a million years from now? Makes today seem short. Repugnance and stepping on toes has been experienced by anyone and everyone. We curse and clamor, yet the wheat in the barn is harvested, and the pitchforks are many.

Broken down and forgotten, the battered car on the road. Who left it there? Don't go back to get it. There are far greater rewards ahead. Don't go back for anything, your reward lies ahead at the forefront in living time. Disgraced and benevolent, the freedom rings on the wedding rings, and pleasure abounds for all. Serious yet destructive are those rotten pickles, and yes, says Baby, let's feed them to the Beast. There is glory in ugliness to the extent that we need not betray it or touch it. Better to let it alone and let the Lord redesign it. So it has been with Baby in all her alone time within herself, the ugly Baby now shines beautifully.

Sinful discouragement brings tears to the eyes. Will we never get out of this mess? Who started it all? Did we ask to be born? Born into an enigma of ever growing billfolds and cracked skulls and giant amnesia lurking just over the horizon? Where is this terrible thing called guilt going to lead us? Who does the authorization of our lives, that those born adopted might peekaboo into the necessities of living elsewhere and dropped like bombs to fertilize endangerment of abandonment issues and rejection from the kingdom? Pure salted disgrace tastes like powder in the mouth, and eats saliva as though it were living water. In hell there is no water. Just fiery brimstone spread all over. Hatred. All. Hell.

Going over again and again what resides in evildoers like the Beast and his son Justin we find there is a partition between grace and retrieval of grace. Going again and again in fortitude of compliance, there is little to think about except that those rotten pickles are the disgust that will feed on rotten pickles. Rotten, rotten, rotten. Kept alive by the rules of nature, forbidden hope ejaculates from it despair and prolonged reserve of justice for the hopeless and the many.

Brought about by despair and conclusive evidence found in betrayal, assault, and battering, the fornication of sin found on the lips of every rapist born in exclusive temptation of hope, the joy feels everything rapists don't in the evil suction of their disgrace.

Impediment by guilt is the fornicating factor found in lucid retrieval and battered rejection. Forming the foundation of sin in luxury, there is a breaking out on the face within those who cannot extend glory to their maker, yet keep glory for their self indulgent selves.

Patterned repetitive betrayal is august in form and faction, tearing at the papers of truth, reading the lie and believing it, and curing tender faculties that race with the occult. Bread and water, fornication and sin. Miraculous recovery in repentance and forgiveness, joy and healing. Fate is destiny to the untoward and those found lost in deceit. Together again, the witch and her accomplice are found with pride in nature and seduction in sin. Miraculously, the overcomer can turn despondency into pride, into neglect of the faculties, yet reformed opinion of the truth. Neglect the truth and you neglect the giant of faith who stands forgiving over the toddler's bed in the night, breathing gently with baby's breath, and curing alternatives to bring healing in later life. Babies remember what it is like to be a baby, and then to grow up later on. It is a foundation, a beginning, where do we go wrong?

Inclusive disgust is found in meaty reparation and tactless betrayal of our instincts. Regurgitated on hope and forgiven in ecstasy, the wine we drink or do not drink at night was made by someone. Jesus performed the miracle of turning water into wine. It heals, it has faith. In conjunction with the tribunal terror of forgiveness, there is little lesson in fate, other than our journey takes us somewhere, but will it ever end? How can remittance of survival cure and end all rapture in itself, where deliberation of opinion obscures hope and traces destiny down like tear streaks on a sad face. Hurting brings joy. There is consequence to healing, and revival in pride. Take pride in the work that you do.

Clenched Fists

Sodden and downtrodden, our hopeful mysteries take us places in pain and danger. Falling down and getting up again is one of the early, early lessons in life. We are trained by the beginning that there is always something more.

Tainted with reprise, our knuckle headed ventures are particular for people like Baby and the Beast, whose version of the growing years is touched by early and submissive death. Created by guilt and science, our loving touch on nature is complicated yet grows with solace in the gesticulating patterns of hope and grace. The anomaly of sin comes with too much sugar and greater expectations than we have of hope. Baby gives too much of herself to her father and her brother, who both need a whopping lesson of indigenous glory. Foundations by betrayal neglect surprise and hint at destiny, or for some, their doomed fate .

Clenched fists in the night pull the skin away from the nail, leaving pain in the morning. Careful not to hit too hard against the wall. It hurts within conclave of its own destiny. This journey that we take makes us sojourners, every time we stop to take stock of our situation. God calls not the wicked but the faithful to his destiny. The sublime rapture gives hope and justice, tearing down and building up that which has been destroyed. Perfunctory and needless of opinion, the grace of the mentally disgraced is not his hope. Pushing and plying against dense forgiveness makes a meal out of the lost, who live parallel to wisdom and cannot give compliance to the nature of reprise.

Hope and forgiveness sometimes come with a fight. We must batter down that which is obstructing us, and configure a faith of glory.

Standing tall in justice, know that the wicked are sublimely rejected by God, in tall conference with his weak ones who wait on him for strength. Suicide, sin, and regression take stock on our accomplices and devices of shattered opinion and disregarding negativity. Please pare the pear, and pare no more. Disgusting in nature and oblivion, the winds outside our windows tell a story, for we know not where they come from, and neither can we tell where they are going. So it is with the newborns of Christ who obtain the Holy Spirit.

Graces exuded by salt, and enough of it, and not too much of it make the silt sticky in the sun that a foot might get stuck in it. Overcoming death is like living too long. For nature forebears her hope in destiny, and our frog like apparitions give guilt to the consequence of sin.

Torn and tattered guilt takes away our bruises yet we remain tender inside. So soft, so sweet, the good ones. There is lecture in deceit, and falsehood in acknowledgment of hope. Torpedoes in the water cause much damage upon hitting a target. Ships, boats on impact are destroyed. A camel in the desert forbears witness with holding water for long periods of time. They are our guides in the distance, holding onto something new, that builds our pardons and gives sin to the unlucky.

Being tested by the enemy, the fruitless fragrance of destroyed oatmeal falling, falling from the air is only an allocation of suggestion, that we all must eat or die.

Sin brings forgiveness, but not hope. Danger is witless, yet true. Broken posits of faith keep supernatural reprise under weakness, where it can be best hidden from the torturers of hell. Meek in compliance with danger brings about a fundamental change. The wicked won't be pardoned, for they cannot change. Wisdom and regression bring opinion to order and give out factions of faith.

Redress and positive, the nail in the wall hurts if we hit our heads against it. Narrow and comely, vibrant yet mutant, so much as for behavior brings about confounding truths of wisdom. Prolonged disgrace, a toy that is in the hands of a toddler.

True turgid acclamation pesters us to get with the program and deny waste within ourselves. It is our job to polish our persons and shine with the glory of God. Getting faith to do this is too hard yet expendable, for it is not an easy task. People spend lives fixing themselves up from before, and taking on what is new. The nest in revoked reprisal figures with withdrawal that attitude which is renewed, new and shiny like a brand new car.

Take care of your car and it will serve you well. God takes care of us, that we might serve Him well. Tunnels in behavioral patterns, chug us through life like a light rail train takes us to and from the city. Conglomerate and destined heroes find help in the power of God, and the truth of the Word of God.

Clenched fists prepare a person for a fight. Defensively or offensively. Bite the flesh of a fish and tear it with clenched teeth and maddened anger. Rip apart a bunny rabbit and throw it onto the freeway out of your car's window. Baby has compared her road in life as having been rejected and cast out of the window of her family's car onto a busy unforgiving freeway. Why did they lose her like that? So helpless, what could she do?

In anger and defense, she recoiled into herself and gave up on getting away. Having been tackled, raped, assaulted, molested, beaten and stowed away from her once happy life, the burden of guilt that she bears does not belong to her. Her molten life of obscurity burst open when God came on the scene and began to preen and carefully wash her wounds with his loving materials of joy, those are, to witness, deny, fake, fraud, mesmerize, appellate, configure, give grace, hop, skip, jump, and go onward.

Defeat is the purpose of guilt, the crimes of destiny bought and paid for with the milk of the nursery. Touched eloquently, those blessed as newborns go through life with a little more grace and tragic removal to eat the syrup of jesting, and to dig holes deeply into the desert that the camels might find water.

Paring the pear peels off its good natured armor and prepares it to be sliced, cored, and cooked or eaten raw. Juices running down from its sweetness affect our demeanor as we smack our lips with a smile. Winced and ready now for more, the taking of soluble fiber into the mouth gives ready a chance for nourishing the body, the body that must have sustenance or else die. Faith is sustenance for our hearts and souls.

Clenched fists loosen up a little when our wiry hearts take faith and we gain strength in the face of the enemy, the enemy who comes to hurt, maim, lie, and destroy. He will kill what he can out of all God's goodness, yet he can never snatch one out of God's protective hands.

Destroy, break, kill, and kill the spirit. No one resists pervading delinquency with regard to the natural kilt of design and suggestive power. Belonging to the mentally aberrant Justin, there is an aura of mean and bitter hatred. Never will he overcome his fate, he is lost already.

Yet God gives him life in death, a long dying death that simpers upon the tea kettle and steams and whistles to be heard. Subjunctive apology comes too late for the witness in the storm. Degraded by popularity, quickened by hatred, and remorseful in despondency comes the refuse of waste, of rotten pickles, and little left to overcome decency.

Twisting words of wisdom left behind in a church unattended, the serial killer emerges who will not live to see God's glory. Fated to despotically emerge and destroy guilty faces left behind in imprisonment, the danger is near to destroy the destroyer with its own guilt and punishment.

Tattered and forsaken, there was never anything good there to take hold of, or this remorseful folly might not have gestated in the hold of oblong security. Security for grace, for the lost with hope, and the needing to go somewhere else.

Gracious and obtrusive in eloquent despair, the feuds in the house of growing up children is often passed off as a phase to go through. Yet some children grow up hating and being hated by compulsory conviction, that God's glory might shine in all of its remittance.

Forever endangered in hell, the wisdom that is lost is foolishness for God, who repairs those he has chosen, and leads them on a path away from all this abject horror.

Pain and destiny come for a cheap price. Long and holding on, brings with it a chance to reap destiny in the Kingdom of God known as Heaven. What child doesn't want to go to heaven some day? Who could teach a child about this? Sunday school? Justin went to Sunday school. Yet he fell away from the faith, and it was all his doing, or something passed down from his idolized, cantankerous father, the forlorn Beast.

Geoffe is now removed from the living. His basement is at eternal death. Gone, now, for glory and disappearance, and hydrated renewal come by waterless surroundings fenced in on all sides with walls of shattered wills and the skulls and skeletons of those to whom this is forever.

Taking tranquility out of peace, there is remorse and agitated regression, simpleton abhorrence and behavioral suicide banking on mass suicidal deficiency for problematic removal in times of distrust.

Holy Saints of heaven lean down on the shoulders of the lost and whisper hope into their ears. This came to Baby in much of her growing up years spent crying in her bedroom. False behavior, similitude and disgraceful faction litter her life with nervousness and dissatisfaction. Yet in rotund trusting, loving, and open arms she is lifted, lifted by grace and glory to the uptake of healing surmised by victory. Changing now in these later days, it is only a beginning of a long journey away from here, to a place she's never been be it in her imagination, her learning, or her hope.

Discrepancy and tabulation of bodily fluids is remorseful in the denying of the skin of itchy scratchy disturbing rashes, falling from sin in denial of sin. Procreated and broken, the gashes in our weakened personalities soothe the sublime and unforgiving tatters of hope. Discrepancy being the only covert design to overcome knitted substance with screaming destiny. Tribulation can count on the fingers how many times it has visited a person, and then many more times ongoing. Tribulation and despairing substance of equality is maturation in the spin of protracted denial and then the blame can't be removed.

Overdone, watchful, suggestive with mercy and hell, the disgraces that convert watching design are figurative and remorseful, digging trenches where water may flow, and building aqueducts where water may run.

Easing our pain, the natural hot water springs are curative and hopeful. In destiny, our finding them after the turbulence of the war is not a belittling sanction. We greet each day with promised help, and all of a sudden it is not so bad or greedy.

Pinpoints on the wall suggest activity and hopefulness endowed. Even then, the taste of victory is sweet, so clench fists and get ready to fight. The wisdom of knowledge comes from within, the tattered and true, the guardians, the saints, the queens and kings, and princes and princesses. Oblong security in the mating of desire with preponderance, necessity in bloom with fortification, the battle is within ourselves.

Neatness, failure, prodigious and swamped disgust is merely repository of the sublime nature of sin. Quick, regard what is uneventful and turn from it. The nature of stagnation is not in good hands. Life needs movement, and movement brings healing.

There is movement in the mind and movement in the body. Movement in the soul and moving of the spirit. Not noxious obedient cultured movement, but discovery and created design which brings about a change every day. Go through your day with design in mind. Focus inward, focus outward, wherever the movement takes you. Baby knows that she is moving up in the ranks of peace, forbidding displeasure and turning away from noxious sin.

Pardoned

Noxious sin is a malignant spoof of knowledge of the wrong things. It is careful to be careful of what you expose yourself to. Bringing bottoms up betrayal, the booby-trap in the guise of a snow goose filtrates to the bottom of the sea. Rampant victory and glowing demonstrations of faith are equal in dissonance and regrettable failure. Astute and benign, the very leverage we use to get to distancing is forthright with fate and eternal glory. Dancing the nebulous quarters of indignant hell keeps peace at variance with torture. Nobody likes torture, some people need it.

To bring an opinion around and necessitate the tallies of hope and nature, we wittingly give disgust to the despairing natures of hell. Blotted, no longer looked upon. Gravitating and giving faith to religious and bottomless failure, the very hope of gravitating upward is in reliance of sin at the bottom. Turning over disgust and remorseful misbehavior, the show down comes with clenched fists in the pockets, and leaning against a wall. Refusing to fight can only go on for so long. Prodded and poked, you feel a little silly after awhile, and bringing in affected growth only puts sand in your shoes.

Gracious and contending obliteration of obsequious and turntable virtue, contending with the just and the unjust, only notating and keeping at large a jar of healing emollients. Satisfaction keeps lingerie hanging to dry, and bringing bitter de-spoofing of spotted denial. Great and necessary turns of events make place for spotted ruin and glowing reprise. Bingo is the jar on the shelf that waits to be opened. The jar of living water in heaven. To drink of it you will never thirst again.

Belligerent and despiteful glory keeps cucumbers on the shelf and pickles in the refrigerator. Or is that too calm for popular events that are charged through with retinal hell and despondency? Failure to betray is necessary and good. Don't go on in qualms of anger. Use anger, but then put it away. It is not good. It finds no home in a peaceful world. We must put away our destinies and deal with the anger that touches us all. Forbidden sin and conjectured breaking of the jar leads to a healing of the mind where everyone is a little bit ruined from living in this world.

Note taking and test takers are oblivious of some things. To really know, you must experience. Reviving qualities of the hit and miss nature, know that you have tried and then retreat. Known that to hit again and again is like beating the dead horse. Victory comes sailing across the seas, the seas of heaven, the oceans of life.

Break through and polish the enigmas, knowing that to follow destiny you are on the right path. Actually meeting Father God some day, the quilt on your bed might look a little brighter. Your hair might be a bit more obedient, your shoes not so scuffed.

Grapefruits on the trees are splurging with sweet desire, the nectar of quality, the vision of the sweet. Her nature and her normal are fitted to desire the good things in life and to avoid the not so good things, like Justin, for Baby. He just puts a tooth and nail in her life whenever he can. He doesn't visit, William won't allow it, but he leaves notes on the porch, pleading for forgiveness. But he hates to do it. He knows he is not welcome there, and this hurts him further. To Baby it is clenched fists, and he will not be pardoned.

Disgraceful in the honey jar, flies deposit their filth and ruin a good thing. Toying with nature is leaving discrepancy with sin and forgiving yet not forgetting, with loving, but consequentially not liking. God says to love your enemies. But throw their filth right back on their heads and walk away. Be determined to do the right thing, to face your tribulations.

God gives us many tribulations, and graphically we respond with torture and offense. Degraded and deficient, the numbness of the torched corpse sits in sickly despair on our doorsteps and front yards. Overcoming we despair and wipe death away from our faces. Never to be again as it once was.

Ointments and jelly soothe our burnt skin when the fire has come too close. Holding onto fate and desperately clinging to righteousness, you will overcome.

Keep notes to tell your neighbor about what you have learned today. The folly in misinformation precludes shaking the tree to get the coconuts to fall. Wizened and shaking with demolition of despair, confabulation brings about the lost and the nuances of nothingness. It is bright and cheery, the smile on a newborn babe.

Delicious and scintillating the true beauty of the Lord shines through on a beautiful and sunny day. The essence of his kingdom turns around in graphic beauty no matter where you go. It is his turn, it is God's turn. This brings Jesus Christ to the forefront of necessity, belaboring and aggressively righting the wrongs with help from the Holy Spirit. Nuances so unforgiveable are graceless in extent of the Word of the Lord. Hoping and hoping, being faithful and waiting and watching we will be ready.

Traumatic dismissal of the disgrace of broken apology means we are in trouble to enlighten the day. Bringing about grace and apology, turning calendar pages every month, the time goes by and people wonder, "why are we living this?" We can be pardoned for our transgressions while we are waiting, waiting and wailing in the wings. Wings of hope and glory, torturous and evil, seductive and ornery. Right when you thought it was over, it begins again, the labor pains of the earth.

Accumulative

Proud and predestined, our natures are forgiving and meant for simply blessing others. Every blessing of hope is fortuitous in profound destiny. Hope builds on hope and remains suggestive in the day. We build our patterns of daily behavior, significant with courting justice. Belaboring patience, a good quality to have, there is doing justice to suicidal sin, a preeminent forgetfulness that breeds happiness and bright, shiny teeth in a big smile on your face. We all have a face. We all face the world.

Smiling in turn brings a smile, and collective reassurance with patterns of behavior and default. Grassy fields are good for running in, chasing, and playing together with balls and rackets and nets. Play, play, play. Life is fun when we get it right, when collective behavior rescinds into a broken and forgotten past. Baby smiles at William when they wake up in the morning and share a cup of coffee together. Each their own, how they like it. The belligerence of picky-picky becomes portent with graceful sweeping of the arms over a great area. Swinging the flag in the wind, going to church on Sundays.

Helpless in love, they can't do enough good for each other, their smiles and hugs fill a large room with gratitude and deliverance. Broken fingers in the past will heal up. The nagging headache will finally subside. Religion will wake up to a world that is ready for it, not one for castrated ignorance, a sideways thought that Baby often has. Just castrate her brother and all would be well.

What will happen? Will he go the way of Geoffe? Rotting in the end to repugnant demise? Blistering away in a barren desert, being stomped on by camels, until finding the courage to reiterate sin only to be zonked on the head by a falling millstone?

What could we requite with good nature? Is it absent without evil? Depository with annihilation of goodness and design on prolific gracious facility? How many questions do you ask to find the truth? What is the truth you are looking for? Perhaps it will present itself to you.

Next in life is the magnanimous virtue of sordid failure. Perhaps you have tasted the sinful nature. God can forgive. Perhaps you have learned to be mean and grasping of destiny. God can forgive and relearn you.

Doing your dirty in the dark, there are lessons to be learned about right and wrong. A nightly walk in the park shouldn't be a frightening experience, but it can be. Regenerative ignorance tabulates love and incendiary patterns that confuse the short sighted with failure of vision. The visionary man goes for long walks, the blind man stays behind.

Usurp apology with forgiveness of sin and know that betrayal is not good. Accumulate the good things not the bad. Give hope to the perfunctory and meaning to the faithless and graceless. Without forgiveness we could not be sorry for our sins, and learning to do that and implement righteousness in our course we deliberate before gestational apology. Required in good hope is humility with grace, and humble pasture to walk upon with reserve of disgrace.

Poking at a piece of pie with the finger brings back a sweet surprise to the mouth. We wait and cry out. We want and can't have. We turn the page and start a new day. Forgiveness in discipline comes with loving your neighbor and loving your enemy. Doing sin on purpose fails to incite a good reaction. Forgotten, broken, then comes somnolence and disfigured regard. Nectar chasing the sweetness of the sin chases away all signs of ignorance being bliss, for the act of love exchanged in a relational manner is not taken respectively. Someone will end up getting hurt.

Congruent Denial

Ever dismember a finger? Break a toe? Tripped going up or down stairs? Falling on your bottom hurts, and it takes time to heal. Internal organs waste away for no good reason. Why? If we flip off someone with the finger, what kind of message is it giving? Do we love to hate? This world is so full of hate, and hateful people. Congruent denial would say that this is ordinary and to be expected, but it doesn't always have to be that way. Give over to love and explicit redundancy. Now it's your turn to close the window and do the work. Breaking free of apology loosens the mad dog's bite on your neck. Humbling and free, give up preposterous guilt and hardened heart, for humbling will bring a wall of stones falling down on you.

Sweet surprise in the Easter egg. Chocolate, coins, money. Sweet surprise under the Christmas tree. Thinking on your imagination. Perplexity, hope, configuration and demolition all in one bite of pumpkin pie.

It is saturated essences of fortuitous nature that expounds the glory of monetary exuberance. List all the things you have to be thankful for and find out you are richer than you thought you were. Obedient to discriminatory badgering, the faces in the walls sometimes speak to you. The shadow in the back alley tortures you with fear, and then you find yourself inside again. It is a gift of sin with reiterating fear, and the plasma finally formulates itself to remove the target with guilt. Happiness in stray form finds exuberance in jealousy and target in the discriminatory ones. Tasting excellency provides guilt for the charged misfortune of others. Pasturing and playing, resting and reviving, the turn of nature brings about destiny.

Congruent denial and utter praise bring significance to the priority of sleeping during the days when nothing else matters.

Oblivious to congruency, the patterned betrayal of mistrust sings the anthems of glory for hope and destiny. Destination is acquittal of our journeys. Where rocks fall hard and branches break on cars, where using others stops the fall and creates conditions of danger. Clattering injunction and patterned betrayal is nebulous and symptomatic. Falling from grace is an endless fall. Riding in the net is a turn about experience for when your feet reach ground again you cannot reason the wit from your faith.

Guaranteed that reaching out blows your own horn, respect and provision of guidance keeps you charmed at wit's end. Prolific and endangered species shake hands on the podium. Nevertheless, one must give and the other receive. Like grace in the night; the pervasive ecstasy of refracted congruent denial splits open the pod and the peas fall out. You can count them, you can eat them. Worship Jesus for he falls for you in your own journey. He eats away the crabs that gather around your toes and saturates himself with pleasure from your love.

Disgraceful conundrums are articulate where grace was never meant to be. Falling from grace is a situation that no one wants to face. It is like Justin, it is like the Beast, Geoffe. Parallel factors of unnatural phantoms calls remittance with the favor to help. Expediency brings rise to encouragement and favors design on the helpless. The pinprick will hurt, yet the dominos fall where they will. We pick them up, we eat them like candy, and we hurt our sensitive teeth. Count the numbers, count the efficiency. Demise and perplexing spirits call to the tortured and the numbers in hell prolific and gone.

The warthog destines favor and desire on the ego, and marches to its own beating drum. Within it is cherished, without it holds a deformed nature. Pestilence and pride shake together and implant wisdom on our skin. Thanks be to God we all have our own leather.

Singing in the shower again is tolerable and sporadic. Forgetful to look and step, we may fall over. Topple out. End up sore and hurting. Bemused, humiliated, and stupid in and out. Eclectic design and forbidden nature are capitalistic in function and grace. Keep holding onto the good things, keep letting go of the not so good things, and definitely hurl the bad things away from you. With apology and incendiary prolific demise, the function of congruent behavior is within the smile on the tortured one, giving up faith for favor.

Despotic and deceitful, the rise in intolerance is respective to our natures. Confabulation and demise disgrace the lost and futile. Jesus holds out his hands to those lost ones, and cries when they slip away. So many geniuses, yet so many failures.

Carrion and road-kill justify the symptoms of the greedy who are carnal enough to spare notation into apology. Wicked in deceit, leave the carnage to the harpies, the vultures, the coyotes and wolves. Face death and don't smile at it. It is better to turn away.

Face dignity instead, and elaborate on your own resurgence of the faith and manner of dignity. Paralyze your watches, and keep track of the sun, the moon, and the stars. Why do we culture our days into boxed out and saturated moments of time kept track of hypnotically? Oh well. It is better not to guess.

In times of reprise, the nail on the coffin should not be retracted out of its stern position. Populated with demise and culture, our ribbons of failures and falling destinies only lead us to the proud and momentous.

Thatched roofs and broken windows keep a storm at bay, and in doing so shine grace and mercy on the broken. Despair may fail, yet failing despair is like cartooned disgrace, broken up and laughing. Utter hopelessness and despair shines through the shiny windows on our cars. Where to go that keeps clean the naughty and the nice? Who was bad before Christmas time, and who wasn't? Are you following your Father's decree? Or are you celebrating in the face of your enemy? Fortune demised, and failed on a celebratory note of infamous departure shine neglected with hope and blessings and notes to the poor. Everyone falls down sometimes and now it is just about that time when we need to stand up tall and take on our foe with the reserves we have ready for the fight.

Wisdom is necessary, and so is truthfulness. Broken hearts can heal, and many have, many times. But to put your faith in Christ, you will never fall down for he will always catch you. Simpleton in heart, and crafty in the mind feeds wisdom a good turn. Simplicity is enough empowerment to start taking steps to that which is more complex. Building buildings starts from the ground. There is a corner stone, and that rock we build our houses on, in our mortal bodies is Christ. The graveyard ensues with pardons and gleeful remembrance. Pitiless and penniless, too many pardons are disgraceful in petulance. Preserve hope and strangle wickedness, and don't ever stop doing this until it needs not to be done anymore.

Graceful indigenous and founding fluid on disgrace, gives graphic portrayal of destiny and the coming to be at destination found. Splurging anonymity cries out with bitter retraces, and people like Justin are long forgotten. Geoffe is long gone and forgotten. Just a taste there of what once was, and then we can spit it out. Splurging in anonymity belies the forgotten with trust and remembrance. No more volcanoes blowing up in our backyard.

Those are dangerous. Mean, nasty, and merciless. Forbidden anger and repulsive ignorance lead to morbid betrayal and sinful ignorance. Reprieve and destination fall through with the founding of repugnance and turned over resolve.

Battered and beaten, Mom is recovering from her long journey on the road with the Beast. Yet looking back someday it will be a long way back and one day will be totally forgotten like a period at the end of a sentence.

Rude and disgraced, the noxious puzzles of nervous intent are badgered with the weary and disgusting. Paling in the face of danger is totally normal. Turn around and run! Sometimes it is the best you can do. Yet a formalist might say you're a coward. Not so, the lessons learned on our feet are not arbitrary or convivial. Being backwards and broken is not so much fun as out running your enemy and dodging it once again. Tremulous fingers drink in repository sin, for the fact that decency disrupts action only portrays to the ludicrous that fate and design can be put together like the pieces on a puzzle. The end result is a framed illustration that you can glue together and hang on the wall, framed.

Bitchy, bitchy, bitchy. Icky, Icky, Icky. Formal design pokes and prods at nature, and bites back at the bark of a dog. So, do you run away? Or fall back and face your enemy? Courage takes imminent precedence in that case. Courage, wit, knowledge, bravery, and trust in an all knowing, all forgiving savior. Blended with pride, and covered with armor that fits, there is danger in letting go.

The supernatural are wiry and proud. The ignorant are foolish in their way. Yet God smiles on both the wise and the slow ones. Pittance and plurality. Sinful victory... and acceptance. At last, a nominal entity. For God chose the weak to put to shame the strong. The path is long and sometimes empty, yet pervasive technology breaks the design of hope. Cherish the future, know the past.

Embitterment

Foul mouthed and potato headed, the mystery of indignant service with washed out resurgence gives grace to the mercy and endless forking up to the small and lonesome ones. Being free on the other end of jealousy, there is betrayal in the elegance of service and forked over peanut butter. Bitter to the taste, dark, dark chocolate is not as much "fun" to eat as milkier chocolate. Yet sugar and fat take their toll on a body worn out with too much eating and not enough exercise. Forlorn and fastidious people are at a loss with the peanut butter, it is so, so, good. Everything in moderation, including moderation. Suggestive anomaly pirates in a boat load of mercantile and wanted products at hand. Enervating and preposterous witty and indecent hunger fail to feed the hungry and house the poor.

Careful with calming down because the baby doesn't tell you exactly when it will be born. Some fall out into destiny. Baby fell out into the hands of Mom, and taken swiftly from her birth mother.

Gestational knowledge and inspiration take hold from human to human with love. Aberrant and incisive discriminatory aberration perplexed and intimate takes time to heal and grow together, like a branch grafted into a tree. Accepted by all, and supported by all, there is a gentle breeze that blows through the branches of growing older, and finding fascination with fury.

Constable recreated and necessitated stands by the fruit of forgiveness, the delicate grapefruit. Bitter and sweet, juicy and divine. To be eaten with a grapefruit spoon and a grapefruit knife. Pleasure in sin, eating it too fast. Expressed love and appreciation for the demeanor of the inhabitants. Not included and separated yet volleying all the time for mortification and indulgent reprise.

Faith grows with nectar grows with sweetness. Paramount futuristic ambivalence is sitting on our right hands today. Bitter, bitter, bitter. Convalescence and torpedoes in our back yards bring home a lesson. You can get hurt at home as well and much as you can out there. Don't thirst for attention, you will find laughter and folly in your face. Drink your cupful. Taste your mark on humanity. Judge yourself, but not too harshly. Ask yourself if what you are doing is right. Pick up your fingers and put them in your pocket. Grace and true, inebriation and hopelessness.

Embitterment grows in the face of eternal envy and pride. Notorious outgrowth from our arms and legs leaves scars where the wrong has been evicted by the right. Scientific mortification and ambivalence collide with the heavenly and divine. Saturated in ignorance, the complex behavior is living with a simplistic attitude. Behavioral apology is well accepted. Perhaps bring a gift next time?

Berating the oblong and intrusive keeps onlookers at bay. Even in the night of horrific shame and harm, it takes its toll and grants truancy to a prideful shacking up behavior.

Singing the songs of the sad makes music in the hearts of listeners. Anything to ease the pain. Anything to bring about contrition. Places in value are sought after. The sunset on an ocean beach, and the sunrise across the many seas.

Luckless

Parallel imperative judgment finds falsehood with false fingers. Failing to find out in eager necessity brings obliteration to the meek and short of courage. Backing out is also a way of dealing with the enemy, yet to what repose? Confabulate the nectar in your teeth and eek out your cavernous cavities. Subjunctive and formal in opinion, luckless mad hatters can't count congruent denial on fingertips for it smashes all at once and then you can't run away and you must be there all the time while the raping takes place. There it is, forever in your midst. But God promises a way out. The future. It is forever coming to you, and no matter what you look like, in your popular condition you might someday be there to face eternal glory and reticent condemnation.

Pervasive continuance and upended retaliation are the chance that we all have after being knocked down and kicked about. Deliverance is sin, yet justice must keep stepped in to take her toll. Grace for the affected, and joyful in the faces of maligned hope and hypocritical distention. Popularity is not a contest, it is a means of pushing each other ahead, so that those left behind might join in the race, the ensuing race to freedom.

Luckless, but chosen, you are born to fulfill your destiny, and God has chosen you right to be where you are right now. Turning tables on endless factions of growth, the dignity of fortitude comes with efficiency and growth. Fat in the face of fury, yet destined to recover.

Foremost and uttermost beliefs carry us across waters with wind in our sails. Hefty to lift, yet comfortable upon us are our burdens. Graceful in the night, and in times of resting.

Belonging to prolific glory and hopeless demise, the falling of the citizen to purposes of beauty sinks with the sunken ship. Grace protrudes from every drowning, yet those lost at sea can be saved during the Rapture. Which is here, upon us, now. So, prepare for great changes, miracles and woeful remorse. Coagulate with servitude and match the endless with the lost. Don't flavor the chocolate with cinnamon, and give grace for fun in the face of technicality. Lost and at sea, found and recovered, the Lord smiling into your face at last. Gruesome retort is ignorant with reprise, yet the flavor of sin is no longer so sweet. Hurtful reconnaissance betrays the battered, and symbolically shines to the future. We must go, the time is now.

Forgetting forever, you need only to look ahead and be reminded of the endless glory to come. Falling, falling, falling, we are always falling from head to toe. The gravitational pull of the earth is a strange feature if you think about it. So, people gain and lose weight again. Picking a spot on the horizon, you fill yourself with glee and focus. Bring to a pinpoint that spot and narrow your eyes. Trust in the confidence and concentration that you can have. Bring about a sorted piece of puzzle making to remember that all the pieces will fit, and not all of the finished puzzle will be beautiful. Our lives like a tapestry on the wall, are embroidered with feelings, emotions, thoughts, intellect, fun experiences, and hateful ones.

During the time of intellect, you are vouching for yourself in a manner that is conjunctive and upsetting. You are yourself. You can be whatever you want to be. God parted the Red Sea for Moses, he can part the world for you to walk on through.

Singing disgrace and soluble entity provides incendiary perplexity that faces vociferous countenance. Shining on glory, the smile on your face is positive and uplifting. Carrion is better left behind, so decency may be protracted in your face. The destiny, the falling letters, the hurtful ambivalence and pride. All goes for the purporting of symbiotic fluid change in the pieces of faith falling for the catch all end all. Pretend it is ignorance, foolishness, or witless, and find that nature absolves every rectal pain you will ever have ever.

Beseeching love, counting on glory and hope, the enervating circumstances are humble and mild. Yet God causes you to feel everything, that you might comfort those in need. Paling in the face of danger can regressively give speed to your walk, that you might break out into a run. Run, run, run away and don't feel bad about it. You can fail to lose, but is that really so bad?

Vectors and planes reach out with significance in lost or regressive behavior. Justin, the slow one, is significantly out of his court and hitting his balls into the bushes. Safe and sound, his cherry tree memories fall to the ground. Then came pushing and pulling, and Rexi got out okay. She was the only one who was "normal" yet she finds sorrow in that.

Her hat is too big to wear, so Baby leaves it for her. Nutritionally bound, they give each other advice on what to eat, and how to make this and that. It is arbitrary conclave with indifference that communicates end hope with the folly.

Frozen in denial, they enervate random repose and luxury on the sinful disappearance of the Beast. He is gone, gone, gone! Rexi is glad at last. She tried to take his side too many times, and fell from his grasp at last. The Beast had no mercy on whom he picked, nor what he said in judgment of them, mercilessly. Concupiscence and sordid design kept him king of the household until he fell lost into the sunken pit of despair that was to be his end at last. Behavioral samples of his deceitful despair collided with the sanctuary of gloating that he made for himself, never to know the sacrifice of Mom, nor the ratted calling for grace that gave up on servitude.

Faith in the frozen, choking on utter sin, yet defeating the purpose of recovery, his only hope was to watch the watch on his wrist and keep track of the hours every day. Endless hours doing nothing in the end.

Gravy on his beard was disgusting to all, never was anyone so hated. As for Justin, well, the apple fell close to the tree. Baby is not sure if she hates Justin or just terminates her thoughts when it comes to him. It is better not to worry and have faith than to reach out to him. Being her brother or cousin or whatever, she almost feels obligated to reach out to him. Yet she knows from experience how that will go. A shouting match, and then a slammed door as Baby leaves him and walks stoutly away in seething anger.

He is sneaky though, and finds a way to implant himself into her imagination, and she does find herself thinking and worrying about him. She hopes for the best, yet can't find it in herself to be worriless or pardonable about him. William thinks it's a waste of time to even think about him, nonetheless, go and visit him like he pleads in the letters he leaves on their porch.

Let him be. Forgive and forget. She doesn't want to forgive, she hates him and holds a grudge, the very thing she's not "supposed" to do. Did Jesus hate Judas Iscariot? Or did he never give him another thought? The thought of his betrayal was significant in resulting anger and intuitive blame. Portrayal of beauty on the counter in the kitchen sits a grapefruit ready for tomorrow's breakfast. Along with eggs and bacon. William and Baby are exploratory in their day-to-day diet. Sometimes it's hard to figure out, other times it's a creative delicacy.

Luckless and lost, Judas Iscariot was doomed to hell, for betraying his master, his teacher, his friend and savior Jesus, and giving up on the holy ghost. Pittance in retardation, and danger in hell. Justin never thinks about Jesus, and if he does, he ushers the thought right out of there. Be gone, Jesus! The worst sin of all, blaspheming the holy spirit in remittance of Christ the savior. Fooling around, giving ground to glory and frustration to death.

Pots and pans in the sink, work clothes on the floor in the living room of his studio apartment, Justin cries to himself and rubs his tummy, mourning the loss of his Dad. Critically acclaimed, he is a national super star in his mind, for being the greatest man on earth that nobody loves, needs or cares about. He has no friends, just people from work.

Needless to say, he is a rotting enigma, and nobody should concern themselves with him. Everything about his home speaks of a rotten pickle. The stink, the stench, the poisonous odor and dirt on the floor. He never cleans, just enough to keep dishes usable and laundry done now and then.

Morose and hurting from a visit to Justin leaves Baby vowing to never do it again. Finally, out of her system, and she *can* forgive him, yet she still pities him and watching she feels sorry for him. Never another worry. Soon she will move away. But what about Mom, and Lila and her family? She's caught in a bind, and sees no real reason for leaving after all. She loves her church, loves her job, loves her Mom and assimilates Satan's death to Justin.

Apologetically, Baby comes to William with the truth about her forgiveness of that brother of hers. Last she saw of him he was breaking out in a rash all over his face. Probably due to the putrid conditions of his home.

William is glad that she is done with him. Fruitless survival and anatomic reprieve give glory to Jesus. Jesus who stops it before it happens. He doesn't give Justin the chance to commit suicide, instead, one day on the way home from work, he drives head on into a fast moving, oncoming car and spins around several times, his car exploding and killing him within. Luckless Justin. Turn favor for truth, and explosiveness for regression of sin. Tables upside down, he is gone. Mom, Baby, William, and Rexi with her family go to the funeral. The aftermath is forgotten, and God seals up that leaky viciousness that poured into Baby's brain, over and over again.

Luckless lost one.

Broken

Times like these, people get together and celebrate the life of the deceased. So they do, and have a cake in his remembrance. German chocolate cake, it was his favorite. William is overjoyed but keeps it to himself. It's not in him to say I told you so to Baby. Lost and gone, this never-ending knife in the arch of his foot is finally done lacerating him.

His ego shined up and mature, he decides to propose to Baby in their living room that night. She agrees adamantly and falls into his arms.

Mom comes over the next evening at their invitation and wallows in the good news. She cries some tears, still in shock at the death of her only son who had so failed in his life. Maybe he's with Geoffe, she thinks, but doesn't know that in hell they have no neighbors. It's worse than everybody thinks it is. That's why most people don't go around with hell on their minds.

Gone at last, the sinister poison in her family has expunged itself. Baby knows not why she needed to suffer so much at their hands, and she's not sure how to deal with this new life of hers, going hand in hand with William and stepping with a much lighter step.

Lila and Rusty and their kids come by for dinner now and then. They agree that it's better not to move for them right now, but to stay put where they are planted.

Baby works with Mom in her garden on the weekends. They don't say much, but the feeling of love and relief is strong. They are both in recovery, they are both needing to overcome and leave the past behind.

Baby tells Mom that she's agreed with William to have a tubal ligation. She doesn't think she could manage another miscarriage. Mom tells her it's a wise decision, and agrees to go to the hospital with her.

Baby makes an appointment for the operation in two weeks. William will go as well. There is a secret silence of peace in the decision. Everyone is proud and understanding of Baby. She needs support now. She is nervous.

Knowing that the rapture has come, it begins for them with this weeding out the weeds in the family. Peaceful resolve descends upon this family. The wedding date is planned for a month away.

Mom and Baby both hobble metaphorically being broken in this broken family. Rexi decides to come for a visit again. She gives praise to Baby for taking this responsibility for herself. Also, she is overjoyed about the upcoming wedding.

Tough stuff it has been. Yet peace is already exuding throughout the world in many different ways. The shifting rains and clouds make way for glorious sunshine, brighter than ever before.

Bent over trees stand up. It is the beginning of the change. The Beast is gone and will never experience the oncoming joy of God's people. Weapons of peace, prayer, and armor of God keep situated with the evidence that there is glory in the mitigating circumstances of wallowing in joy and peace. Grace tingles in the air. Wobbly feet are a little uncertain after many burdens have been lifted. Water now is clean and drinkable everywhere. Flowers stand tall and stout, boasting of their illustrious design.

Dogs and cats play together in the streets. The savior has come to stay.

He has come to stay and take nutrition from everyone in a way that is palatable to society. He briefly enervates custom with design, and gives countenance to the decisions he makes regarding who comes and who goes. Everyone knows that Jesus is the Lord, but does everyone believe in this? Perpetrating indifference toward him belies the very vacation of hell. Never ending, never protruding. Sucks at the very cuffs of the jeans, and winds up penetrating Jesus in all his anomaly. Brief and brilliant, the summer sun is wild in its fury. We hide in caves and under rocks. We swim in the waters and take mercy with faith. Faith without works is dead, and forgiveness of sins overcomes the restitute in compliance with forever living grace.

Grace pins the tail on the donkey. It bobs for apples in a big bucket, and comes home from church in the guise of a goldfish in water in a plastic bag. Resumed hope is forever graceful, and the very indignation of disgust is valiant and true. Forever copulated by intrinsic design, the favor of Jesus is a rich one indeed. In timely death of the overturned and mysterious, there is lacquer in the necessity of forbidden charisma. It is Jehovah's witness that ensues with a library full of downtrodden books of salvation. Get ready, go kill! Kill the ugly and deficient, the lost and the hopeless, the made up of popular death. Inquisition finds true the way of the Lord. Back him up! He commands respect and violently chews on the distasteful, spitting them back out.

Violence in the shower is only a show of ape-wisdom, the wisdom found in apes. Technologically disgusted with us, the usurpers of faith now show indignant surprise to the lost and the eloquent. Reaching out in fun and glorious factions of delight, the remembrance of the lost jellyfish forks over a disappearance of life in the seas. No more whales, sharks, fishes of any type and definitely no more bottom dwellers. Ice skating across seas in the end will be quibbled about and fought over. Forever broken in design, forever rant and forever out of reason.

Negligence despotically finds intrusion on the failure of hope. Turned around waiting, and smothering indecency while obliterating sausages. Sausages and donuts comply with every tasteful resolve, and paints lacquer on the designs upon the walls in our halls of dark tunnels and unending light. Carry on disgrace, it will be matted to the walls and left there to hang. Juices and glory, enigma and sandwiches of mortified forgiveness, the realism of a diploma comes with graded results.

High school education is enough to get by in this world. Much learning can be done on the side and with grace as one follows one's interests. Pick a flower and think on it, and forever give grace to its maker. We have design, we have reiteration and absolve of opinions in lost hope but holding up two thumbs.

Grace and recognizant mutation belies the forgivable with the lost, and the graces and mercies of the true. Willy Wonka and his chocolate factory tests resistance of children around limitless supplies of sugar and sweet things. So much is too much, and there are so many cases of diabetes these days. Intuitive and full of garlic are the mangy debris of disgusted malnutrition and sanctified proliferation that runs with hope in the disgusting eras of our eternity of emblem design.

Quantification and necessary obligation give to us the means to taste juice and respect fruit. Obliteration and satisfaction can be contributed to the meaningless despair of forgotten little ones. The little ones so sound and sweet, so sweet and touched, so touched and developed into big ones. Carefully fortified in nuances of ratified compliance we see bananas on the trees and in the stores. It's a work in progress, making everything available to everybody.

Sacrifice and nurture, the broken down ones are qualitatively insistent. Mutually obscure, and dancing with remittance of sin foregoing ecstasy, this eases the imagination. If sorrowful and bitter, maybe then turn to the sweeter choices of nutrition. Just hang on and don't get lost in that. Degradation hangs on with every toe and every last finger. It purifies the unnecessary with the broken, and calls to service those waiting in the wings.

When it's your turn you will know when to step up. Step up and fork over love and forgiveness. The destitute with the relentless, and satisfaction going against the grain. Too many rules grow old and badger perplexed people that can't remain in the light for too long. In our caves, and under rocks there is safety in numbers.

Mutual Respect

People are tantalized by the rate of affection going out of Jesus Christ unto his world of lost ones. Truly a faith so delicious and divine, that numbers don't count like grains of sand along the sea shore. Imprisoned by decent respect and overwhelming love there is true beauty in the natural reprise of respect. Respect your neighbors, respect your friends. We didn't all get here for no reason at all. Even broken in requite and miserable upon the sewage outposts that process our junk we fail to deliberate how in technology there is a better way. A decent way, and a way of hope. Processing mechanically and efficiently we get lost in time in managing waste cleanly and with purified content.

Nothing comes out so repository as the emblem of defeat when one team beats another. Carefully trained, sportsmen, athletes, show downs gradually give of themselves in bottomless raiment and problematic dissolving chemicals. Together in sin we can agree to turn our backs on this sin and walk forward with respect and charisma. Smiling in the faith of much attested, chagrin. Despised and mortified and indignant of life surpassing beauty there comes a time when all must begin to march on. On and on and on. Letting go is the pigeon toed and much barked at soldier with a defect. We all have defects, some more noticeable than others. Reticent in design and behavior there is eloquent attitude of letting go, and letting your defect be filled by someone's affect, the generalization of flavorless design.

Flavored to opinion and sedition, the grace of the contorted, the paralyzed, the maimed, the discretion at which we keep these ones at bay, to maintain efficiency there is lacquer in hope and it shines brightly.

All of God's little ones have forbidden defects but those are only in need of more care. Don't turn your back on the disabled. Give them a hug and a prayer.

Fine tuned and prolific, we find pasture in the mesmerizing compliance of sin upon death. Deceitful in fury and raging like a queen in the wind, there is sublimation for forgotten apology and a fallen king. Where once there was hope there is now something called destiny.

At faith and distraught among the hopeful and the reasonable in mercy we find love and disrespect for sin. That is the first step in ratting it out. Can a people full of sin be expected to stop sinning all at once, all together? Not where quirks remain and hope falls short of love.

Pediment and preclusive operations keep factories in motion and workers at rest at last. Time to play in the fields of joy, the momentous occasions of love and resistance, respecting each player for whatever input they might have. People win and people lose, yet losing is just giving up on the migration of happy compliance and distended resolve.

Poking at the furniture that now begins to wear thin, we find materials ready to be invented again. Make everything for everybody. Do miracles, and give grace to the lost, but not hopeless. Turning over obedient articles of gratification, the vomiting from a sick stomach is enough to rid one of the flus. Influenza has no hope here, neither does covid nor pneumonia.

Shattering with reprove, the somnolence of disgrace pardons garden variety vegetables in their lacquer and shine. Quotas and grief come in apology for wasted produce. Bring about grace to the solid. Remember, grace cannot be earned, it is a *gift* from God.

He is upset about many things, and sometimes it is good to stay at home. Deliverance of the forgotten emblem shines in the sun sprinkled with water. Water and vegetables and sunshine come in great quantities; we must not forget our natural resources. Thinking on quantities, we think of the fields of our imaginations, and what treasures are found there in implementation. Forgotten cigars and hidden treasures make to believe a compliant nature of saturated sin and done over eggs in the pan. Requisite hope and fostered opinion come with the belonging of faith to the unjust. Just a small seed of faith can be the beginning of mighty insurgence and congruent fat on opinion of the believers. Chase down the reticent gone bad like Justin and stick him in the incinerator. But who is to judge? Why can't we all stand in the way of suggestive inebriation?

Parliamentary discussion quakes in fact with a piece of quality and sin smashed together with great force and entities of divine reparation.

Orders in, there is destitution made of perplexed and compliant characters. "Over the river and through the woods, to Grandmother's house we go…." Sung with abatement at Christmas time in freedom to run and play and dance and make angels in the snow. As well as snowball fights and building snowmen, and crafting ice sculptures to divine point of grief. So pure, so beautiful is suggestive of nectar on a tree in a honeybee's home full of honeycomb.

Disgraced again, we find compliance in the guilt of the "bad seed". Who created one to sin onward in unjust and prolific demeanor? Why the paralysis of the cruel and impediment of the broken hearted? Disbelief and utter discrimination between the beauty and the ugly, even reticent ones have beauty, yet those gone the way of exceeding sun shine bright with the light of the devil. Lucifer, himself, a fallen angel giving glory in respect of malice and hatred. Fallen, burning, desperate now that his time is short. Reaching out to slash and burn everything in consequence of bright blood in the snow.

Recovery, endless love and hope, respect for the demise in all its failures and upended technologies there is danger of losing opinion and being smashed. Subtle yet unique in greatness and unending beauty of lethargic obliteration, opinion smashed and burning emblems create just the target for the unbelievable land confounded ecstasies of goodness. Greatness ensuing and piling up of behavior upon behavior, the acquisition of compliant returns comes with nearness of affection and tender touches of the soft and nurturing.

Upon marital failure and marital success comes the marching drum of forbidden and compliant. Baby looks forward excitedly to her marriage with William and knows for certain that he is the one she wants to go through time with, for ages, and ages yet to be.

Relays and penitence give respect where respect is due. It comes to the good and to the many. The foul mouthed had best shut up and find a way to compliment society, for the breathing of their epithets is heavy and down pulling of migrants to territory and implicit rejection of nature. Stop using the "f" word as though it were a blessing. The forbiddance of such words only maligns danger and essence of perpetration, sending perverts away from their ungraceful due, like so many serial killers in a tub of soap and water.

Yellow rubber "duckies" float high in the water, in their innocence being poisoned by the luckless and the faithless who refuse to change their ways. Impediment and failure stops the breathing of the broken and fallen in eminent repairing to challenge mortification with insolence.

Why, why, why do we cry out when things get disrupting and uncomfortable? It's because we were meant to be put together and released with fabulous energy and meaning of truth and oblivion. Sarcastic phrases mean little in hopes of glory and remittance. Sour tooth and significant design brings us to the needing point of care and watching out for one another. Plus, the need to be free of dominating accusers and amphibious characters who safely design frustration into our daily patterns. Prolific and sinful taste the water of fortuitous grace and purified cleansing for our bodies.

Allowing character to judge hope, we send bones down to the incinerator and watch as life goes by in other directions. Populous and precipice, needing orange and green and red to delight our eyeballs in faith and altruistic love of colors. The daylight grows ever brighter and softer. Quit realizing the sinful, but distort their inefficiencies in oblong mercy of the justified. Justification, found in hope and rescinding equalities among nature and forbidden justice. Qualities pushed past the point of death, and risen again will be justice enough for the many who R.I.P. Well put, the dead in Christ "rest in peace", waiting for the coming of the time when there will be peace on earth as it is in heaven. Clouds fall all around us. Clouds obscure the cleansing process of the earth, making ready for the receiving of Christ in all his mighty glory. Rescind and make ready, the truth is spoken and there is release of forgiveness into the air. Cleaning the apology and wiping all the tears away, the sin and the glory of misfits are brown nosed and trodden upon with big feet made to travel swiftly.

Holding onto congressional optimism, the fight for fire against fire burns our kaleidoscopic refusal to generate prolific wisdom and colorless design. Flavor and forever, the knowledge of Christ like a sweet bit of honeycomb on the tongue. Sweet and justified, with remittance of glory and caring about the unnatural population. There is faith in the "junkies" who need healing in this world. God doesn't expect us to be healed when heaven comes. It will take place slowly at an accelerated rate. Shine from heaven will light our way, the sun no longer sending its crafty rays to us, burning us. The heavenly light will arise from altruistic glory and unburdened penetration of sin. Once alit, it will light forever, and no unheeding consciousness can be over done in place of a forgotten descent.

Everybody everywhere are noticing the differences already, yet not sure what it is they are experiencing. Prolific in grace and understanding the sinful nature, we are absolved from ruination, and the cleaning will be done.

Brilliant and territorial function fills our needs for land and space. Bright and tolerant, bears will no longer attack, but will feed on the grains of the fields.

Baby takes a fall and hits her head. She sinks into a coma. There in a protective somnolence, she dreams of Heaven.

Compromise

Holding out for hope and the radio across the waves there is something called chagrin that will give place to wiry sedition and forgotten misfit attitude. No more cancer, no more kidney disease, no more heart attacks, and everything under the sun that once counted as a disease will be smoothed over with God's absolving light, and in our awkward way of dealing with this eternal goodness, we will bump into many people, some in the guise of those who R.I.P.

Baby face, she is and does understand the conglomerating opinion of spoof and proof. Down again to the enigma, the resourcefulness and exacerbated compromise is what it takes to bring justice to truth. What did you do in life? What will you do now? And forever? Who made us like this? Able to latch onto the goodness of heaven and be healed and recreated completely and without opinion.

The destitute and compromised find falling rain to be tender and acceptable with grace. The grass is green, the roads are smooth.

Oblivion does not remain counterproductive. Deceitful sin is ushered out with immediate destruction. We hold hands with the brave and the true, and the fallen kingdoms of earth as they once were. Grapefruit in all of its bittersweet juiciness comes toddling on to our tongues, holding reprieve and lustful generations to watch and wait and see.

Giving hope for the compromise of destiny with mortification and destined reproof, the insolent are party animals who will find such a nature going awry. Pandemonium and marching in the streets are a confusion, for no one knows what they are marching for. It is a sad way of coping with the grace of the knowledge of the truth. Boring and complacent does not exist. Hunting is no longer necessary; we will treat our neighboring animals with respect that does not compromise them in all efficiency.

Gracious and true knowledge falls where it will as we take steps forward into appropriating destiny, which for now is right here.

Indecent with surprise, the falling nectar of grace and love sweeps away dust and dirt from the streets. We no longer have grace, there is little to respect of the forgotten. Forbidden anger is smoothed out with glory and transcendent appeasing of all appetites. No more greed, no more need, just worshiping of the Lord and carrying out the duties assigned to us. We will all know when it is our turn to move, and gestation is a popular event.

Overgrowth of worms and weeds trouble us no more. We breathe the sweet air of religion come in glory and in aptitude.

Prolific and disgraceful means nothing anymore. There is a pinching of the teeth as all of our dental work gets remade in its own time. Hunting and carrying on with killing will be no more. Dogs are outside of the city on high. Perplexed and disgraced in nullified assertiveness pervades with oblivion and silent remorse. Carrying on with gestation is folly in its own wisdom. Disgruntled nectar we will drink in a timely manner, witnessing to sin that it is no more.

Blasphemous troubles will be destroyed, as everyone who remains will worship the Lord God Almighty, his begotten Son, Jesus, who in truth with the Holy Spirit are ONE. God will be inside every one of us, purporting negativity and crediting us with laughter to boot. Laughter in the streets, and laughter in the garden. Subliminal spoof and proof, Mom no longer worries about "shit and stuff" for the evil will be remedied away and taken far from us, expunged into the universe where waste retrieval is accepting and functioning in sync with earthly orbiting.

Plasma and knowledge make us adept at curating disgust and dusting the surfaces of the planet. Cleanliness will abide, no longer will sweating be obnoxious to the nose, women's periods will be obliterated, and our feces will be waxed away and no more.

Dogs and cats outside of the high city will be on friendly terms with one another. No more will dogs bark and bite. Friendless to no one.

Pitiful escape of fish no more means no more deserts of the oceans. Laughing waters will be clean and beautiful and fun to swim in. To play on with our boats, boards, and speedy windsurfers. Sounds like fun? It's only beginning… abusive behavior is in hindsight, and nobody will drown, for life will be forever. Clean, perfunctory, littleness and cranky demolition will bring to the surface an incendiary problematic opinion of demise. Don't destroy the beauty, because you can't!

God walks with his loved ones in the garden and up and down the city streets. He eats at our tables with us out of pure acceptance and joy. Wiping away our tears, he looks away so that we don't see his.

It's a homecoming so gracious and true that we can't even explain what's happened. Your best day here on ancient earth will not compare to everyday in heaven on earth. Problematic incendiary reward pops up everywhere, giving us the meaning of hazarded disguise and prolific lunacy. No one can believe it, this feeling this place of heaven here at last. Leave behind the wicked ones now for good, and don't give another thought to their disappearance for we are mature and thoughtful.

We will go on and on, leaving the old behind and receiving the new in all of its glory. Abandonment of design gives way to creativity, and abhorrent destruction of the old ways of doing things. Hitting and crying no more, no more deaths, no more suicides. Cars in the streets will be clean and proficiently made new. Driving will be a pastime, and the only thing held in demise is the air we breathe which will open up the lungs and heal all deficiencies.

William knew it was coming, but didn't know how or when. Disturbing or not, he realizes first that the fungus on his toes is gone. Baby notices that the arm she injured no longer pains her, and discrepancies of her miscarriages are no longer depressing for her. There is challenge, there are problems to solve, and the ongoing creation recovers not sin but dashes it away and it never appears again. Baby dreams on in her coma.

Brown nosing is not an apology, and apologies deserve grace. Where there is none, the sin has disappeared. It hangs in the distance; a sightseeing destination for people to look and see how it used to be. Then it will be forgotten.

The compromise in nature will be that affect will be no more in congruent denial of opinion where the rake gathers leaves on the ground and plastic bags are filled with them to be shipped off to the renewal plant. A population of prolific people must have a ruling authority, and God is one and ruling over all, yet he appoints Kings and Queens to Lord over the land and to nullify tensions and constrictions in the media that sweeps the earth. The entire planet is a new creation. People love each other unendingly, and welcome each other into their homes.

Pilgrims are appointed to work at a grass roots level, hands on with the harvesting and upkeep of the forests and rivers and plantations.

Where the sun was, it is no more. A new and different light shines and obscures darkness, which exists no more. The compromise of destiny with blackened darkness left behind, the earth goes swinging into a new orbit, and touches in greeting the other planets in our hereditary solar system.

Who is there? Did we not see them before? Enlarged opinion shatters the construing nature of the seductress who is no more, that faith in Jesus Christ will rise forever.

Who was that seductress? She was once of silence and curtsying, deceiving, untruth with problematic remission into the oblivion of nature. She was the waste, the problem, the malevolent distrust in God. The Tree of Life rises up with its passionate and delectable fruit. It necessitates truth and spears the ingratiated ignorant people with aggravated, ongoing despair and revitalization. Showered and inspired by anomaly, the people will douse themselves with uprising fountains, springs of faith. Deliberate, electric, possessive behavior brings peace to the outcome of ambivalence and to the outcome of repudiated hatchlings, nestled on seats of opinion and frustration. With regard to peace, resolve, and patterns of rhythm there comes together a time that has neither day nor night. Thump, thump, thump. No regrets. Christian warriors marching on.

Respective of our differences, the blending of all kinds of people will be spiced in the reserve of appreciation. Demolition can no more split differences, but instead we will gravitate toward them. Being different is being special, and no one looks after those who are pitiless and subjunctive in character. Proliferating circumstances come in the guise of never-ending trust and things we can rely on. We can still go get our pedicures, manicures, and do our hair appointments. Funny how the clothes in the stores fit exactly perfectly and without compromise. The indifference to sin hangs on the very glory of its falling out to be forever annihilated.

Pure decision making makes it easy to go about day to day lives, there are no "poor" decisions, it is all an ecstasy of creative powers that we live with. Destination foregone; the beauty of the pilgrims is that they have a place to be. Don't be alarmed if you find yourself to be a pilgrim. These must go forward and take charge, taking orders from ranks above them.

Be a king or an inducement for generative despair. Always the forgiveness is there, even in reserve of a pardon. Things can be done wrong, and things can be done right. The populace of fathomed opinion comes with understanding with joy. The joy of learning, the joy of respect. The joy of friendship and family on occasion.

Disrespect toward leniency construes opinion as being common knowledge and not a deficit. We can egg and gird each other onward, but really the Lord makes all the difference. Those in heaven don't do wrong, for it leaves a bad taste in your mouth. Nobody likes to feel hurt or cheated, and nobody forgives upon an apology. It just is. Related and chiming with decency, the characteristic hope of redundancy comes clear and clean with the operative respect we each are due. Not to be traumatized at others who appear better, but accepting of ourselves in nocturnal celestial magnificence. Spinning on wheels, the donkey carts go up and down the streets. Someone might ride the donkey, a postal system.

Aggravated demise is found in conjunction with our "failures", which are actually just attempts that come up somewhere other than expected. Failures are change, allowance and comforted in internal pastures of healing and making big changes that haven't come yet.

Acquittal of anomalies that once were decrepit with hatred and disgust become matter of fact discarded with the pleasure of being renewed. Devices slain upon target are those we now need not anymore. Difficult decisions keep operative the many pastimes due to creativity. Problematic somnolence is no more, for it doesn't matter if you're late for appointments, everything happens at the right time so that obliterating nuisances might adjust in the common conjunction of cogs working together by design.

Lacerative and unending on policy brings about the police who only humanely protect citizens that get stuck and can't go on. These are renewed in "jail'", a place to reside with happiness and joy as changes are made and everyone receives new instructions.

The planet is pious and so are all of its inhabitants. Those who are true will walk with Jesus Christ, yet the many who doubt and disrupt will be let go. To be no more. To be agitating in revival against seditious threats and forgiveness. For God does not thwart his called ones, wherever they are in whatever condition they find themselves.

Middle East destiny comes with peace and justification. The dead who remain there will be judged according to the laws of the Bible, the only source of remembrance that needs to be remembered.

Clarification, justification, and coagulation becomes perverted with nuisances of stubborn and ornery contempt. No more forgiveness for those who deny Christ and who he is, the one who died that forgiveness would be ready for all who are ready for it.

Mopping and glowing in the in-transcendent nuptials of agreement flow with nutritional ecstasy that our once mortal bodies never had. Our immortal bodies know when and what to eat wherever. Who cooks? What kind of food is in heaven? Prepared differently with the right ingredients, everything becomes satiating, and glorification of ardor combines with every needed element for joy and the ratification of problematic gestation in the guise of a happy digestive job for the body to position itself by and with.

Nuptials in forgiveness of contempt and aggressive behaviors means throwing rebels into the sports arenas to work out their differences. Orbiting with many indeed forgotten opinions, the nature of death is no more so there can be no more killing nor dying due to disease or despondence. Depression willfully creates denial that something is wrong. Those tied to depression in life will be blessed by joyous and overcoming experiences of achievement and suicidal bliss. No more suicides, their complacent resolve will be remembered no more.

Those who committed suicide in the past life will be reckoned before the savior who judges all and in all with respect to acceptance. Forgiving and overcoming for those who were faithless but true, and denial of those who came out of the walls of disgrace and decided that life was too good for them. A disrespect of nature, and a congruent surprise for many whom we thought were gone.

Paralysis, justice, motivation. Congruent love and enigma. Failure to buy, failure to sell, there will be nothing without hope. Forever broken and downtrodden are the bad memories we have of this place. Our new positions in this affected area of demise gives hope for the conglomerate beseeching of negligence and no sin. Who needs a lawyer? What did you do wrong, or was wrong done to you?

Practicing faithless and disgusted, the people of the earth will judge one another in response to the admitting of the Lord in his fathomless gestures. The Bible says that we will even sit in judgment of angels. Bordering on hell, the difference of saving goes hand in hand with punishment. A righteous punishment can be born with pride. Forgiving and overcoming difficulties only means we are proud to be who we are.

Cleansing and renewal in the faith and grace of deficiency, only obligates opinion to mature faster and to give oblong resistance to the naughty and the true. Who makes the rules, and who Lords over all?

Jesus Christ is first in the coming kingdom, and his disgrace will be overlooked for we had him killed in order to submit to judgment the allocating of renewed pressure and despotic surmising of hateful indignation. The opinion of fast and resolving opinions is hatred to what was done to him. He holds a candle to the light, for he is deemed greater than all. He knows nothing that his father did not teach him, and he is perfect in regard to all significance.

Jesus Christ is love above all love. His insistence on enervating malignance is only a quarter of opinion that matches the true resolve. Hope and destiny, remittance and malformation. Doing dirty to the trick of demise becomes oblong nature and naturalistic surprise. Forgiving and overcoming all, he knows not to be with the wrong people, for only those who God has chosen will reach his outstretched hands.

Reservation for those in order of deceit is found in integral fortification and national alliance. Perpetrated and misguided are the attempts at peace where there is no peace. It will be forgotten; it will be gone. Altruistic of nature is the surprised one who dominates regression with a simplistic attitude of joy. Differences manufacture joy and appreciation. A little here and some over there…. We will all find perversion a thing of the past. Some of your mortal enemies will be gone. Others God might justify in deed and in truth of expectancy.

Caring, judging, incriminating, and causing violence to war at peace with the preponderance of peace drastically hedges the forbidden in all but the dominated sources of conjuncture. Never again will there be the lost at sea, the lost in the forest and the lost maintained within the mind.

Congruent denial precipitates judgment and gives to us a formation of opinion that is tattered but true. Beginning to absolve differences means that justice is taking place at last.

Immortal Glory

Vegetable gardens in all of their once questionable series become hereditary in decency of nominative construction and pervading negligence of lost opinion. Gravitating towards insolence and coming out on top means that pervading goodness has become reckless after all. We meet in peace and conjure up danger. We give free will to the majority and stand guard on a few perpetrated with injustice and somnolent disguise.

Factions on the enigma of faith becomes questionable. Who gives faith and where does it come from? What is it? Do we so know each other that we give faith freely and upend sin when it is not there? There comes a seed of faith planted in joy that once had no home to call home with fragrant and illustrious design. Quaking with denial, the reticent and the introverted criminals can be forgiven in justification of things that went wrong but weren't meant to go wrong. Suited to blame, these inefficiencies give ardor to peace and solace. Contemplative design is like the cucumber on the shelf, and the jar of pickles that no more has to rot. Only beneficial mold will work in heaven, to trim the lost and broken by eating up mistakes and conjuring over the image of redundancy when lost faith in the end is lost hope.

Never ending demise, and soap on the countertop next to the sink keeps the little bacterial bugs at bay, so that they only find habitation on the lost or wasted particles in trust of cleanliness and safety.

Perpetration and over girding insolence becomes ready for the nature of all and in all, the presence of the Lord who betrays nothing and loves his church with interminable strata and uplifting oblivion. Gourds of implementation are efficient with plausible guilt and forgiveness in a grapefruit manner of surmise. Confabulation gives justice to the people, the lost and found, the beaten, the weak, and those manifesting joy with hope as they realize this place is really coming to be the kingdom of God, better known as "Heaven", a place for the gracious and the true.

Those who killed in anger are unreachable. Those who stopped the killing are a misfortune to society. Even those who did not kill can be forgiven with those who did kill in mercy and in grace. Creative sustenance sings songs of retributive harm. A saturated opinion fortified with obliterated hope and undying insurrection of the lost and mysterious is sordid in pummeled redundance.

Equitable to the redundancy of plastered and broken opinions, the judgment of hope is released at last. First, we were not to judge. Now, judgment remains upon all of God's kingdom, and nobody gets by without knowledge in all impediment of sloppy forbiddance. Construed at last, in a changing opinion of the lost and indifferent, there is no saying goodbye to those lost in their wicked ways. Contemplative redundancy remains matter of fact with the necessitating brokenness of losing hope forever. Keep hope. It gives courage and restraint. It builds forever on opinions of joy, and reticently knows that constraint and obligation are justified in the danger of equating hell with a hand basket. Burnt to sin, ashes be gone.

Equitable in narcissistic judgment and despised nature, only the weak can overcome where the lost have lost their footing. Slipping, falling, breaking and bleeding, the domineering blatant monsters who served as "bullies" in this last world were trodden at last between a justified "nerd" and one whose obliteration of the past is beyond necessity.

Sanctified in guilt, healthy guilt, not despised guilt, the touch of the weakness in all of its enumeration and calculated genre of reprieve denies suicidal knowledge and borderline graphic control problems.

There is change in oblivion, and a turnaround of blatant disguise. Characteristic of wealth and untimely overcoming of a blasted disguise which dramatically changes in reparation and disgust, the futile rebelliousness and given redundancy to faith is like a feather on the wind. It blows here and there with no control over where it goes or where it might finally land. In Church, in faith, those led astray will be absolved for searching for the truth. The truth in all its profound agreement with ascertained oblivion partakes of desire and can be found only in the spirit of Jesus Christ, the Holy Spirit.

Unfathomable guilt and denial by decency protrudes with exotic defiance with uncharted perpetration, and forgotten pieces of joy. Under turned pride and enigma of faith are forgotten. Joy touches all in a renewed sense of pride, which at one time found nature to be configured with senses of achievement and moving forward in life. To bloom where you are planted is respectable indeed.

"Nerds" carry a trophy wherever they go; lost to the bitterness of embarrassment and feelings of not measuring up in faith and in sound intelligence. Faith is a meekness that graces all souls in sound judgment and a seeking of the truth in Spirit. Demise and projection can incinerate a lost or incumbent soul, projected with the camera to make mistakes and look stupid. Faith is annihilating and exacerbating with diminished disapproval and fated whinnies of trust and admiration. We can meow like a cat, "neigh" like a horse, and bark like a dog, but that doesn't change who we are and what we were made for. Digging in the dirt displaces agitation and morose involvement by implementing disgust where once was disguise.

Oblivion is long lost in the truth of forever. There is no room for it, and there isn't left a beseeching quality of induction. To be truthful, the grace lost in internment becomes part of a river of hope that flows through the lands of adjustment and the peace-making barriers of hell. Trying again and again to be seditious in nature makes a bowl of fries seem like a purported design and a nebulous undertaking to be digested and prompted in heat and grease.

Characters of heat and grease only make ready those who are too weak to carry on on their own, and the listlessness of arbitrating action with resolve.

Tender resolve equates destiny with encouragement to those meant to give who felt meaningless in the past but have gifts to share in the future or onward without oblivion.

Basking in disgrace like weeds on a knoll, near an ocean, and by the sea, there dissimilates fragrant opinion with noxious embezzlement of sin and joy mixed together. No more faith in a pattern, for the devil is gone, let alone one thousand years. It's a pattern of making in betrayal a letting go of the evil one who sinned upon sin to become sin alive in sin with sin and because of sin, all dead.

Porcupines and diseases don't belong together. One is there to disregard safety, while the other one will be no more fruitful. Crafting and equating justice with miserable portrayal of nuisances dissolved in factions of overgrowth, and the lard filled mines of mineral deposits. Proclaiming heroism and banking on a sharp turn, the faithless fall yet those with hope can keep them hanging on until they have been explained the path of their destiny.

Goodness and hope for those without faith is oblivious and gregarious in sapping sin from the cedar tree. Burning in a forest of obliteration, the soil is nourished. Barking up that tree might fake guise of the illiterate, yet the tremulous fear found in those who reject the faith can only be pitied.

Found in the lost and filled with gestational clarity, goodness pervades in hope of the justice for the sinners who sinned like everybody else but didn't believe in Christ Jesus our Lord and Savior. They either didn't believe because they weren't exposed to him, or they were exposed to him and didn't believe in him. So, the lost man says… "Help my unbelief!" And this equates him with a ticket in.

Before we reprise the evil, the evildoers who hold contempt to the faith are resistant to pardon and don't believe on Christ because they reject and abscond him to the terror of all that stand by to watch their doom. It's a terrific evil to say "no" to Christ when judgment takes its turn with each one of us. Sublime and negligent impediment of faith also falls in the category of hope. Some are too simple to understand what faith in Jesus is all about. They are simple minded and do not make notation in their minds about those who have justice and those who have faith.

Splitting the deficiencies with a Father who is slow to anger and quick to overlook a disseminated matter changes everything. For He shows mercy to the ambivalent and disgusted with pleasure for sin. He makes right the wrongs of those misguided, and those who weren't reached in time. So, we have one thousand years to make things right, yet we do not all live forever.

A disagreement with this pardon is an ecstasy of lost forgiveness and overturned despondency clearly betrayed by a stupid shit who had no eager memories to dissolve webs of proclamation and stupid, stupid mistakes. Letting go and hanging on at the same time makes sense if you have two arms. Swinging in the trees like Tarzan trains you to understand the environment and to learn not to fall.

So, heaven can be like an educational course for the malignant and the benign. Both have an acidic course for nature and burn the mistakes created by the lost to forgive their upset and overflow their design.

May peace have mercy on all, and heroic despicable flavors of lost and meaningless hopelessness, the aggravated intrinsic design of portent suction into the gates of hell, mutated by nobody.

Imprisonment

Cat got your tongue? Too many things to say and you just can't get it out? Hold onto the flame, for it will not hurt you. Hang on like monkeys in the trees, and dance with the lions on the ground. Nectar, faith, nectar. Fast approaching disqualification and imprisonment. Desire is found in hope and belittlement, obtrusive with despair and fondling with disgrace. Patterns of negativity don't believe in eternity, of the joy of nature absolved by opinion to create or destroy at will.

Fortification and finding faith are all equated with a destiny of hope and joy, making faith a stand all and end all power to obtain and keep. Keep the faith that you have and enjoy the power that it gives you. Sublime and forgotten, the tendencies to resolve with nature the fetish of denying grace and casting evil into the waters, there will be a lake of fire where all the evil things will go. No matter what they do, they can't escape. It's a hot, hot brine full of minerals that eat and destroy all life that comes in touch with them. Minerals that are eager to consume those who are thrown to them, their burning toes being the first to be consumed.

Paralyzed people will move again. They will rejoice in their new and immortal bodies, they will run, and jump, and throw their hands in the air. Breathing air in and out like never before, before their bodies stopped.

Freedom to sing will come to those who worship God. To sing with joy and clarity, in the event of a stupendous visit by the Savior. He will wilt no more, will not be subjected to useless cursing by his name, and won't be accepting of disrespect and mocking anymore. He has the weapons of the Father, and in all guilt, those mockers will be destroyed by a stroke of faith and perpetration to be killed.

Thanks be to God and we have the religion of no mercy to all that drag Jesus' name in the dirt, who wound him with despise and guilt and shame, even mortification to the wounds he bore for all his people, a forbidden shame to mock, test, disgrace, and forbid.

Incendiary fools are forbidden for showing him no humility and humbleness of heart. The disgrace thrown at him is hateful, stupid, and not of art or opinion. No one can know him and not love him. For the viper snaps up those who mock Christ, they are most delicious to them. Falling, falling from remorse and attitude of opinion, the love of grace in Christ finds remorse with resolving of opinion and falling out of destiny. A tiny bit here, and a tiny bit over there, the faithless is truthful in bearing witness to the sinner who overcomes sin, and the loser who follies in it and destroys himself as others watch him die while they again are reborn.

Rebirth is eminent in Christ Jesus. He shows a new body, a new form, and the difficulties that reason in him show a magnitude of justice that can be found no where else than in the world around him, this world of oncoming joy and complicated matter.

Abstract technology and deeming the future as lost is imprisonment here on earth. Losing to failures is the art of sin, for it is a practice made by many and lost to some. Altitude in faith and judgment finds a curse on the mountains of shame that exist here in nominative somnolence. Regarded with true shame, the embarrassment of joy, the forgiving of the riddance, and the mopping up of the floor by truth gives radiance to the implied and distrusting nature of lost pervasiveness. Only in entity and disgrace do we find the lost in the prisons of hell, waiting to be shamed before all of glory. Revised, changed, terrorized, and fearing a fear of all fears overflowing with remorse, terror, and loss of a foothold on grace gives arbitrary congestion to tremulous annoyance at hell.

It is a password to the negative and those who don't measure up to the grain of the wood. Lost in carving images to represent other Gods is a mere nuisance to the Lord, yet he will oust the lights of those wretched idolaters with the flick of his wrist, and they will no more stand in the perversion of the truth and the meek and tame people of the earth who are trying to find their way. He is the Way; Jesus is the way.

Pounding on faith and giving remittance to hell, the joy factoring in grace protrudes from the remorse of hellish creatures watching the time approach of their sins in idolatry and the practicing of foreign and strange customs. If it doesn't align with the Words of the Bible, it isn't true. Glossy, and shiny I know, yet the destiny of truth is to forbid all falseness. There is reality of grace in the Bible that cannot cause foreign opinion in malicious despise. There is truth outside of the Bible, not mentioned, that find a hereditary descent of the Word. It is complicated, but not grotesque, for times have changed many realities in the emblem of grace as servitude and positioning has brought about all realities, even those of disgrace.

Profound opinion and judgment might bring the questions to bear, about "What is right?" For we are lost in the seditious falling out of betrayal in disguise of what might and might not be right. Who is to judge, and why? God appoints the judges of this world. They maintain the glory of justice and transfuse the wrong words out of reality where faith grows like lichen on a tree. Out of the wind it grows and flourishes, marking our paths and showing where to go.

The forbidding of hell to take place in our natures is a good and hearty grace of suggestion made in rampant despicability of hell and its saucy lake of fiery brimstone, which does not look inviting at all. It is hell. No one wants to go there, but some will. Others don't care one way or the other. They will go for they are fools on a fence and can't mind their own manners. Lashing out to hurt someone is dangerous and unwarranted. No one had the right to put down a "nerd", although some protect themselves by remaining out of sight.

Projection of the forbiddance of nature belongs with all recall to a renewing of the mind, the accepting of a new heart, and bodies turned immortal and sinless.

Wanting to do good, and wanting to do right bring about a question of apology. Good natured sin is sin judged out of sight of justice. To this many times, God has winked an eye, yet no more will he accept these borderline deficits to his kingdom.

Crowns will not be worn without heady knowledge strong enough to support them. Even in grace, even in truth, and even in mercy there is an outgrowth of wit that degenerates a particular person from wanting to fit in. Feeling different and despised has been an imprisonment for some people all their lives long. Mocked and persecuted for reading the Bible in public, those of the learned will continue in heavenly regard. Those upholding the faith will not die. There is no problematic procedure that witnesses as the faithless do in their due regard of degenerate craziness. The unfounded opinion of witches and slavery may give a padlock undue for their freedom and their clarity and their witnesses to grace.

Set free from hell fire on earth, these slaves and witches have been persecuted all their lives and yet it remains on. Yet no more, for the faction of truth is alive in our minds and imprints on the negativity found in foundering rapture and demise at the same time. Give glorification for their remorse, for their misunderstanding, for their mentally ill. How the truth holds steady for those who have suffered affliction all of their lives, for their reward in heaven will be of grand design. Even in the yesterdays of yesterday, the will to go on has kept many alive from self-torture, mutilation, and self-contempt. Craziness is found in the fear of pain, for all know pain and justice. The enigma of the serial killer in prison cannot be deduced by the replica of their unwarranted habits and portrayal. Give grace to God, for he excludes all of the unworthy, and comforts those who lose their loved ones unnaturally.

Forsaken and despised, holding for years upon years, correctional facilities give remorse to those who hazard them a thought. Sometimes it is better not to know, but to be prepared for the worst to come.

Breaking up in the courtroom of justice and despair is the great countenance of joy found in the coming of justice in truth.

Immobile nature transfuses frustration with guilt and common justice. Perpetrated by design, by followers of the wicked and those who walk in their paths by means of hurting the innocent are greedy for gain. Adding to the faith of denial brings a foreign opinion of mild retard and generative ignorance. Random portrayal of mistrust and reward brings the medallion to the loser on the far end. The loser is lost not because of justice, but to maintain dignity where forever we are stretching our toes and fingers.

Deep in the dirt of weeding and plucking, saints breed their hope and pass on the faith in what once was wicked but is no more. Defiantly based upon religion in relinquishment of forebode, disgusting nature sins with oblivion. Polished trust and ongoing faith can only find corrupt and undeserving calculated traumatic appeal. Grace for the older and grace for the younger, and then to all who fall in between. Last but not least, the first shall be last, and the last shall be first in line waiting for their judgment. Stupid and forgetful, we meander in and out of line, not walking the straight path put before us. But God knows this is a weakness in our civilization of beautiful heads on necks on bodies overcoming despair.

Indignant retrial forgives even the sinner who sinned in line with faith. Temptations abound all about us, and to those who are enticed there is forgiveness to the lost who come forward in hope and in sorrow. Melt down in faction zero of malignant political destruction betrays only those greedy for power, yet there will be no power given astray of the meek and the weak and those prolific in dynamite internment.

Pleasing preposterous and empty acquittal in design, the judges of the truth stand straight and tall in eminent disguise so as not to shock the weak and meek ones but to tailor their approval of delinquent and forever absolved integrity. Caricature and nebulous construction of congruent design are aligned in nature and in the falling flames of hell fire that confuse the weak and the poor, and those who have no spirit left to call their own. Broken spirits and broken hearts are bound together with toxins of faith in broken powers of broken lords that roam brokenly and spattered on the edges of the earth proclaimed to all renewal and the fire of justice.

Place the young ones in the churches and provide the faith they need with prayer. Coax the young ones to follow in righteousness and faith, the doing of good and the being of a loving neighbor. Witnesses of faith and disgust together can see where a dunk in a pool of holy water would cleanse altogether the weaknesses that keep us from standing up tall and to falling down in the dirt.

Bitterness and reprieve, coagulate guilt and practices that shame us unto one another. Better than not at all, the practice of righteousness is a show of faith. Bitterness and construction of the lost with the despairing shows a mere coating of sin put over a reality of wickedness that copes in its ugly disdain but forever acquits from hell. Hell. Hell. There is hell and forbearance to the underworld that shoots from below and punctures our bellies with wounds that drip snot from the nose and call on kaleidoscopic adventures to mutate disgust with reprieve.

And so, we call it mal-assurance, the assurance that you won't come home tomorrow if you are hidden in a cave somewhere, trying to hide from falling debris and hellfire indignant but putrid and noxious.

Crying out can sometimes be a downfall, and forbidden pleasure might rock the crib, yet in all damnation of the lost and wicked, the truth is they will be no more. Too many people in the world? Unfortunately, many will be lost to damnation. To hellfire, and darkness and guaranteed destruction.

Dissonance and indifference squeals in terror at the changing times ahead of us. We procreate, and that is good. Yet wired opinion and justice are just hypocritical and unbeknownst to the fathomlessness of reprieve. Dancing in the darkness with strangers is not worshiping the Lord, who is in all with light, light of the eyes, and light of the soul, illuminated with a holy light that is soft and gentle to every eye. Those being lost will reach toward the light, but it is too late. Everyone who missed their opportunity to do good instead of bad begins to realize their error in many ways. True, God can be persuaded to make room for more, for overcomers who are just coming in at this late hour. Preventing solace from neighbors and upending difficulties found together with fun. Fun is to be had by everyone everywhere in the kingdom of Heaven. Some know not the meaning of fun, for affliction had terrorized them all through life. Some understand, and many are quick to learn.

Boring and recalcitrant in negative betrayal of apology abounds a non-ending predisposed letter of significance to the wrong. Careful to undo the wrong and make it right again, such attention to detail is pleasing to the Lord and he will make allowance in respect to passing qualms of envy.

Speedy recovery equates newborn with reborn, possessive of ignorance, and dancing in the wind on a blustery day. It is unimaginable, what we will see and experience soon. Where the hopeful brush their teeth, and the many drink their coffee, the endless repose of repair brings about building blocks of creation that stand in the erection of great architectural design. Mortification of the lost who have lost many, like the elephants will repair and be renewed in numbers. Forever bliss will remain contained.

Critical indulgence and opulent disgust are creative in spunky and aggressive implementation. Pleasure is sin if it is enjoyed wrongfully. The wrong foods, the wrong drugs, the failure of fitting in consequentially so rebellion takes place in messes of despair.

Retroactive and failing altogether, in time in mortification of zest and the willing amendment to life that lives in disgust with betrayal, a bribery would suffice if only there was food and pleasure to betray insult.

Caring design and overcoming populace and pervading torture can bring about a new and resplendent joy that makes good all that is bad and turns the leaf over of a new page. Ink in the pen, and then all is lost.

Burning the lost with hellfire is indignant of the nature of hell. It is imprisonment with terror and defiant radiance of conglomerate images, bestowing truth upon a nation of lost ones who bitterly cry out in uselessness, unlearning despair, and putting effort into redemption. Can a whole nation be despairing in folly and reprieve? Whosoever does not fail in terror and fails in restitute proclamation, discovers a life lost to no one and taken on by many who give faith where faith is deserved and implemented by grace and a down falling of mercy and justice.

The Lord knows every language spoken here on earth, and brings us together as a populace who diplomatically are sealed with redemption. Reaching out to the lost and imprisoned ones, who do cry out and *are* heard, bring beauty and simplicity to a recalcitrant oddity that factions into domestic policy.

In the fading light of yesterday, there comes a new light of today and tomorrow. Imprisoned or set free, we can still hold out our small inner candles and shine a light to Christ who has made his home within. Torturous and divine palpitations give credence to the new world of egotistic justice and despair.

Topsy turvy inclination to swing from side to side of the despairing road of justice, sinning is no more, no more meant to be. Agitating, aggressive denial of faith merely pops like a pimple off of the planet into the nowhere of out there. Faith and fragrance of flowers cry out to be rewarded by the Lord. And he shall give and give abundantly to those who in all effort have failed him yet in all spite have endeavored to love him. This is what counts the most, for it is the first of the laws in the New Testament of the Bible. Again, the laws say to love the Lord your God with all your heart, mind, and soul, and to love your neighbor as yourself. If these two laws are present and alive in an "alive and kicking" person, there will be a downfall of eternal glee onto persons of such prevalence.

Grateful of opinion and resurgent in directives of lost faith give over a bitter remorse of grasping to hold on, and to come forward in the place of your judgment. Then what will you say?

Baby Pollyanna will fall into her Father's arms and weep upon his shoulder, for all the evil done to her in this life, that is wrong, painful, and head splitting. Her demeanor is faith in her Father's trust, and trusting him in her faith.

Quilted down and soft approval forever lie in sync with the replenishment of goodness and soft approval of forever. In between lie the twin towers of insolence and the misjudgment of illusory hatred and foreign despise. Healing comes swiftly and mercifully. For Baby loved the Lord with all her heart in this life, and served him and worshiped him to no end. Baby's Mom stands quivering at her turn in line and transcends decency to admit to recovery of the small child at birth and her harsh and challenging life to raise the tiny tot with no end to her brother's and Dad's mercy that did not exist. It was with foreign foreclosure and eminent despise that she inserted herself between Geoffe and his mandatory possession of Baby. Baby and the Beast were a trauma in her mindful life and piling ambition of resource upon resourceful trauma and exotic faith. Baby and the Beast mutated. Baby won and the Beast mutated away from Christ and in the direction of darkness in acquittal. Baby and the Beast were an eternal source of friction for her in this life, and she did her best to live on. The Beast gone forever.

Reward

The Beast is no more, and Baby rejoices with her Mother. In all sanctimonious blending of perverted circumstances, the recall of faith upon foreclosure signifies a hatred so deep it cannot be explained. And for this there is forgiveness, it is out of control. Rewards fall implicitly and with easy forgiveness to the tune of a beating drum in all of its rhythm and melodic dancing. The tunes of a beating drum, falling in step with a line that is moving forward. Forward, forward, forward. Step, step, step, and then dancing on the other side of judgment in heavenly appeal.

Paralyzed are dancing, the eternally shy and beat up ones are dancing. Well-wishers are dancing, and kings and queens are dancing.

It is a false alarm for nothing, it is the beginning of the end and a newness that in faith comes with leisurely denial and consequence of lost partitions of elegance and bloody murder.

Blood spilled in self-defense will no longer stain the earth. God has a cleanup crew for every death on every account. In mercy and in danger, the plotting of distress symbolizes fragrant opinion with the nature of the lost who have been found lying and hiding in darkness for there being no other explanation in sight. Curses to hiding deficiencies that have taught shame and cowardice. Soon these will bloom with self-opinion that both distresses nature and flowers like the daffodil on a warm spring day.

Saying goodbye to the past, and hello to a future beyond anything we can imagine is a possibility. There is place for the hopeless, and place for the lost. Incongruent nature and split infinity puts a sour taste in the mouths of those in line that grow ever more fidgety as their time for judgment arrives.

And then it's all over and done with. Wickedness gone, and righteousness recovered, over and over and over again.

Little witnesses are called forward in the court of appeals and directives. Subliming nature with opinion, the judged are deemed innocent or guilty. Where reward is due it shall be dispensed, and for the guilty, there is suitable punishment, if not hell, than bitter servitude for a long time before faith is learned. These are the "grunt" workers in ambivalence building a new civilization with adamant talent and artistic creativity. They will have plenty to eat and no undue burdens to bear during their ongoing service to the King.

Plenitude and exacerbation call for a forgiveness in justification and undeserved guilt. Those stepped all over in life might believe they did something wrong to have suffered so immensely. Yet bruising leaves scars that heal and equate indifference with paltry surmise and disbelieving evidence.

Evidence brought forward by the meek and by the weary who have witnessed such undeserved destruction. Very acclimated to repose and undue nature, the opinions of faith and justice bring about an eternal song. A song that will be sung around campfires forever.

A lagoon is but a quiet preserved area along the waters on a shore that encloses it with blue hue, and white sands on a poplar tree beach with insidious pinching crabs and stinging jellyfish. Preserved without the crabs and the jellyfish, it is a jewel in between cliffs, and inordinate creation. Dispelled by the truth, it is a private get away for those who visit intermittently in exchange of others. The lagoon to our new world will put to shame what once was thought to be beautiful. It is a reward, a place of rest and recovery, and a sought after semblance of perpetrated coagulation and peace. There is inside, and there is outside. There is tame, and there is wild. Yet insignificance of reaching forward to dime the banked-on truth gives forbiddance to despair. A trip to the lagoon nearby wherever, is a place of solace and despairing justice that meets the ongoing challenge of forbidding pleasure with sin. Lying on the sand beside diamond clear waters in ecstasy of living light falling gently to the undeserved, forgiveness makes it right again. All paths will be illuminated, no one will fall in the dark or hide in the darkness.

Pain upon humiliation brings about the seedy opinion of joy surmised by water that is clean and beautiful, it is nice to swim in the lagoon, or put your toes in the water. Visiting predatory animals mince by here and there, no longer interested in blood, but living happily along the flora that avails itself in the wild of nature.

New plants, new discoveries, no stress, and where there is tension one can take a trip to the nearby lagoon and resolve what is wrong by going deep into thought. For we are now a people of prosperous problem solving, to make things better and keep building onto what the Lord has prepared in all magnificence and beauty. Clearly there is a reason to remain calm, free of anxiety and depression, and as we get used to this freedom there is a forgiveness that goes along with sins made inadvertently. Diffused and properly dispended, the truth of what remains in the waters is a mix of healing elements that curtsy out the death of the evil and remind one another of the inordinate despair that once claimed their lives.

Properly dispensed, and put up for observation are the finished products of joy that are achieved in this world and maintained into the next. Superior to all projects taken on in the old world, those that perpetrate grace, peace, and mercy on a gentle note now, beginning as it does, the time of renewal and of a new world with unimaginable glories and feudal repetitions that create disease, and these create disgust and rejection, keeping the things of the old world at bay. Like a boat coming into harbor, the uniqueness of faith in battered renewal gives peace to an aching heart of justice. No more common colds, broken bones, or torn muscles and tendinitis. Grace on absolving opinions of popularity disguises new and uprising meshed recovery, where people of all kinds mesh together and work at will.

The glorification factor is at work in all that the Lord does, says, and predisposes. Unction upon unction in grace and leadership, giving hope and merciless truth about the torn and the lost ones, soon to be remembered no more. Enough about the lost ones, for they are no more, in sense of time remitting with retrieval and guilt. Pardoned and duplicity acted upon repeated grace induces the justice found by the Father. Equally in times of faith and justice, the exploration of the new, the immortal, the challenged achievers procure adamant displeasure and forgotten dysfunction. No more achy bones and hurting shoulders or ankles. Strong and healthy hearts, blood that flows with new life and energy. Muscles strong and taut, even of those who choose to remain indoors.

Everyone will have their own mansion; it is a promise. Disreputable and insolent, those who procure homes in apartment housing live happily in an apartment building which, in itself is a mansion with many rooms. Monetary issues become second nature to the absolved and the technically worn sin. Above and beyond, created and belied, dignity with grace and the oncoming of newness in a new light.

For the light shines everywhere, and we are always at peace in the tender mercies of Christ who shows the way especially for the timid who know not what to expect.

Our reward is a new light that shines, dignified and respectful, not hurting anything or anyone. Credit where credit is due there is work for everyone.

Prosperous Problem Solving

Ignorant of worry, and lost to faith, the justice that comes to all bends on God's promise that he will avenge the wronged in this life. "Vengeance is Mine," says the Lord, "I will repay." And he will give due to what is due for those who forsook peace and did danger to other people, properties or lands. Discovery of nature in a working truth gives us the last laughs. We can laugh in the faces of those who hurt us shamefully, in all new unfairness and trepidation departed from anomaly. Coagulant truth and all its despondency, mutates the untrustworthy and cycles them out into despondent despair, even in lack of forgiveness. The Bible says to love your enemies and do good to them. Can we intrinsically do this? To hold a grudge gives base judgment to the unobserved forgiveness that is rapture in disgust and dismayed by abhorrent faults and misaligned hatred and behavior.

Quizzically made fair versus unfair judgments places names on the list to do the justice and faith that predispose the despair shrieked at by merciless cruelty repaid.

Baby Pollyanna is never again to be deceived by monsters like the Beast, and his heady crafty son, Justin. Baby doesn't have a bone to pick with anyone other than those two. She merely forgave and forgot all others. In decency, she can't find it in her heart to love them, yet all is okay with that. If she diffuses their danger to her person, she can if she tries and she does. Yet her heart does not go with them, it stays on this side.

Prosperous problem solving is the ease and protected nature of doing good things out of will and judgment. Where there is an obstacle, it can be removed, and tainted waters shall never be tainted again, concerning oil spills and other irresponsible issues that have polluted our seas, and then to come back to the new lagoons, we find rest and peace and ongoing graciousness and obliteration of folly. Chemically charged for our benefits, the reaction to the meaning of glory comes with the fixing of faith that has been misled and gone wrong. Absolving the issues of love and forgiveness, it is easier to be done out of sight of the wrong doers. So, we may forgive and pardon, but the Lord is the judge overall and all will receive their due for what is due to them.

Gestational wisdom complicates the suicides, and the homicides based on glory and good will. God will judge to the tee of bone divided from marrow, through the spirit that will pierce the soul and give cause to cry out. Fingers in the dirt and plants along the row, it is cursed justice to walk where you do not belong.

Living in sedition with wilderness and overcoming disputed territories of the heart and soul, we are beating in revival of a new and different way, which is the Way of Christ who founds love with trust and merciful forgiveness, the lust of denial, and the forbidden pleasure of standing among ice blocks on a warm day.

Vaccinations are no longer necessary, against diseases that harm and kill for they are no more. We observe practices, washing of hands and a clean shower when needed, yet in all truths there is no dirty substance remaining, no more deodorant, brushing of teeth, and optional laundry practices. We will have many of the garments that we want, and everybody will look so nice. Pleasing to the eye, warm, not, cold, not hot.

To sit down and read a book is not a problem, especially if it is the Bible wherein you will learn all you need to know to get around in this new world, God's upending Kingdom that sacrifices jealousy for not being forgiven.

Radical improvements and gesticulating harmonies of light and truth and forbidden judgment allotted to sinful nature and the recovery of those who lost their way, yet called out to the Lord while despairing. Falling in truth from the purported faith of negligence, we who have wisdom are none the greater. Even in the night we can sleep and dream and have visions, that will absolve all problems prosperously that the new beginnings for a show of hands are those who remain faithful and loving. Quaking in love and joy. Tantalizing love and mercy and grace and hope. Surprised by negligence in despairing attitudes and alternate demise of frozen solid opinions who do not come about with gratitude in the end.

Replenishing substances in moments of glory are like stopping at a gas station for gas for your car. Your automobile is a problem to be solved. We are to run on faith and forgiveness and elements of surprise. Noxious behaviors and talented reprieve, the new creation will be brought about by true believers who will be instructed on how to overcome the problem, the issue of newness made whole and retractable. Joyousness and beloved problem solving are a mercy given to us by the Lord. For we will not sit around doing nothing all the time. There will be problems everywhere to fix and to grow into complications that don't matter anymore. First, there is the cleanup crew, after a mass extinction of unbelieving sinners who laughed in the face of glory and murdered the little ones.

Your punishment for doing evil to only one of the little ones will be cause for you to wish you hadn't been born, to fall into the sea with a millstone about your neck. Those who didn't lead children astray will be magnified in grace. Truth and justice make allowance for those too weak to fight back.

Intrinsic design and bottomless behavior is seductive to the juicy elements of reprieve and denial purported on the negativity of slipping and sliding down a bank of shale, falling, hurting, bleeding. Disgust surmises the guilt of these ones, trying to get away, and reaching out to hurt God's chosen ones who have no despair, for the Lord is with them. Christ be to God as what sinners have to despair in truth and naughty opinions. Factors in regeneration of acquittal and newness please the Father for he forgets nothing and not a soul escapes him and his determining judgment.

Justification for truth on the elements of disposed and patterned denial, the face that looks into the face that forgives will receive a smile with symptoms maladjusted and despicably refused. Playing around with justice and despair is a privilege of the populace, and the inverted syndrome of aching peaches and splitting grapefruits.

Sublime and functional, the destiny of heartaches plagiarized by opinions not sought after quakes with denial of arbitrary slapping of conclusion upon waste. Waste, denial or arbitrary, falls all around us in this living, breathing world, totally dysfunctional and acquitted of all mercy disputing despair.

It is cleansed and reaped, fixed, made new, put to work. Aligned with these creations is the embarked on journey into the new world with smiles of glee and soon to be forgotten tears. Obliterated and punctual, the timing of all is all in God, who is the Alpha and Omega, the first and the last.

Protrusion from difficulties arises with the sin of replenishing the lost with lost memories, and betrayal by pardon in the night. Factories swoosh and vroom, making lots of clatter, and on and on into the night they work, building, building, and turning new into old, and old into new. Progressive production of the following issues mandates a retracting policy of patterned nebula and upturned forks and spoons.

Relating to the palate is the consequent denial of forgiveness of sins in gestures. Mandating reprove that begins with the glory of those who no longer call out. Yet God sees all, knows all, and does all that is good. Those who do good both seek him, and aid Him as he works through them, giving them responsibility to work their own way. It is this ambivalent system of calling on the spice of the weary to weave this world together with creativity and generous internal programs like guilt in squabbling restitution and glory. Better not to call on Jesus with a false guilt to remind him of his death. Duly done with partition to faith gives guise to the replica of nuisances and deprived subjunctive failure. Falling in a bucket full of insects, which make up a part of the cleanup crew would be a heady experience indeed. Yet insects in the new world have no need to bite or suck blood. They clean up our messes equating them with fear undone. Procuring obliteration of defeat, no nutrition is quite as enticing to the insects as the dead, and then our physical debris and defecation.

Problematic and belonging to undone repose, we find that the enigma of carnal wisdom is no longer a study of science. Medicinal pharmacology will be replaced by elements of beneficial qualities that will give rise and pleasure to bodies worked out in "the gym" where people go to exercise indoors. Of course, there are cliffs and mountains for the great hearted to climb and pivot and float in the natural world of glee and heart rending glory beyond all significant glory that we have seen in this old world, which soon will pass away.

Effective in arbitrary guilt by design, the significance of grace and mobility is dispensed to all in differing quantities based on hearts' desires, and plugged incorporate stand up. Glazing in the intention of despair upon demise, the prolific or prosperous repose of problem solving in disgrace shines newly in the ones who play with lions and tigers. The food chain as we knew it is completely uprooted and demolished in a way of peace and carnal acquittal of beauty. Destined to demolish the ways and means of a clarion call for true beauty, the sound of ambivalence is soon heard no more. Equated with disaster and upended repose of a falling oblivion, the nature of despair gives rise to a new and foundering quality, the genetically disposed. Lost in ourselves again, procreation brings untimely event to the lost without giving into diplomacy. Recreated and significantly reduced in population, there is room to move on, keeping only the best of the best. Some will be sent another way, to other homes out there that exist in much the same manner as we do, only our opinions are ignorant for we have no experience of such a matter. Safe to say, there will always be enough room for everybody.

Significant sin in obligation of jealousy and jealous reprieve disguises chewed up tattered messes of false creations where normative clattering sounds signal the turning of the factories from doom to new and better creations.

Sucking blood, no more, the vampire bats will live in the trees near lakes and ponds and protective caves. Ladies will no longer scream at the sight of bats, for they only want to get away and go back to nature. Our houses of course were not meant to house bats, but sometimes the empty ones do. Critically acclaimed we are not all here yet. Those women who are pregnant and nursing will have the hardest time of all in the adjustment phase of new world religion. Bearing gifts from the old world, they must be seeded out and remain in seclusion while they gestate their infants who are one of a kind. In cantankerous consternation, those concerned with birthing issues will be taken care of to the tee. Grace and sound oblivion reach out to all, for all who get pregnant do it in the natural way of which we are privy. Embanked on the narcissistic repose of carrying an infant through the renewal process, these gems of the old world will be honored with dignity far above the normal realm of people. These infants will grow up to be leaders in the great new world we now know as Heaven, the coming, and the here and worldly now.

Embanked on the retrieval of grape vine knowledge and the manufacture of wine more delicious than any we have *ever* tasted is globular in the event that vineyards grow and flourish sporadically upon the earth, which is our steppingstone into heaven. Prolifically, engendered to be our home, some will always stay home with practice and reversion of truth and guilt. No more fear, anxiety attacks, panic attacks, or any sort of anti-peace or depressive issue will remain, and we will come and go as we please. No more waiting in lines, untimely catastrophes, or uncharted mutations of our species for we will go out into the world and make changes wherever we go. Infinite and final, yet flexible and malleable.

Enervating and sublime religion is the maximal quality upon this new and beloved world. To worship the Lord, Jesus Christ, and to serve him upon all base and forbidden procedure, the service to him is obliged by all. The electric truth of that disgrace for those who slipped in and refuse to worship the Father, in Jesus, in the Holy Spirit there will be paramedics brought in to exit them out to nothingness and despair, a prolific equation of hell.

Expanding knowledge will overwhelm the many learned of university professors who will be done in by the manufacture and study of our new creational home and amendment to the structure of the grace and good will of desired study and design. Carrying onward, the truth of good will, will be spread out all along the seashores, and the mutated landscape which will cause creative desire to explore and make note of and write down each new discovery, of which there will be endless, for the world will be a generative and busy, and revealing display of gratitude to its inhabitants; the world is alive.

Talking

Recreating what is well known knowledge to us is significant endangerment of not knowing how to record it superciliously. Changes in the environment will not be stressful, but relieving and exciting for us. Those who were deemed "smart" among the people will be as though they were "dumb". To judge the "dumb" of this world we recreate a mess, so they are given scientific pleasure and a grasp on words and technology.

Belittled by many, those who were stumped in this world did not know how to express the many thoughts that they have. So will it be as the Bible says, "the dumb will speak" without fear but in eternal glee and glorification. Renewal of our times and our instruments only go on to say that the newness of grace in disruption of territory absolves the hatred of what once was and is no more. For Satan, that great old devil of old, will be locked away for a thousand years, to be released at that time once more into the world. Here comes the final judgment on God's people who will or will not succumb to temptations in greed, power, and usurping rebelliousness.

Flavor in rebelliousness is not permissible, for God is the King of Kings and Lord of Lords who reigns over everyone. He will tweak those who wander, and touch those who slouch. There is no laziness here, but still, we have peace and rest. Contemplative glory gives recluse to the aberrant and destructive qualities of grace that protrudes with an ugly eye meant to be withdrawn. It is better to lose an eye or a limb than for the whole body to be cast into hellfire for eternal damnation.

Cluttering about in despair, comes the naturalization of nutritious and disgusted incubation of terror for the malignant and the graceless. Forgotten aboard, they will be ferreted out like so many unwanted mice, and given over to the cleanup crew for the disgraceful many who disguised themselves in white robes that never could get quite clean.

Knowledge is for the many and grace for the young. Those partaking in credible enigmas like before have become overcomers in the joy of pardon and acceptance. Those lost hiding in fear at the quaking of the planet will be jerked up by the collar of their shirts and dropped into cleansing hot springs to be welcomed with happiness and reassurance. No more to be afraid. The Lord misses not one, no, not one.

Incendiary detrimental reprieve falls on no one. For the Lord rewards the graceful with the time to talk with him one on one. Yes, we get to talk with God, not only to him, but with Him. We have conversations with him as we walk through the forests, hills, mountains, valleys, and all places of the earth brought to bear.

For once in all our history of knowing ourselves, God will have a talk with the many and the few. Those who on earth hated their lives, will now be brought to glory and condemnation of judgment for those that did them wrong.

Fallopian tubes might well be severed for many will not yet have time to raise children in the face of this new recovery and discovery of graces and fallen reprove of denial in the face of many who have been heard but remain unanswered in the face of growing old. Growing old to bear no more children will be no more. But we shall get used to this place first.

Uncomely and forgotten in disgrace the particular habitation of globular languages purported about the world will be understood by everyone, until at once and in all time, the heavenly language will appear that no one has at any time ever heard. Qualifications for certain positions will be suitable for all who apply to them, for there is a place for every last one of us.

There shall be a unity of the spirit in the bond of peace. (Ephesians 4:3) For unlike the people of Babel, long ago, there is no longer any greed or desire to rise up to heaven and overcome God by uniquely speaking all of one language. It was at this time that God sent confusion upon them to garble up our communications by giving each nominal group of peoples their own unique language, each unlike any other one. In heaven there will be no greed, for it is a fallen disgrace that is no more.

Profound insolence and disgrace shall inhabit those who speak forbidden words that shall be no more received. It was Satan's doing to pepper our speeches with violence and evil, misdoing, and undoing.

Grace shall be sufficient for all, and all will have grace among them. Despicable displeasure will be no more, for our work will fulfill us, we were meant to work without stress, but creatively and with design. Loved ones will fall together and join together in happiness and joy, with superfluous animation and haphazard opinion. Meekness of suffering shall be there to remember the joy of pleasure and righteousness. All healing shall come to a head, and no more will the minds of the weak be disturbed.

Purported and consolidated efficiency makes marrow for bone and sufficient emblem for requite. Patterned and forgiven, the lost and the foundling are disguised in ignorance for the shame of their glory. Confused and wretched, the alimony of payment given upon a marital separation shall induce others to take place for the lost and to provide for the children. The children are first. For the Bible says to enter the Kingdom of heaven, you do so as a child. Simplistic and ready to learn, to be craven and disputed over, the naturalistic way of reasoning beyond knowledge and above the absolved numeration of sex offenders. Problematic and purposeful, the enmity within wagering parties gives enough hope for all to learn to live in peace.

Though a natural argument is normal and happens in conversation intermittently, the betrayal of a pattern of all likelihoods gives up on nature with hapless debate. It is good to exercise opinion in the broken nature of fixing apology. Crammed into a space too small, the bitter argument will pop out into everything and be judged by everyone in the court of law. Resending implications mean nothing to the destitute and forlorn, for the waking up of problematic demise secures a sugary and tasteful resting of apology upon sin.

Created to be haphazard in all analogous temptations, the belief that God is good cannot be disputed. Also, God is good *all the time*. Bearing witness on contemplation and subjugation of analogy upon sin rides the knowledge of equating goodness with evil, yet only goodness will overcome. The jolly hope of a better today, and an even better tomorrow succumbs to the grace of oblivious shining in the heavenly light, and the overturned disgrace of forgotten apology.

We are wrecked upon the shores of a new world, and now it is time to go out and discover it. Oil probably needs not to be forsaken in all of its gracious indignities, and the fallen halo of the broken angel will disguise us in frequent abode habitations like the learning of how and where to cook food, and just what makes a meal for the palate with regressive nature and new-found procurements.

Eating in heaven might be a normal practice, as we are used to in the old world, yet finding food shall have a new name on it. No more eating of pigs, cows, birds, and many other old-world foods shall be needed for God has provided us with something much better. It is a natural opinion of grace versus despair, and the overcoming of somnolence with disputed behavior. Collecting the goodness of the trees and the forests, the fish in the seas are no more. Juncture upon a forgotten iniquity, the reason for failing fisheries provides clues of despondent behavior and a new breed of fish shall appear. The seas will be filled with new breeds of everything, for the old has gone and the new is arising.

Fish shall be enjoyed for their beauty by divers and people who wade in the waters and get massaged by schools of happy fish who live to be grateful to God, and to the people who harness them for outlived circumference. Broken and besought, there is an outlived ability to see and appreciate the beauty in nature, the discovery and reporting of discoveries sublime in age and new age, giving and reporting in decency and overcoming derisiveness and contemplation of glory and repose, a sea is for beauty, play, and enjoyment. Wet water in its own meaning is soft and healing to the skin. Aberrant and unordinary, the skin tickles to be touched, and remains within reach of symbiotic displeasure, forgotten and denied.

Perplexing and dominant behavior confounds the opinions of food and its icy smooth sheen, oily to the touch, a rainbow to the palate.

Dominant aggressive behavior is naturalized and obliterating as fear leaves all and leaves no scars on our hated bodies. Those who hated their lives in the old world shall be in love with their new lives. Those who loved their lives in the old world have lost them. Yet there is preeminent return for the resistance of surprise and gesticulating speech mannerisms. Talking, talking, talking shall be a luxury to all, for there is so much to talk about in all of our prosperous problem solving. A guarantee to forbidden pleasure, no longer used to harm one another is gone for decency of surprise.

Dysfunctional habitation is for the lost and the dirty, who do not answer to the laws of the Kingdom. Pleasure and detriment leave all on an inclusive and repository semblance of nature, upset and caricatured by negative somnolence and a waking of the senses to new and different features on display. Coagulating circumstances devise different and anatomically forbidden creatures to nestle in device and procurement. Long lasting and never forbidding the castles of the regal in opinion of largesse. Contra-indicating features of a latitudinal structure in the observation of hidden take over and loving remorse, we see with our own eyes what God has made, and we deliver ourselves over to it.

In finding peace among the subjunctive and emotional delivery patterns, the qualm of seeking a new neighborhood is open to all for all to assume. Congratulations come with a new habitation, for all have worked hard to get here. Now we are here, and the beginning has begun. Riding nature with opinion to structure waits in deficiency and applies needed pressure to absolved skin and forgotten remittance of apology. Enough about apology? Not yet. It is beautiful, a part of speech that all should be uniquely acquainted with. Talking provides an outlet for apology, for we are not at all without our inborn clumsiness and forgotten lassitude or inebriation on sight of overjoyed angel dust as the beginning of hallucinatory experiences. These can be good and for the adjustment of all nature and expediency.

Critical and trustworthy people have much to differ on and don't keep badgering one another with forgotten demise and prolific inebriation. What once was drugs and narcotics in the old world are now new and fashionable recreational substances that are non-addicting and highly enjoyable, similar to a cup of coffee.

Reaching the point of glee and incendiary production, the wise and terrified no longer point fingers at the small and repudiate little or nothing to the fashion of talking together in groups or intimately. This fashionable language that we now will be speaking is a surprise for all and includes all the differences and nuances that once graced our tables of foreign declarations and munitions. Forgotten behavior can be calculated and remembered, and passed on down in stories told to one another. Much of talking is a disgrace to be without, for the forming of opinions ought to be shared to discover the lost and attempted failures of destruction.

Caring about the nature of reprieve, we are gesticulating with our hands and our thoughts. We reach out, but unless we talk with the eternal language there is no hope of reaching agreement on all knowledge and differing points of view.

Purgatory

We seek to be found. We give to be gotten. We suggest being discovered, and we wait for our blessings and reward. Listless and true beginnings are natural in a natural world, where the joint of attainder splits negativity with a bath in the waters of healing joints and forgiven inconveniences. Saying "sorry" gets you a far distance in the world of colloquial misunderstanding and farfetched diplomacy. No one knows without saying how things are going to turn out.

Perplexed and demised like darting schools of fish to be had for their smooth and healing massage of our bodies, we acquaint ourselves with trouble when we indignantly create a mess of absolved quantities of lost aberration and dignified repair. Schooling ourselves together with the knowledge found in public situations, the conglomerate retrieval of nasty unfounded grief are overturned with seditious warnings. Naturalized and forbidden induction to the equating of the fear for the nasty and lubricating spouts of spigot enhanced retribution, we formalize our opinions based upon those awaiting judgment in between the two worlds. Emaciated and far fetching turbulence tries to elongate the stretch of truth without apology. Gracious retrieve belongs to the hope of those waiting in purgatory, ending in retreat from imprisoned burning of fiery brimstone.

Blossoming with weeds and destructive animal habitation, there is consideration of the waiting and the worn. No one wants to stay there. Where are they and why are they there? Those who have a kaleidoscopic experience of becoming productive and encamped within justice and belonging to the figurative of goodness in all appellate derived sequences give forbidden hope to those who dare to crave it. Without a lost hope, the once disparate and subjunctive people like the prodigal son in the Bible who spent all their goods on conferring and legalistically wrong practices see the folly of their ways and travel home to the Father who waits with open arms and ardor for his lost sons and daughters who strayed from home in search of stolen, foreign goods and greedy betrayal of responsibility.

The Lord has waited, and now his prodigal children must make their way home, and it is here that they remain in purgatory. Sinless and sorry, they expunge their defeat and confess to the wrongness of their ways. Yet they always remembered their Father being there for them at that time, before embarking on fatty reprieve and fatty liberation at the other end of their route.

So it is that those who got a seed of faith planted in them in the early years, that had not the chance to grow and put in roots upon a slow-moving stream, created in alliance with a justification factor that moves the noteworthy with the fastidious and underling motives of subjunctive despair. This alliance with God based on a memory of something special and good is created to bring home his loved ones and their special spicy tempers.

Tempers of indignant and merciless release of fat blown creations live to grow into the nature of the Father for all he has done. They turned away but turned back. This is a great compliment for the Father, and he longs after his lost and hurting ones who have gone astray in meaningless faith. Despite opinions of lustful waste of goods and total revoking of becoming an heir, these rebellious sons and daughters remain in purgatory on their way home, as a way to remind them to never leave their Father again.

These are the criminals who robbed convenience stores and banks. Those who stole from houses, removed property like boats and cars, stealing things not belonging to them. These are those who squandered their goods gambling in casinos, who bid at silent auctions, and also stabbed their brother in the back, metaphorically.

Insidious despicable despair hangs like spider webs all about them, while spiders gnaw at their flesh and leeches suck on their legs. Mosquitos buzz about their ears and fleas pepper their skin.

Upon reaching the Father at last, he will yank them out of all suffering and plop them down in hot springs of water to be healed and overcome of deficiency. Fabulous, enthralling awakenings overcome them desperately, for the Father is overjoyed that they have returned home.

Making a conscious decision to return to the Father that they learned about long ago, despite the innocence of reprieve, the justification of lucidity, and harmonizing of tickling melodies bring back the goodness that once was. These are exploratory creatures made in the image of God, who passed the test of total obscuring from grace and put in to practice the abatement of negative construal and blazed trails in mountains high and valleys low.

Balanced on repaired modules of once were the naughty and indifferent, capable of doing righteousness and choosing not to, we deliberate on forgotten confection and reiterated bar code decency. Never say the "666" to a forgotten one, never get it tattooed on your body, nor sing it in a song. The Bible says that "666" is the number of a man. Yet it awaits in aggressive apology to the seditious belongings of mankind. Mankind can mean "womankind" as well. Those two unceremoniously prevalent and inhabitant of long going forces with fallen figures, we nestle in our little holes in the wall and watch as the dangers go by and give decency to our sins. Learning and lusting, lusting and learning, we perceive differences between forgotten promises and broken squabbles of detrimental failure in chains.

Progressively decent, the number fades away, yet do not take it, for it is the mark of the beast. All who take the number upon themselves shall not make it into heaven. It is a situational factor that keeps nonchalance at bay and disqualified from perdition. Unknown and not belonging, the criticism of forgotten decency becomes portrayed as a broken branch of knowledge left hanging on the tree of absolved history. Family trees, and so on, are remarkable in their tendencies to reiterate forgotten pasts, and broken tablets of forgotten insolence.

Qualified and indignant resuscitation makes new the recklessness of absolved features and nuances which decide for us which way to go. Not all will go the right way, there are those who choose death over pardon and forgiveness of sin. Weak and terrified, they cling to one another in listless grasping behaviors, tunneling through sedition into the might of knowledge and overcoming practices of decency. Blanked out and forgotten, the remittance of sin destroys that sin until it is no more. Forgotten apologies continue to work their healing magic. Redundancy of faith gives weakness to goodness in the saving of the proprietary and sudden awakenings of joy.

Salivating and waiting longingly for nutritional envy to fail, there shall no longer be hunger in sin, no temptation in its lateral frequency of design, and the behooved of the innocent lost upon qualities of wretched turn over and oblong deceit.

Craving nothingness brings about a cure for the reticent and unbelieving saturated misfits who tend to balk at technology and find it hard to learn all that it avails. Saturated apology and meekness in foundation is found on earth and will always be there to those who have neglected to study the Bible in this life. There is much learning to be had, in apology and in discrimination. Tottering on empty promises and forbidden demise, the waking up to our sins in apology brings about a spontaneously quibbling infrequency that gives logic a hand on history. Capable of nothing less, we can always do something more.

Acidity and prevalent nothingness can give the mote in your eye a grounding technology of perception. Our eyes were meant to see and cause understanding with equated equidistance on confused and colorful palates.

Sugar coated ecstasy and foundering devilish compliance only signifies that remote and total oblivion can't be achieved but must be had in order to be gotten. Spontaneous surprise, and enervating dysplasia, curtail the opinion of forgotten "neatness" and good organizing of our thoughts and opinions, our hatred and demise. God gave us hatred to learn upon the past and to overcome the tired with deficiency and abrogation. Belonging in all apologies to aggressive permission, we are goaded into a new and happy atmosphere that chokes no one on breath, and that involves the capitulated demolition of structure and sporadic surprise.

Logan berries and narcissistic raspberries are in flavor with the tuned and pleasurable palate. Significant in number, and equated with design, there is something forgotten and ambivalent about a missing feature that derides apology and magnifies the goodness of distress. Distress can be like spurs to the stubborn donkey, burdened and complaining, spilling out mutated tears and cuffing the ground with broken hooves. Clattering along in front of a cart, our mules and donkeys make happenstance of an intermittent vacation. Coagulate with disgust the anomaly and partition of mutated surprise, and dump our loads at our destinations. So it is to factual surprise, that the loaded colt pulling the load must be guided with loving hands and not forced to go along.

Purgatory remains in the blend of sacrificing sin for technology, and intermittent design with formations of new and sound production eloquent to despair. Formulating and necessitating the guise of given juncture gives hatred a resounding kick in the rear, for it does not belong in heaven, and those in purgatory cannot enter until such hatred and design is forgotten and left behind. It is like the mill, which refuses to process the harvest, because it sees decency over the next knoll, and despairing of nature and presence, their need for deficiency is not so illuminating as mature and present danger.

Functional decency gives pleasure to the possessor, and leaves behind unmated danger and forgiveness of sins and wrongdoings. God gives ultimate danger to the lost, and keeps them walking along next to their donkeys that bear their loads upon their muscular backs. Bearing and stubborn, these give demise to the problematic, and weariness to the next subjugation that illuminates properly and forgives adamantly. Pervasive and destructive, the lives of those who are "prodigal" both men and women, recovers in unanswered apology and somnolent permission to revoke hatred and count numbers backward in our minds. Belonging to remission and forgotten in insolence, the "mentally impeded" are so labeled for a deficiency in thought process. Not in the new world, where the way not in is the way of "wickedness". Interminable distress and despair gives allocated judgment to the opinionated and overturned dysplasia of forgotten incidences. Lucky is important if by nature it is designed in fortuitous pleasure belonging to the good and satiating witnesses which provoke keepsake circumstances of certain opinionated and distressed attitudes. These are articulate of circumstances made necessary to provoke design in alternate thinking capacities, brought forward with discipline and forgotten with decency.

Superfluous and overcoming despondency is ratified in heaven as a natural quality that brings death to the maker who will no longer absolve a sin. Great in all poignancy and militant design, the "go figure" initiative has been given to respond to those spurs and to necessitate our futures.

Tranquil and restful, peaceful and lost is okay, for there is no lost in heaven, only where you were meant to be for all time at every moment. So comes the obituary of displeasure and productive policy.

Waiting in the wings, turbulent despair. Broken and forgotten, nebulous and mortal, avenged despair and forgotten losses, there is nature in nuances and betterment of getting successful in qualified nature. Thank you, Jesus, for what you have done and given for us. There is redemption around every turn and every corner, mating with the desire to replicate the suddenness of salvation, the equidistant and procreated dysfunction followed by saturated rotten pickles in the jars of discarded giving of lost despair and turned over mentions of equal jealousy to remote provision of cleanup crews and the insects who define them.

Equatorial

Tabulate and function your disgrace upon denial, for forgiveness of sin follows the world in all of its circulating of the sun. Living with suggestive circumstances that populate betrayal, there is forgetting of the lost and the greater of no more. Not all are going to get into Heaven. Some are lost by despair. In equatorial designs that betray nothing, the coming of new earthly patterns will slowly surround our planet and overcome the rotten pickles of society. Rotten pickles like the Beast, and Justin. They were not meant to go, for they denied any fickle attitude about faith and meaningless dysfunction.

Popularity gives hope to the meaningless, for their design is functioned to equate nature with design, and to cause equatorial patterns that remiss in tortured evilness. Spontaneous design and certain forgiven and forgotten supplements to the aggravated design of destined failure, keep on rescinding in copulate positions and do not give up on respectful design, yet continue to dismember it.

Faith, quality, design, and superfluous unction of perdition cries out with a whale of a design to perpetrate indifference and copulating seduction. Normal design, yet found in the lost and those filled with hatred, are ambivalent with suggestion of immersed position and defiant behavior. Broken, forgotten, sinful, the earth spins so fast that negativity is arched out into space and eternity where it gives displeasure and then it is eaten by monumental creatures seduced into eating pain, and suffering by procreating goodness and wellness to be.

Dilapidated and construed opinion with technology gives graciousness to those populated on oblivion, taken to the new place, the somewhere that pops up out there. Kissing the faces of the lost and missing, there is sadness in the way of letting go. Even with incarnate apology and overcoming of unstable ways, we forget to give God the glory, and He is our destiny.

Equating equal with good and turning about in a revolving room, there is mishap in every corner, until corners have been polished into the circular mishap of greater control and understanding watch dog retrograde. Biting at the stranger, the watchdog keeps at bay all who go near, and don't participate in frequencies of sins, but avail themselves to opportunistic surprises. Facing danger is one thing, but overcoming it is something completely other than. Cryptic necessity and faulty reasoning don't belong in the trouser drawer, nor hanging in the closet. Forgiving nuances of alternate incisions make the Beast hungry for kindness, but there is no such thing for him. For he is evil, and his turning of the corners in the room of forsaken oblivion makes him a bit disoriented, nauseated, sick.

Ranging along the way, we desire to let go of it at last, for the time had come for two faced apologies to be uncovered for what they are. Lost people, losing the way, never coming out, and failing to have a just persuasion of truth between all enigmas that face destiny.

Turntable and about, there is a vehicular design upon disgrace and pardoning of sin. To distrust is to alienate upon disfavor and ruinous magnificent places of evil service and aggressive loss. Turn around and face the nature of revolution, for it undercuts the motions of the earth being alit all of the time, in unending joy and peace.

Aggressive natures of nuances and surprises all start with a startled reaction and a new face on the faces of the hellions and those who batter destruction. Facing the dangers along the way, and mediating terminology of the divine with the lost, it is obvious as they slip away that they are no longer wanted in this world, and especially not in the next world. Those who want to hang on and specify this, have service for the goodness of all in justice and failure to equate justice by design.

Giving up hope is the last thing to do in losing out on forbidden ecstasy to those who don't deserve it. Failure and compliance reiterates the steam engine that needs to go on a turned wheel, for the expectations of the lost grow further and further away from us as we go along with that steam engine and remember to not lose hope in so doing.

Gratification, by design, is an outlet for our thankfulness when we see what our reward shall be in heaven, equated with technology. Spoofing opinions and warthog countenance becomes apologetic with the fool. For the fool has no place in a world he denies, with profound forgotten production of sin. Lying in the midst of apology there is a sleepy place to go where no fools have ever been. Who is the forgotten and wicked by design? Those who deny that Jesus Christ is Lord and Savior to our world, those who don't believe that he came, lived, and died in the flesh as the Son of man and Son of God. Growing in prediction of all events, we are soon to be exposed to a new and differentiating nature that belongs so encrypted in science that niceties are needed no longer, and attitudes of malignant design go faster and faster towards nothingness until all is lost about them and they have no remembrance with us, nor of us. Forsaken, lost, denied the privilege of disgrace yet whetted with appetite of despair, pure hatred and knowledge of a strangely dysfunctional speech. Those are fools who are regressive by nature and into significance where despising those who despair is a cumulative behavior on regression of sin above all knowledge.

Failure to deny the opportunity of disgrace, we who are so sodden are provisional in despair and incompatible sorrow reflected by demise. Forgiveness and failure forgotten on the nub of the hill, we tried to see but could not envisage that which lies over it.

Over the hill and across the plains of perdition, absconded in truth and denial, overturned like a fallen donkey cart and aimed at a forbidden piece of knowledge. Who God is. No one knows who God is. People know him, and he knows us, but not each other, for persuasive demise formulates opinions with counterbalanced alienation and the wisdom of a forked tongue that speaks in balance of nature all the time.

Forgiven and opinionated, we malingering people of walled in countries find that peace is not meant to be had just yet. We are overcoming difficulties all the time, and pretending to be knowledgeable over which we are not. Fallen and forgotten, the wisdom of once interminable sin is foolishness with all created destruction. Going on and on again, the means of lying in wait of a newer and better "something" we know that there is always hope in looking forward, even to the lost who don't know any better. But who can look at God in the face and deny that he is God? Moses did look, and came back down a mountain for meeting of him with a veiled face that shone so brightly he needed to cover it for a while, people generally don't look at God in the face, but some do, some have, and some will. Actually, they all will, all the creatures He created that live and breathe shall bow down before Him and worship Him.

Breaking news of apologies lunges at the throats of upset criminals and brokenly held prisoners. Sometimes God takes the worst and makes them the best, like he did with Paul, the apostle, who turned affectionately toward God and away from a life of persecuting God: The Father, the Son, and the Holy Ghost. Who breathe the same atmosphere that we will one day breathe, not lost, and not forgotten.

Equatorial demise is a prolific pension for the serving of God and the giving to God in this life. Happenstance of delivered momentum creates gestational figures of obsolete hatred that doesn't mean anything anymore, for there is no longer anything to hate, and nothing to be hated for in the self as positioned in this world. Problematic procedure gives love to all, and to all a good life. Awakening in despair, and prolific of sin, sometimes it clings to us in all things attempted and achieved. Wherefore the judgment of evil brings remittance to the table and a pulling apart of a species upon the table to examine exactly what went on in this life. Poking, prodding, fishing and hooking our bodies clings with regard to remembrance. The body has memories that we only now understand are ever present and sometimes a burden. Other times, there is a flow of pleasure surrounding a being, and distraught and hated remembrance gives up only on rendition of nominal gestation.

Giving and living, we can't hide from God. He will face us, and we shall answer to him. We don't collide with God, yet we recognize him as being all the beauty we have had in this world.

Denying ourselves, we, some of us, are found lying to God in order to cover up guilt and shame. Borders of creation give over a meaningless and perceptive branch on the tree, the one that gets most of the nutrients, and floats higher above than the lower, costlier ones. Measuring ourselves against trees, we find behavioral science to be in retrograde obstinacy, forlorn and without love or decency. The test is to bare all to God, and come out on the other side in relational decency, and quagmires of deceit fall away from inside and all around us.

Hapless and hopeless, many are surprised by forgiveness for that which they have done in knowledge of wrongness. Those who think they don't deserve a chance, are best fitted to succeed into the greater world above the old world and beyond it in all decency.

Ground and lost, like the heel of a shoe smashing the ground beneath it, our faith exudes with glory that comes into contact with the Father, who loves the Son, and gave us the Holy Spirit. Shining in all detrimental agreement, the problems of yesterday have once again floated away from us, leaving a peppered trail to the lost and hiding who don't deserve to succeed, and who leave marks of science on the rendition of purported gregarious and militant rambunctiousness, seeking to be eloquent and not knowing where to begin, for there is no place for the wicked, and the wicked cannot hide from God. They may try, but only end up hurting each other more, in disgust, blame, and saturated connivance.

Hidden in sin, fallen in blame, and gone for good, the wicked who have peppered our way with cheating, stealing, and defrauding, have chosen to follow the devil, Lucifer, although they may not yet know it. But to follow Lucifer to his defeat only ends with him in the eternal lake of fiery brimstone. Liquidating redundancy and diminutive apology cannot help now. For even in the forgotten, there is much evil to be found. Fornicating, incest, mongers of both mothers and fathers, salutary and traditional exotic reprieve and denial, there is liquid to be had that portrays all as lost. No more water gives us an end to earthly water and the introduction to holy water. To drink of the water of life, they shall no longer thirst. There is forgiveness in sin, but ruination without apology.

Turbulence

The enervating circumstance to die for is the obstacle of romance in suggestion. Here we enjoy battered and bruised opinions about behavior and despair. Relish the incendiary productive disguise, and found a new site, a place of repose, similar to the lagoon in peace and glory. Rectifying such gorgeous and opportunistic problems as may arise in acquitting souls from danger, and applying pressure to hatred. Growing old in death, like the life of the Beast, wasted and not picked up again, imagine his face, his evil ugly face when he sees ahead what is in store for him.

Bouncing around on a turbulent plane, the transfiguration of processed hope and disfigured apology comes quickly to the lost who will soon be no more. There is still evil in the world, and it breathes and resuscitates on our bodily auras and implicated disgusting ruin.

Tattered and broken victims, soft to the touch and open to healing from above can be denied any truthful place to be in acquitting of brutality and force from against the soft and lost, weak and meek, kind and gentle.

Suppose the postulate of rumination brings terror to those who have experienced grave harm and terror from helpless situations and despicable truths. Overturned and prodded to death as the Lord separates bone from marrow to overcome what has been done, for every cell will tell him a story that we could no longer bear.

Imprisoned and squashed, bearing down on vengeance with the Lord, the lost and overturned will again see light and justice. Becoming smaller and smaller to ourselves, we will see the light of mortification switched off into immortality. A breaking of truth to the mortified sin of apology leaves fallen leaves where they have fallen, until someone comes to rake them up.

Baby does enough raking of leaves around the middle of fall to interject hatred into a born loser. Her disgust with her father still rises up sometimes in a certain reminder of ache and ruin, yet she doesn't postulate the enervating circumstances of reprieve. She dominates herself by working hard in her landscaping, and she remains fit and trim. William is working his way into a position to minister the church that they go to with Mom, Lila and Rusty, their kids and occasional visits from Rexi and family.

The Church is a grand structure, suitable for heaven, to maintain and pamper young Christians and provide places of learning from the inspiration of the new world and all of its suggestive places.

Baby in her nonchalant way, had just had a bad fall, and landed on her head, and gave way to a hallucination while in a coma in the hospital. Here she dreamed and dreamed about heaven, and that heaven was coming, and what it would be like. She had visions and experiences in her body that taught her about what was coming and what they should do to prepare for the return of the Lord. His touch on her body would heal her, she knows, but for now she rests comfortably with an illumined mind and a suicidal faith for glory. Her presupposition that things would change in a great way remained with her, even after waking back up to this world. Mom was in tatters, fawning over her daughter, and flitting back and forth from her home and the hospital.

Baby remained in her utterly somnolent state for three weeks, in which the Lord spoke to her and achieved her imagination with a spite of grace. Upon wakening, there was William there, planted beside her bed and holding onto her hand. She turned softly and smiled at him, and knew in an instant that he was a gift from the Lord to her. She squeezed his hand gently and he rubbed her fingers. He took her right hand into both of his, and prayed to the Lord over her, giving thanks for her recovery, and his merciful treatment of them all. William texted Mom and told her that Baby had come awake from the coma.

Nurses and doctors filed into the room and ran tests on her, lifting the bed into an upright position. She smiled and talked about nothing much, but held a huge story of love within her chest that she had dreamed about while "gone". Her eyes fluttered open and closed, she was in a dreamlike state. William hovered over her and made way for the hospital staff to adjust equipment all around her that had maintained her vitals and registered her brain functions. Although she had been unconscious, there had been much brain activity. For three weeks she had been fed by a tube to her mouth and emptied her bladder by a catheter. She was weak, yet her resolve remained strong, and she smiled into William's eyes.

Mom and William were so overjoyed at this awakening that they ran out to get coffee, flavored espressos and came back, returning with force and happiness. It transfigured her repose, but in waking up, Baby Pollyanna had a huge smile on her face and was nodding to everybody, garbling words, unable to talk decently.

Mom needed to go home and feed Strawberry, but William waited, and he slept next to Baby all night on a cot. The hospital deemed it best to keep her for another week, to analyze her speech problem, and make sure there was no relapse into the comatose state. So, she got better and stronger each day, taking small walks around her floor and from the nurse's station to the windows that overlooked the parking lot. She got tired easily and didn't stay up for very long.

She smiled as she remembered her dreams, and couldn't wait to tell William about all the heavenly apparitions that had come to her. She was slow in her recovery, and stayed in the hospital an extra four days before William brought her home. Too weak to work, she found herself painting portraits of everyone she ever knew who had affected her life. She painted Mom, and then an ugly Justin, and an even uglier Beast. Her painting of William was regal, and he wore a crown. Rexi was a beautiful image, and so was Lila. She was proud of her work, and rested a lot, and read a lot, and watched movies on her Netflix station.

Tired eyes looked at William across the living room as she sat reminiscing and enjoying her eggs and bacon and coffee for breakfast. After the first two days at home, she fell into a leadership role, taking care of herself. William availed himself to her spontaneously and awkwardly, he was used to her benevolent nature, not this wild woman who had come home spurting scripture and praying out loud in a domineering way. William was uncomfortable at first, but grew lustfully attracted to her new way of being, and made sure not to disappoint her in any way. So, he cooked her meals and did her laundry, and kept the apartment spotless and clean.

After two weeks Baby made mention of wanting to go walking outside. She hadn't been outside in what seemed like forever. Her muscles were sore after the first walk, and she cut her walking short due to her weakness. She was placid and remained uneventful, except for her painting and reading, and she painted landscapes too, creating gardens and recreational areas that she could put forward to her boss when she went back to work.

Her turbulent life these new days was effectual and unordinary. Once upon a time she had been a little girl. The girl grew up singing songs and pushing people around. She was no ordinary thing, and William was blessed to have her. She remained in his thinking all the time. He knew of her abusive past. She knew how special she was to him. She doted on him as he doted on her. Respective personalities, they were kind to each other and rarely had a disagreement.

Baby began going on longer and longer walks, sometimes now by herself, and she remembered her past of doing marathons and running long distances for pleasure and to deal with the effects of the Beast and her brother/cousin. Now she knew what would become of them, and her antsy little seat had no problem flaunting itself in front of William, who brought up again the subject of their marriage. They hadn't talked about it since before the accident. As newlyweds, they would make an estranged couple, keeping to themselves and leaving their footprints on this world and on into the future. Waking up to William was like a nice, soft, peppermint cookie in her face. So sweet and good and charming.

They thought about getting a cat. They decided against a fish tank. And no dog. William wanted to travel. He made this known, and she realized that unless he worked too, this would never be possible with their income. But William was adamant and suggested a weekend camping trip outside in the hills to start with. This wasn't too costly, and they had all the equipment they would need.

The ride to the campground was afire with Baby's new and exciting personality flitting around the car and pointing at "who knows what" outside the windows. Their first night they saw the sun set behind the hills, and they cooked hamburgers on the camp stove. Squirrels and various birds visited their site, and the air was warm. Tranquility rested upon their outing, and they went for a long nature hike in the hills beyond the campground. Baby relished the fresh air, watching the slow-moving stream that graced their campsite, and sleeping together with William. Together they made love during the nights and woke fondly in the steamy tent in the morning to a nice dark, hot cup of coffee. She watched the steam come out of her mug and circled the air in front of her with the coffee cup, watching the coffee dancing in the cup, and bringing it to her lips. Each sip was kaleidoscopic, and the caffeine went straight to her head.

Baby talked to William, and laughed and talked and talked and laughed through the morning and into the evening. And when it was time to leave, they packed up and made sure there wasn't anything lost. They left their site clean and ready for the next campers.

When Baby talked to Mom about their camping adventure, she was provocatively graceful in her listening, and made sure that Baby was okay concerning her revival from the coma. Baby reassured her that all was well with her mind and body, and her heart, spirit, and soul were alight with the manufacture of solace in her mind, and that she had had some strange revelations in her three weeks of being comatose. Mom was just happy she was okay, and took all her bubbly excitement as a new energy coming from a long rest and a healing recovery.

Residual and complacent in her enervating circumstance, she saw no reason why not to go back to her job and to show off her prints and new drawings. She did, and her boss was amused at first but upon a second study, she realized the potential that lied before her. Baby was excited and explained her drawings to her boss, suggesting where and with what they could use them in the near future.

She got a raise, and the awkward attention of her co-workers, who were slightly jealous at the newfound elation in their usual old Baby who was significantly spiritual, yet never in such a bright and bubbly manner.

Grace brought her through, and she found a new great fondness for pizza. Pizza became her favorite dinner, easy to fix and totally delightful to eat. She took to making her own dough, pizza sauce, and selected yummy additions to put on her own pizzas. Her most favorite was a simple pizza with black olives, mushrooms, sausage, and pepperoni, along with onions and garlic and mozzarella cheese. William stalled and stammered at first, but took a liking to this new and aggressive Baby, who ate like she hadn't eaten in years, and selected a new recipe each time she made one.

Turbulence, at first seemed like a block in their paths to William, who soon became accustomed to her new and happy nature, and accepted the challenge with a dignity that became him. Grace and knowledge exuded to him from her bright and dainty mouth, and she privileged him each day with a new thought or idea, that she had gleaned from her sleepy dreams. Baby held onto her new life like a cat clinging to a tree that didn't want to come down. Her claws were razor sharp, in readiness to fend off any attack of the enemy. She smiled at William extensively and put him off with a shy and gentle laughter. Mediating himself very carefully, he asked small and unnoticeable questions, one after another throughout their days, and when Baby went back to work, he turned to God in prayer for understanding, and how to make his yearning to marry her a vibrant reality.

Insignificant appeal, and extraordinary care went from William to his fiancé everyday bringing him closer and closer to bringing up his desires to her with elated curiosity. She knew he was a good catch, and he knew that she knew, which gave him confidence in reprieve when he finally mentioned it to her like a wild stallion nudging his mare… he bent over and laughed at himself. "Why am I so nervous?" he thought eagerly. His eager nature procured an adamant response as the energies shifted turbulently around the room. The closet area was closed off from the kitchen, but the door was open for some reason today, and he realized that Baby had put her boots in without shutting it. This reminded him about Baby's mention to him of getting some work to join into their income. He could only make promises at this point, yet he still felt embittered and repugnant at his loss of footing. With disgrace he challenged her.

One night, William brought up the subject of marriage over pizza, with sun dried tomatoes, onions, and pepperoni. She looked at him insolently and shoved her foot at him under the table. Why hadn't he talked about it before now? He seemed cross, but secretly pleased.

His animation took turn and a new proud and happy William slowly turned the handle and new words came out of his mouth to her. Easy does it, he thought, and knew in total glee that she wanted it too.

So she gesticulated in all recognizance and minored in detail to get to the point of what he was saying to her so elaborately and curiously. It was as though his amusement only flavored the conversation with heady spices and complete maturity.

No longer dismal, he took her hand and decided that tomorrow they should go pick out wedding bands for each of them. Tomorrow was Saturday and Baby didn't work that day. Sometimes she did, but tomorrow she had off.

Quietly she screamed and then louder and louder. "Oh yes!" she cried and shuddered in her benevolent laughter and quizzical impertinence, making him known to her for sure in all his seriousness and anticipation. Then they were kissing on the couch, and the night unfolded onward from that. Peace rested over their tired and resting bodies that night, and Baby dreamed again of Heaven, and thought to herself, "Is it really here?"

They untangled themselves in the morning after another spout of copulation, and made breakfast and made coffee, and took showers and got dressed with heady dreams of picking out rings together.

The morning came swiftly, and they got up to have breakfast before going to the jewelry store that day. Once there, their eyes opened wide at the selection, and even wider at the prices. So, they picked out a couple of low end rings, hers gold with a small diamond, and his a simple band of gold. They needed to get their rings sized for each of them, and they held them, and they gnawed at their teeth, not wanting to wait for the rings to be sized, and wanting to be gratified instantly and over the counter. But, alas, it would take a week for the rings to be fitted for them, so they conscientiously went to church the next day with the rings a little cloud in their minds. Believe it or not, they almost enjoyed the waiting period, and gave tithes that Sunday and alms for the collection box. Weeping in their minds at how happy they were, Baby told Mom about the proposal and the rings. She was super happy and couldn't stop feeling joy for her daughter. Baby texted Rexi that day and told her they had picked out rings.

Finally, a week went by, Baby working at her job and William taking care of some details at the church. When they awakened that next Saturday, William called to see if the rings were ready. They were. They paid for their rings with insurance, and joyfully put them on. They wore them out of the store, feeling elated and ready for marriage. At last, thought William securely, at last they would be wed.

Everyone enjoyed their joyous states of being, and they set the date for the wedding to be held in their church, where the associate pastor would perform the ceremony.

Baby, Rexi, and Lila all went shopping together for the perfect bridal gown. They tried on several before one fit perfectly for her. Mom would help with the cost of payment, and Baby would keep the dress packed away after wearing it for her wedding. It seemed almost a waste of money to her, for only one occasion, but Baby let herself be nudged into buying it to wear for that dreamy occasion.

Baby and William realized that no Dad would walk her down the aisle. Nor a brother. Not even a cousin. Uncle Sandy, Mom's brother, finally agreed to walking with Baby to complete the ceremony. Baby cried on his shoulder with thanksgiving, and told him the decorative colors she'd picked out, royal blue and pink. Uncle Sandy was delighted to take part in Baby's wedding, and even talked to Mom about staying in touch more often. He was happy to participate, and was aggressively impressed at Mom's own home and Strawberry, whom he hadn't yet met.

Rexi, Lila, and Mom decided to plan a small bridal shower for Baby Pollyanna. She agreed, though a little hesitant, not sure she wanted to be the center of attention. It came about, Baby took part, and enjoyed herself and the cheerful gifts she received. Rachel was there with all her good will and well wishing.

For the most part Baby received some books, clothing, money, and more paint and canvasses for her to do her work on again, like she had after coming out of the hospital.

She thanked everyone affectionately, and went home to William with a butterfly in her chest.

Dreams and Visions

Partaking of nothing else celebratory before the wedding, the two of them took snatches of endearment with one another, making sure they were ready, and how they wanted to proceed once the beautiful wedding took place. A honeymoon? Where should they go? Baby wanted to go to something like the lagoon she had dreamed about, or the hot mineral water springs. William listened to her solemnly and decided that Hawaii would be their best bet. They could go, stay in a hotel, and spend many happy hours on the beach beneath palm trees. In the meantime, William had had a bachelor's party with a handful of close friends, and received quite an equitable amount of money as gifts, so now they could afford to do it.

Baby looked lovingly at her fiancé, and fell into his arms. Hawaii would be perfect she said, meaning to stay just one week. One week would be fine with William, and they made all the proper arrangements, to be leaving three days after the wedding. Mom was delighted when she heard the news, and couldn't help being excited for her daughter, who deserved such a magical event after a long life of suffering and intrusion.

She was even proud that Baby had gotten a raise at work and was using her own designs to help organize the upcoming projects to which she had paid close attention. Mom's life was going well. She continued to go to her support group for battered women, and she was with the same book club, and yoga class. She knew that the worst part of her life was over with, gone. The same thing held with Baby, and they continued to see each other, meeting for coffee once a week.

They talked about all kinds of things, about Geoffe, and what a Beast he had been. And then Justin, who had parried a lot of blows yet never came out of his august personality traits and forbidden calculations to do with the viper he was to Baby. Both agreed that it was for the best that these two were deceased. And Baby knew in her heart that their demise was fixed and final. They were two very wicked men, and men like that had no place in heaven.

Baby talked to Mom about heaven, and the glee she had felt in her coma when she dreamed and had visions about it. She told her about the lagoon, a quiet and beautiful place to go, and how this had swayed their honeymoon decision making to land on Hawaii. When Mom offered to help pay for the trip, but Baby declined and told her about the money they had been given, and that it was plentiful. In fact, their plans were already made.

Her dreams came back with violent repose and struck her in bed one day as she slept in on a weekend. The beauty and absolvent tenacious responses to her made up version of ecstasy complied with the beauty and gorgeous aptitude of her life as it now stood before her. She swooned and told William about the rapture, as it had come to her in a dream, and that it had already begun.

William witnessed without a hard heart, and glorifying defeat of the Beast and Justin who now lingered in long gone hell, unable to ever be reached by anyone again, ever. In fact, they were dead in a burning lake of brimstone, which would burn them for all eternity, and into nothingness.

Baby told him that they all stood in line to be judged by the Father, and Mom and Rexi and Paul and the kids had made it in, and Baby and William also. She was sure that Lila and Rusty and their kids were also on the ticket. Also, Rachel and her children were happily knocking at the door. But the Beast and Justin stood not a chance to even raise their eyes for resolution, for resolution would not be had.

She remembered wanting to talk with God, and he spoke with her about many things. There was the hint he had made for her to get her tubal ligation done, as now was not a good time to bear children, for the cross over had to be made, yet he was indignant that perhaps down the line new babies would be conceived and born in heaven. She was long recovered from the operation.

William chose his best friend John to be his best man for the wedding ceremony, and Lila was Baby's maid of honor. Uncle Sandy was ready to do his part, and to play it with pride, for he had been there when Baby was born, and his sister had died in childbirth. Not sure why he hadn't been closer to them all, he knew there had been ongoing issues with Geoffe being a violent husband and father, as well as Justin, who walked in his father's shoes.

He apologized and promised to be around more often. He was a loving brother to Mom, and became a regular visitor at her cozy home for tea or coffee and then there were the family dinners.

But the wedding was near, and everyone was excited, cheerfully anticipating the event. Baby deserved someone so wonderful as William, and vice versa. Two very high-quality people, equipped and versed in the Lord Jesus.

Baby's dress was ready, and she looked absolutely gorgeous outfitted in it. William wore a tuxedo with a royal blue bow tie. Everyone dressed up, and the wedding was a clear success. All were blessed at the happy ceremony. When Uncle Sandy walked her down the aisle, the organ played the wedding march, and she stepped lightly and gingerly next to her uncle. William stood ready to receive her from her uncle's arm and they stood facing each other. The minister spoke and they repeated their vows, and were proudly pronounced husband and wife. He lifted her veil, and they kissed quietly and softly. Baby hung onto her husband and looked into his eyes. She smiled and whispered, "thank you", and he thanked her in return.

The wedding was complete with an enormous cake boasting bride and groom statues. William cut the cake, and they fed each other a piece with the dreamy frosting. Rexi, to surprise all, stood up to make a speech. She based it on family, courage, overcoming and success in life, and what a super and wonderful sister she had. Everyone cheered and the champagne was poured. Glassy eyes filled with tears as everyone cried with Baby who wept in utter joy and unbelief, that something so wonderful could happen to her.

Finally, she let her emotions out, and the whole sanctuary swelled with a song as she sang to her husband, "I Can Only Imagine" by the popular group, MercyMe. William hadn't the guts to do the same thing for her, but he followed her around the room greeting all the guests. He held her hand and continued to whisper things in her ears. The tears were done with now, and simple, gentle smiles lit faces as this tender and gentle wedding took place. Everyone admired Baby and William, for never before had there been a more deserving couple. Punch was served, and everyone's tongues loosened a little bit. Baby thought about the rapture, and decided to herself that it had already begun then. And now she had some idea of how it should progress because of her hallucinatory visions and dreams from her hospital stay in the coma. Finally, guests began to leave, until there was just the close family and friends. Baby and William showed everyone their wedding bands, and all admired them. So now they had three days before embarking on their honeymoon. Saturated with happiness and peace in their souls they no longer wondered if sex was permissible. Now that they were wed, there were no more imaginative roadblocks, just in case the Lord didn't approve. They had decided it was appropriate in any case, and didn't believe that their lovemaking had been wrong. Now being married, they gleefully had no second thoughts.

Secluded together in their apartment, they spent the next three days talking about Baby's dreams and visions, and William listened with all amazement. So, it really had started, he thought to himself, and looked at Baby and celebrated with her, knowing for sure that they were saved. Which was much more important than the fact of being married, with lustful guilt and overcoming forgiveness. The Lord had made it clear to Baby that she was innocent, and definitely saved, even before their marriage, so circumstances weren't as glum as they had started to think. Going out to pasture was okay, and they played by the little streams of imagination in their heads, and tickled each other, and said nice things to each other, and kissed, and ate pizza and drank coffee and made love again and again. This was a test, the two of them spending a block of time together like this in their own small space, newlyweds. And it worked! There was no awkwardness or pushing or pulling. They agreed and disagreed all to good cause, and overcame every problem with an angelic smile.

Then the day came for their dream get away. Not much of a traveler, and unsure how she felt about flying, Baby followed close behind William in line with their tickets after checking their luggage.

They found window seats next to each other. They sat and prepared for takeoff. The plane backed out and turned and traveled to the start of the runway. Then they were on their way, speeding down the runway and lifting up and up and up into the air, circling around so that Baby and William had a great view of the city below them. Then up and over the ocean they flew for the next five hours. Baby giggled incessantly and held William's hand in her excitement and shocking guise of fear. She was amazed at the feeling of being high above the clouds with the blue sky all around them, and then the sun shining in.

Their week in Hawaii went by too fast, and soon it was over. They had eaten to their hearts' desires, and lollygagged on the beach every day, doing some small touristy things like a visit to the pineapple farm, and a bout of snorkeling in the blue water where they saw colored fishes and held hands as they swam. They kicked and swam and had fun together. They also visited a giant flea market, picking out gifts to bring home, and buying little mementos for themselves. Baby wore a freshwater pearl necklace, and William found a silver crucifix on a chain, which was a blessing because he'd been searching for a new one since the old one had broken off and been lost. They took a myriad of pictures and some at Sea Life Park where they watched the dolphins do the tricks they had been trained to do.

They bought Kona coffee to bring home as gifts and for themselves. Scuffing around in sandals, they sunburned their feet and bodies from lying in the sun every day, and swimming in the waves at the "lagoon" like beach. They were elated, and found truth and hopes in the forgiveness of letting each other be who they were, and compromising together on what they should do each day. They were reluctant to leave when the last day had come, but taxied to the airport making sure they had all their belongings.

Mom picked them up on the other side, and brought them home, where they walked into the apartment with a new air, and a new way of beholding one another. Baby took all their gifts and wrapped them in colored tissue paper. She had purchased four silver dolphin necklaces, for Mom, Rexi, Lila, and Rachel. Then two little shot glasses with painted designs of fish and turtles for Rusty and Paul.

Stepping out into the world together that next day, they had new and grand expectations about what the Lord was going to do. Baby ran a marathon two weeks later and came home to William feeling great about herself and the astonishing achievement of her goal.

William finally was invited to preach at their church, so he spent some time putting together a sermon. He talked it through with Baby and came up with a grand idea to use for this opportunity to spread God's word.

Mom, Lila and Rusty and kids, and Baby waited eagerly through the first songs of worship and praise. Then William took the pulpit and began by making eye contact with his wife. Then, swelling with energy from the Lord, he began to spew words of inspiration and hope and encouragement. He talked about the rapture, and told the church that it had already begun. How could he support this? He cited blessings that had come recently, and talked about the dreams his wife had had while in a coma, from which she had miraculously recovered.

The trees were green, he said, and the flowers blooming. It was to be expected that the Lord would come in a present and dangerous mission, absolving those who would and wouldn't be making it to heaven. He urged the congregation to make things right with the Lord before it was too late. To forgive, and to love others before him in traces of glee and enjoyment, knowing that things might get different, but a lot better.

He reached out for testimonies that people had recently had, that could only be explained by a new and different coming of the world in all of its amazing patterns. Letting go, he prayed for the church and then dismissed them as the music started up again. The people went home thinking and digesting this new material. Had the rapture really begun? Soon after, people began experiencing small and evident miracles. The time had come to new birth fulfillment.

After the sermon, Baby ran to William and held him in her arms, praising him and blessing him. He smiled and winked before thanking her and moving on to talk to a multitude of gathered people. There was a great and tumultuous spirit in the air, and people realized that William was right. The world was changing, and many people had had miraculous and unexplained differences in their lives. Now they knew to expect even more and great happenstances deliberated by the Lord, who speaks to his people in many ways, but now was conversing with some of the people who held onto this experience with overcoming love and joy and acceptance.

Everybody knew about Geoffe and his terrible graces and offensive, standoffish and abusive nature. The same with Justin, and people were almost relieved that they had disappeared into nothing. Baby knew with gentle reprieve that these two were not forgiven and that the world was better off without their wicked appeal.

Graces fell on everyone at church that day. William was invited to speak again on this matter, and many people wanted to hear what he had to say.

Believe it or not, the little princess Baby Pollyanna was taken into arms at her new marital status. Older women who knew of Geoffe's behavior, and Justin, were fulfilled in her happiness and glorification of God who would have the vengeance. "Dearly beloved, avenge not yourselves, but *rather* give place unto wrath: for it is written, Vengeance *is* mine, I will repay, saith the Lord." (Romans 12:19)

Ridiculed to all the ends of the earth, Satan would be soon no more for a thousand years under the earth, and then released once more before the new world took its final position, only to be swept into the lake of burning brimstone reserved for his judgment and his punishment for having led so many people astray. In all of his grumpy despair, people need not fear him in consequence of guilt, nor of having been led astray. The Lord Jesus would rule with all of his saints, judging the world, and even judging angels.

Baby and the Beast was no more, neither the son of the Beast, Justin. Her shining beauty overcame all resolve, and she could already feel the Lord's shining presence and his sweetness for her in her stout and stubborn faith. For having been tortured all her life due to ungrateful situations and bodily invasions, the ugly emotions were disappearing for good and final repose.

Questions about faith have never bothered her. She knew, that if she hung on, things would eventually change. She was adamant in her love for the Lord, and the decency and respect he gave her at her lowest points. And now, her three weeks of dreaming had prepared her on how to deal with a new and oncoming world on earth. Absolved of everything wicked.

Creatures

Baby continued to have dreams about the coming of Heaven, and sometimes woke up William to draw him in. "You speak like a prophet," he said to her. "I need to witness to you and spread your words wherever I go." Together they made signs to put on posts, warning, "the rapture is here! Get right with God!" Complete with hearts and crosses. Then they recruited a handful of people from the church, including Lila, and they all made signs to go march with downtown and to talk to strangers about their witness to the rapture. Eyewitnesses, for many people were seeing changes already.

We are creatures of faith, thought William to himself as he talked more and more with his wife and her nightly visions. They marched for two weeks before taking a break, and talked to many people who asked about the rapture and what it was. They fed and edified these people with the truth, and the blessings of God that would shower the world in all of its translucent apparitions, hands on changes that would benefit all of the world's creatures and hands on people. Significant to failure, those lost to the faith and ignorant no longer needed to be in the dark. God would shine his light on all creatures, and all creatures that had breath could worship him.

Faithful compliance and acrimonious plunder of envisioning and overcoming destiny began to range about all over the globe. William still wanted to travel but realized now that his calling was right here and in this church.

Faithful reprise and significant danger falling from wicked people was being put to a stop. There was much clamor everywhere, and precious miracles taking place. Local food banks were overstocked again and again, providing food for many needy families. The weather was mild and warm, even during the fall, so that the air was likely to that which they had experienced in Hawaii. Clouds stretched across the sky in strange and celebratory forms. Ambivalent homeless people began to cry out in their visions and vicious observations. Intriguing and prolific, medical services were found for more and more people who didn't have reliable insurance.

New dental offices opened up that were covered by most insurance companies. Gas prices went down significantly, which was a welcomed change. People waiting in lines found that their waiting times were swift and easy. God was ushering in his companions, those who saw heaven and came down to minister on earth. His republic was decently accepting of the nature of new beginnings. Changes were happening slowly. Mom noticed the skin on her hands and arms was firming up and looking smooth and young. The destitute muscle pain in her ankles was giving away to painlessness and strong health, incorporated with a healthy appetite, and a desire to exercise more.

Mom testified in church about these miracles along with many other people who were noticing changes. The rapture would go on awhile, yet God would make a short work of it.

Baby spoke of the cleanup crew. And insects that would devour garbage and waste. She said that not all people would die during this change of worlds, but would grow younger and younger, changing into an immortal body. Death was not the certain end for every life. As the Lord said to Peter about John in (John 21:23), "If I will that he tarry till I come, what *is that* to thee?"

The book of Revelation tells the story of the rapture and all the strange creatures that would appear. Some are monsters, and others have a body full of eyes, or various heads in the form of certain creatures all on one body. It is a privilege to see it and read it, though we can't truly understand what is meant by it. Baby had read the book many times, and she tried to graph in her visions with the words of the Bible. It was hard to do, and she realized that so many changes would go on everywhere that it would be hard to see the equations taking place.

Filtered through necessity and wrought violence, the wicked were plucked up and discarded just like tares sewn among the seeds of wheat. Violence pervaded for many days, as the wicked resisted the pressure of the Lord on their condemned bodies. They broke out in horrible boils all over themselves, and couldn't find food with which to feed them. With no nutrition, they grew weaker and weaker in heaven sent love, which discarded them like rotten pickles. Humorous and of grand design, they filtered out into the open, and lectures on the great beast to be had by design failed to frighten them. Many churches began speaking on the book of Revelation, the last book of the Bible that told about the New Jerusalem, which was to be the new and precious habitat for God and his children.

There was a definite division between the good and the evil, for where the good people got blessed, those who were evil were cursed even more, abating in great suffering with tangents of hope spiraling up and away from them. For what you treasured in this life will be brought to the new world, while those who precociously sought evil resolve would be tossed away, for nothing evil can enter the kingdom of God anew.

The talk on every television was about this new and different change that was to come about, for you to hold onto your hats! In conjunction with reprieve and belittlement the sacred virus of hope could not be judged evil, for hope looks for the future to deliver up its elegance with mercy and surprise. Focusing on deliverance, there was little to be done, except what many Christians were saying, "Get right with God!" Some people laughed and scoffed, while others took the advice seriously and pondered Jesus in their souls.

Petulance and dignity became a wasteful procession for an eagerly turning world that held onto the notes of tomorrow and the regression of disdain. Particularly in somnolence and walking behavior, they walked all over the place making messes here and messes there to clean up. Abstract promises poured from the churches all over the world, and Sunday services became so packed that most churches offered up multiple services during the week as well.

Thanks to Jesus, many souls meandered the road that led to heaven, and clung to his happy hands that knew who was wrong and who was right. For his discipline had been just, and forgiveness found its way into the souls of many lucid and arbitrary creatures. Pictures came easily and many people dug into closets to retrieve paints and canvasses on which to describe their joyful feelings and experiences that couldn't be explained as other than a miracle. Sodden and down-trodden, poor people all over the planet opened doors to the ambivalent who were confused and didn't understand what was happening. Figurative and obsolescent demeanors were torn from the truths that were happening, for there was no turning back now. What had begun would go on interminably. Right or wrong, black or white, it was insignificant.

Nations sang songs about superfluous creatures that inhabit the earth and always will. Christian musicians developed massive arrays of new music, and secular bands began to write religious songs as well, in much confusion and disdain, being repulsed by a myriad of messages in the media and on every street in every house.

Procuring diseases without pleasantries, there was talk of a healer who was traversing the world and performing miracles in the sick and diseased, the broken and the pardoned. Sinfulness could not overcome duty with recognition, for the falling of dust in the air took time to ingest itself into the lungs of fallen corpses and endangered species. So the world was saved, but not for all. And it would take some time for God to clean out his closet for meandering Neanderthals couldn't keep up with the cost of cleaning laundry and badgering truth.

Forgiven and obsessed, there was much delight in the hearts of those who knew they were saved. Clinging to the goodness and the messages of the Bible, they found assurance as to forgiveness and multiple healing agendas. Talk of the healer went on and on and people murmured and wondered if this was Jesus? Clueless to the remarks of the sordid began to be explained in all tarrying of all obsolescent design and recreation to be had. Even nuptials from death began to appear so that many people thought they saw their loved ones who had passed away, come back to earth and made whole and new. But these they only saw in passing, for the agenda of the world was not to impress the deceased, but to forgive the forgiver, the mighty hand of God.

Traces of eloquence rose up and appeared before the world in all of its elegant reprieve. There was a sect that arose of people only wearing white clothing. But not to everybody, for people worshiped in different ways. Overcoming guilt with pardon, the singing of church songs in the streets and over the radio brought joy and happiness to the hearts of many people who worshiped along with the music.

No one betrayed anyone anymore, for all was given over for lost and in control where demise planted seeds of forgiveness, yet controllable abstinence came to be in the sedition of overflow and fallen countenance procured in general. Passed away and gone, like flowers dying in the fields, forgiveness clung to those who had been betrayed, and so many were saved due to arbitrary conditions. Glowing with reprieve, the nectar of society squeezed out from one world to another, bringing destiny into forgiveness and righting many wrongs.

Older and older they became, the wicked who clung to their obstinate and insolent ways and dying various types of painful deaths. Once a wicked one was snuffed out, at least two or three people became converted to the religion of Christianity. To believe in Jesus, (wasn't it Jesus who was healing everyone all over the world?) as the Son of God who designed creation and creatures from the beginning of time. As it were, it was not Jesus who was doing the healing in person, but an adamant apostle of Christ. And there was not just one, but many who were sited doing their works of miraculous nature, bringing even the dead back to life. Creations were ambivalent to the surprise of nature, for God had created it as well. Every tree was subject to new growth. Grassy fields were burned up, but new and original grass took its place.

Seditious awakenings happened to the unconscious all over the world, who woke up spewing visions much like Baby had. Baby who kept dreaming and dreaming with God in his Son Jesus Christ. While the Holy Spirit worked in her body and began to transform it into something immortal. Brand spanking new! William felt the changes in his body as well, and wondered why some people were changing yet others still died.

Perhaps, he thought, there was a common destiny with a separate path. For only those in Christ could enter in, yet many turned to him later in life but had not served as mediators of the truths they had found. In criminal cases, there were many who disappeared unexplainably, for these were inmates who found God while serving time in correctional facilities. Yet where did they go? There were many coming who had served time in prison and awkwardly got thrown out by passing of good behavior. Some of these knew Jesus, yet did not achieve the status of in line immortality. Because of nature, the retribution of solemn revival began in the decency of forgivable substances and uncanny resistance.

Holding onto thoughts of reprieve there was ascension and descent going on from earth and heaven above. The Bible says that the meek shall inherit the earth (Matthew 5:5). Who are the meek, if not those who speak about Christ Jesus and stand up with and for him? For every word concerning his visionary strength was either obsolete or true. Envisioning danger and retributive beating of the head against the wall, only waking up to religion would require a death to get in that way. Only upon waking up again could these forgiven and unworthy souls be saved.

Could it then be said that a measure of time was the ruling factor for those who died and were saved, or those who were saved and became immortal on earth, never dying but being made new. Configurative analogy would incriminate hope as a diseased factor traded for apology upon death and remittance. Beautiful, but yet forsaken only in losing life for new life, while acquainted with those who gained new life through seditious reprieve.

Eternal Glory

Bending over backwards to see the other side of the globe would be back breaking indeed. For as the earth turns with growing and growing agitating with mass, the trading of religion with copious disaster becomes negligent without meaning. For turning over the new leaf on a new day, the remittance of sin falls far from the tree.

Forgotten and betrayed, new lovers found insight into one another that had never before been shared. People talked about their past hurts and pains, things that had long been held within and covered. There was elation in eternal glory, as the foundations of Christ became all and for all. It was destructive to the wicked and undeserving, while lacing the doilies of fragrant opinion. Finding design upon approach, people were given their assignments via a visit from God the Father himself. Protected and mediated became normal functioning for the lost and the unholy yet broken and serving the Lord. For those who had served the Lord in this life were considered worthy, with exception of those who serve the Lord and then turned their backs on him.

For they had left their first love with a kick in the chest, and gone on to procreate evil destined for killing and destruction.

Careful and violent, unholy yet deserving so the harvest is ripe and ready to be reaped. Yet even those who have fallen from the arms of salvation could be gleaned by followers in the faith, and picked up without being trodden upon. Soulful believers like Mother Theresa were still witnessing to the lost and distant, who had not heard of Jesus Christ. Who came to the world to die and be raised again, and now was returning again a final time. Patience and trust in the Lord would save many souls who would otherwise be looked over, us knowing that Jesus is the Way, the Truth, and the Life. He is the destiny, he is the survival, and he gives those who need it the hope that they deserve, for having unknowingly served the Lord all their lives by way of righteous behavior.

Conclusions would come with a bout of sin that emits from the mouths of those denying the truth and persecuting Christians everywhere who were speaking the voice of the rapture, falling upon the unworthy and disgraceful, the failed and ugly, the gone and already forgotten.

Those absolved and ready for life to live in immortality only now seeing hints, bare hints of the glory that is to come as we reign together with Christ for one thousand years. Only after that will the "New Jerusalem" come to be interpreted by genius and design, responsibly communicating with death over behavior.

In conclusion those who are deprived of their innocence with wicked design shall be rescued and transmitted to the new world ready to heal and make ready to worship the Lord forever.

Crying out for peace and destruction, the annihilation of those deserving hell fire will be witnessed in their shady and unspeakably wicked ways as the Lord has vengeance for the wronged and the destitute. Contributing to destiny, the "others" who were not likened to us who are saved would spell defeat for their own sinister ways.

Nourishment

…And the hungry shall eat. No more starvation, both physical and spiritual. Lost teenagers who cut their arms with razor blades would stop inflicting such punishment on their depressed and sordid bodies. Nobody hopes like the sinner who knows he is wrong in his doing. Shaping up the world in a matter of a few seconds, God would send his mighty angels to bestow grief upon those who were saturated with Heaven, and negligible for grief and abstaining of humor. Knots tied in stomachs held despair for those who were truly, truly sorry but did not take it upon themselves to give intermittent design to the republic of nature.

Foreign species, like endangered wild animals would ride out the storm with much relief. For their numbers would again grow to the aptitude of full-fledged immortality. Yes, even animals could become immortal. Significant and trustworthy, the design of nature was for her creatures to live onward into the new world. No more would they be meat eaters, the same likeness with humans. Fish of the sea might be eaten and consumed, but no four footed or winged creature was ever again meant to be consumed.

Lost and eternal, the fish of the seas would remain in numbers lost and numbers renewed, so that a shortage could never be. Friendly fish who played with swimmers, yet also got caught in their nets. Preliminary phantoms could be seen in the deep, but no one would ever again harpoon or kill a whale. In fact, communicating with them would be a grand pastime, instead of going fishing. Playing with whales was a magnificent way to interact with nature. Playing with dolphins brought surprised smiles to the faces of abject and hurting people, for all are not healed in an instant.

Subjugated decency brought preliminary behavior to us and all the animals of the earth. Mutual respect and love causes great swellings of love in our hearts, and some people would ride elephants, camels, and even lions.

The lion-hearted man cave agendas relied on picture taking, not trophy taking. Grounds for knowledge about hope and procedure would not take on a juncture for forbidding mercy and adventure. Little babies played with tigers in their back yards. Snakes were no more. And not to be missed. Satan the serpent had done enough evil for his kind to be forever put out of the New Jerusalem.

Baskets of bread and bottles of wine were spread from neighbor to neighbor, in love and joy, in sharing and satiation. Bread and fruits and vegetables remained in their strongest forms and made sustenance for happy people eating happily, never again to go hungry, as many people have.

Even the tradition of popcorn swelled through in the new world, and delightful dancing with music.

Tasting of fruit and water was nourishment enough, for fruit trees produced such nectar in their fruits that every thinkable nutrient we might need could be had in the fruit of life. No more temptations to eat of the hidden and forbidden fruits in the "garden". For that eternal sin was provoked and walked over. Man had paid for his sacrifice and given goodness to evil enough times that evil became plain and boring to see, and never could there be temptation to be had. Humans had meandered through their kingdoms on earth being plagued by evil because of the sin we had brought onto ourselves. Carefully, and ardently the love of life became worthy on the cross where Jesus died. His single and worthy temptation was to lure people to God and to walk in his ways, that man could redeem himself from the fallen sin and despotic characteristic paroxysms. Paroxysms that lasted through the whole history of mankind, up to the moment when Christ would return again from heaven.

Obedient to his Father, he was made sin for loving it and doing it in all of its reprieve and symbiotic refuse for delinquent pasture and forgotten goodness. Received in the beginning, it was procured till the end.

Happenstance and enervating circumstances brought religion through as an offspring of the Creation that went wrong. Jesus paid for this wrong with his own body. That mankind would be eternally brought again to its Creator who created life on earth in the beginning.

Flavored appeal and broken-hearted trembling kisses death with the violence of man betraying his savior. We did it to him, and now he is here for us. Total turn around. A drop in the bucket of faith, and a paroxysm of grand design and utter conclusive reptilian sanctification, the oxygen lost to the devil will never despair again. For trees and plants make oxygen for our needy bodies, and we are repaired with hope, knowing that God loves us, enough to reward us benevolently after years and years of ongoing suffering in payment for that cardinal sin that turned us the wrong way. Payment, forgotten, despair used for justice, and wrongdoing annihilated.

Lemon on lemon trees, sweet and sour, but no longer bitter. Tomatoes on the vine ripe and swelling. Apples "the forbidden fruit", sweeter, juicier and tarter than ever before. Many kinds of apples, and pears, and peaches, and apricots, and even figs plus redemption of every fruit on earth brought to perfection.

Equitable and strange, the manufacturing of sweets is redundant and perplexed, yet still good, for no more is too much sugar a possibility. If you've dreamed of it, it's there, even cheesecake, and endless possibilities.

It's a land of milk and honey, where our cream and butter are no longer a health hazard, and honeybees make honey as they pollinate plants to give them ongoing life and nutrient immersion.

The catastrophe of hope versus fertilization incorporates pumpkins, and all squashes. Beans, and much, much more.

Chocolate a divine and ecstatic experience every time.

Food enough for everybody of every kind, and to eat an animal is totally unthinkable other than fish. Genomic mutations are no longer possible, for hormones and steroids are no longer in catch. For our bodies so now perfected need not bolster themselves for competition or falsehood in strength. Never will a disease or weakness hinder us.

Oblong frustration in mediating hope lingers with our fruitfulness and pregnant talents, gifts, and failures too weak to be seen. Obsolete and unprepared differences only bring beauty to the fate of the human being. God made us in his image, and finally we get to look at him. Stunning and aspiring to give as much love as possible.

Training in significance versus failure, the deceit of the wicked can no longer fool us, or pull the wool over our eyes. No longer are we sheep, lost, and needing a shepherd, but we are found, discovered, and prolific with hope and new design.

Brought betrayal is dusted off into the end times, and none of it remains. No one has to look over his shoulder with fear anymore of being stalked, for jealousy has disappeared in her forbidden darkness where the smile never dies, and the tears never cry, and bodies are wrought with stiffness and pounded in doom until all that remains is a dust. Assimilated in hell and destroyed in the lake of hell fire.

Expunged forever into eternity, without a god and without a life, cremated in copious guilt and frozen despair. Burnt to a crisp. Hazy and unrecognizable. Baby and the Beast are no more. Now lives Baby Pollyanna and many, many people she would like to get to know. Pollen in the flowers no more brings an allergy. The honeybees are sweet and busy. And they don't sting.

Music plays on various instruments and everyone can learn to play. Such music as has rarely graced the ears of the listeners.

Baby and William can only cry now and then of this disbelief that Heaven has finally come to them. And to Mom, and Rexi and her family, and Lila and Rusty and family, and Rachel and kids, and even Uncle Sandy who was one of those converted in the last time. Rape and despair are out of the picture, and cause not even a spasm of guilt, shame, and memories.

Conclusive desire comes with sex in all of its most glorious and beautiful ardor. More powerful than it has ever been known, without shame, without disrespect. Forbidden failure disgusts the newborns who must venture into this new world having gestated on their way through the gates to heaven. Quizzical and warm blooded, our saturated bodies still procreate, and giving birth is a beautiful thing. Baby knows that not now, but in the future, she will bear children to bring up in this awesome new world found in feature and found in obligation. We pay our respects and give divisive gestures to the man and the woman who joins to the man. In equatorial disgrace, this remains a function of deliberation. Unnatural sexual practices are not committed for they are no more. Rambunctious displeasure and forsaken design give life to those who had no life (seeds of abortion). Perpetrated disgust gives hope to the lost, and healing to the misaligned who deprave not love but cost in sexual exploitation. Maybe Baby's miscarried children have a life somewhere up here in heaven. Forgotten yet always remembered, the pain she went through in losing her unborn ones.

Then there is Mom who is ripe and ready to find a good, kind man and settle down. As the grafting takes place, and the old is made new, a world is born in perfection with no more pain and suffering. No more alcohol to get drunk on. Not to mention wine, for wine is traditional and beautiful.

No more guns, for they are no longer needed nor wanted but there is archery for sport.

Untamed tongues speak now only the truth, and the truth is made known to all who hear. And all do hear, for the deaf shall hear, and the dumb shall speak. Then there is writing which was used for communication. The Bible is the written work that saw us all through.

Everyone who is in heaven has been utterly and totally forgiven for all past wrongs and crimes and misdemeanors. No more are the oblivious forsaken and the weak walked over. For there is stagnation in the forbidden qualities of rotten pickles which are no longer given as gifts.

Torn to pieces, the survival of guilt disrespects quality and remains stoppable and frustrated in careening qualities of aggravated dissonance.

Everyone can pray and talk to his neighbor. God knows all and sees all. He can sit back down with a big, good sigh of relief.

EPILOGUE

Baby and the Beast may not be what you expected to find in a book with such a title. Enamored with glory and hope and expectation, it takes you on a journey highlighting the realities posit of heaven and hell.

After meeting Geoffe, Mom, Justin, Rexi, and Baby Pollyanna, you may have cringed at the horrible outlook that faces those who are wicked and disgraced. Rightly so for the distraught, when justice is done, she really *is done*. Nobody looks out for hell who might not be headed there already.

God made it clear that this life is full of choices to make, being wrong or right. When justice is done, forgiveness is saturated with hope. Some turn away from God, and that is their wrongful decision. *Baby and the Beast* qualifies truth and adamant revival between deliverance of sin sought for heavenly inhalation. Baby breathes freedom to be away eternally from her atrocious and abusive father and brother, who walk the way of the evil and wicked losers. Not to be redone or renewed. Heaven welcomes those who show mercy and live well by loving and observing kindness, thanksgiving, forgiveness, and humility. God given grace opens a wide path into a narrow gate. Formulating Heaven, he cares for the lucid and proud, who uphold destiny and give division to the faultiness of loss and decrepit, being lost and no more.

An enlightening Heavenly vision comes to Baby Pollyanna as she spends three Heavenly weeks in her coma dreaming about Heaven and the arrival of the "Rapture" on earth. This may or may not be true, depending upon what you believe. According to this book, the "Rapture" has come upon us, and Baby and the Beast, as this world evolves into the next—Heaven.

Love God with all your heart, mind, and strength, as well as love your neighbor as–yourself. Accept Jesus Christ as your Lord and Savior. Worship the One true and living God. Forgive others, apply your faith, and walk a right and respectfully diligent path. Heaven is yours for the taking, if you don't miss this chance. Thank you for reading *Baby and the Beast*. Your response is for God. He is waiting.

www.ingramcontent.com/pod-product-compliance
Lightning Source LLC
Chambersburg PA
CBHW060438310726
48977CB00001B/243